A Sticky Situation

A Sticky Situation

PIPER IRELAND

A STICKY SITUATION

A Mountain Valley Entrepreneurial Romance

Copyright © 2025 by Piper Ireland
All rights reserved.

No part of this book may be reproduced, distributed, or transmitted in any form or by any means, including photocopying, recording, or other electronic or mechanical methods, without the prior written permission of the publisher, except in the case of brief quotations embodied in critical reviews and certain other noncommercial uses permitted by copyright law.

Published by Piper Ireland Press

ISBN: 978-1-966216-00-1

This is a work of fiction. Names, characters, places, and incidents are either the product of the author's imagination or used fictitiously. Any resemblance to actual persons, living or dead, events, or locales is entirely coincidental.

First Edition

Printed in USA

To those who believe in love and to
Philip Michael Delmolino who showed me what love is.

CONTENTS

Chapter One	3
Chapter Two	9
Chapter Three	15
Chapter Four	26
Chapter Five	35
Chapter Six	44
Chapter Seven	49
Chapter Eight	56
Chapter Nine	67
Chapter Ten	75
Chapter Eleven	83
Chapter Twelve	93
Chapter Thirteen	102
Chapter Fourteen	108
Chapter Fifteen	121
Chapter Sixteen	131
Chapter Seventeen	137
Chapter Eighteen	145
Chapter Nineteen	156
Chapter Twenty	161
Chapter Twenty-One	168
Chapter Twenty-Two	173
Chapter Twenty-Three	181
Chapter Twenty-Four	190
Epilogue	198
More Entrepreneurial Romances	202
Acknowledgments	205

A STICKY SITUATION

A STICKY
SITUATION

CHAPTER ONE

Jamie Parry's gum popped like a tommy gun.

"What was that?" her uncle asked.

"What do you mean I'll have to get on a plane?" Jamie gripped the cell phone. "I do NOT have to get on a plane. That's what you're for."

"Oh, honey," he said, and she could hear him rustling through something as he spoke. "I can't do this for you forever. We've talked about this."

She knew this day would come, but she had no idea it'd be so soon. She started to fit the key into the glass door of her shop. Above her, the printed sign read, *The Cuckoo Cl*ck*. When she and her mother had planned this store, her mother had done all the procuring. Jamie hadn't been afraid then, just busy with school. But after the incident—

OK. We don't talk about the incident. Just breathe, she told herself as she unlocked the door and walked through it. Above her head a bundle of carved penis-shaped amulets knocked against each other like wind chimes. They were called Palad khik and they were from Thailand. No crying this morning, she coached herself. She inhaled through her nose and blew out into a gum bubble. It relaxed her to steady her breath and hold the bubble's shape. She sucked the bubble back into her mouth and tried to reason with her uncle.

"Uncle Norman. How am I supposed to get stock for my store if you don't go get it for me? You know I can't get on a plane. Not after what happened. Are you saying my store needs to close down?"

Ugh. She hated even mentioning what happened, but she was desperate. He couldn't ignore facts! And he couldn't exactly expect she'd get on a plane. Like for real. Maybe on a rollercoaster shaped like a plane. She'd get on that. Maybe. But not a plane, a real plane with its engines and its engine failures and its rare but very real chance of crash landing. She reached in her pocket for more gum—this one guava.

She could hear him getting out of his creaky chair and start shuffling somewhere as he spoke. "This is my last trip. At least for the store. I'll go with you to the Peruvian Amazon. I'll hold your hand on the plane. There's nothing to worry about. Planes are the safest travel there is, honey dear. I promise. And there's so much to see. I've planned out the whole trip so we can meet the artisans and also get tours of the Amazon. I've even booked a little hut village in the rainforest and we would stay there for a few days, swimming in the Amazon, hiking through the jungle, meeting the locals. And the food! I heard it's fantastic. C'mon, I mean, how can you resist? Hot weather, hot men, cold drinks, and a dip in one of the world's most famous rivers. What I say is take your destiny into your own hands. You can't live forever. Morning, Carl. Can you make sure that the bins are appropriately separated? I found some cardboard in the plastic dumpster on Friday. Sorry, honey. I'm just doing my rounds. Anyway. You're twenty-one—"

"Twenty-two. How can you forget when you made me a cake?"

"See? I'm too old to be traveling all over the world and brokering deals. Oh, honey," he said and sighed dramatically. "I'm nearing the end, darling. And I can tell you, as someone who has lived a full life, an expense-free trip to Peru is nothing to turn your nose up at. And you are my only grand-niece—"

"—great-niece," she corrected.

"I prefer it grand, though you are right. You are great. I don't know anyone else who has the stones to open a sex store next to a Bullseye in a dead mall in a dead town."

"Cultural erotica shop," she corrected again.

"Darling, the point is, I can't just let you wallow away in the dark. Your mother would haunt me."

That last sentence hit her a bit hard and she blew a bubble and then sucked it back into her mouth to pop silently.

This whole time, while he spoke, she began to prep the store for opening. Jamie started by dusting. She went to each set of shelves and dusted every object she found there from figurine to sculpture to book. This is how every morning of hers started. The store was quiet and all she could hear was the rustling of her feather duster on her wares and her uncle chattering away on

A STICKY SITUATION

the line. She listened to him, listened to his vain attempts at convincing her on a plane, but kept dusting. The opening ritual kept her calm, and she chewed her gum quietly, no longer blowing bubbles. It was easy to tell if Jamie was upset by something, she'd start blowing gum bubbles like crazy. Most of the time, however, her gum chewing stayed discreet and subtle. You could have a whole conversation with her without realizing she was chewing away the whole time. She was quite expert. The habit ingrained itself in her when she was a child still and her mother had told her, rather suddenly, that her father had left to pursue his career and wouldn't be back. She never saw him again, and he was replaced by the incessant gum chewing. Despite her mother's many protestations about Jamie's oral health, the dentist had claimed that her teeth were sparkling, probably because of the constant chewing. So the chewing was going nowhere.

"Wait, what?" she asked. "You're not well?" She started to blow small bubbles again.

"Nothing to worry about. It's just normal wear and tear."

"You keep saying you don't have much more time."

"Well, yes, but relatively. Compared to you I'm almost out the door. I'm not sure if I can hold on much longer. Maybe I've got another ten years in me if I'm lucky. I mean the way life has treated me, I wouldn't be surprised if I dropped dead any moment. Life—that you know what, she hates me. Oh, don't get me wrong, she loves me too, but God knows what mood she's in every day and even he doesn't have the stones to ask her. That's why I'm retiring. I decided today. It's time to pass the crown on to someone younger. My district manager has been throwing out hints that my time is near anyway, so I guess I'll just beat her to it. That's me—the first. You know I'm the first person to manage a Bullseye at seventy-five years old. I'm a legend, honey. And it's nothing new. I was the first boy to win the Sunshine Sprouts pageant when I was only two. Granted they couldn't tell me from a girl, but that doesn't change the facts."

"Yes, uncle. I can't argue with that."

She could. She could tell him that he was the last person that had a spot in her heart for family. If he left too, that particular region of her heart marked "family" might stay empty forever. She kept this to herself as she dusted the testicles of a Mexican saltshaker.

PIPER IRELAND

"You do know that I'm old, don't you?"

Actually, Jamie hadn't thought of it much. She supposed he was old. He did walk with a cane, but...it was a sparkling carved wood cane, encrusted with gem-like stones. The man had always seemed like such a big source of energy. For her it definitely seemed that way. When her mother had died, he had been there, helping her sort through things, visit lawyers, drive to donation centers, do all the paperwork that for a few months might as well have been written in gibberish for as much sense as it made to her. He had held her as she cried and had kept watch of her like a father. To call him a source of energy was right. He had been a sun, keeping a very dark night from completely taking over. Thus, it seemed strange to think of him now—though it struck Jamie as obvious at the moment—as someone close to dying. "I guess technically you're a senior citizen, yes," she said.

Her Uncle Norman laughed. Then she heard him calling janitorial staff through his walkie-talkie because of vomit in an aisle. "I don't know how this got past someone last night," she heard him saying as she continued dusting.

Next, she wiped down the counters and the register. She could still hear the small drama continue through the phone. The janitor showed up without any cleaning supplies and her uncle sent him back with a gentle quip. She uncovered the bins of gum she kept near the counter, dusting the surface of them, while her uncle complained that people hadn't drank their coffee that morning. She loved this gum, sourced it from all over the world. Jamie couldn't resist, and, as her uncle, apparently, got down on his knees to wipe up the vomit himself, Jamie put a few choice pieces of gum into her pocket.

"Uncle Norman, shouldn't he be cleaning that up? Like you said, you're seventy-whatever."

"Darling, darling," she heard him say as he struggled to get back up. "I had something else to talk to you about, but that requires being face-to-face. I also have to tell you, first of all, the things I discovered about that little corner of the Amazon that you're going to visit with me..."

While her uncle went on about the adventures awaiting them in the rain forest, Jamie retrieved a broom from the back, continuing her opening routine. As she swept, she heard shuffling, as if someone were approaching fast and then the door swung open wide and crashed against the plate glass window. "Uncle

A Sticky Situation

Norman, I'll call you back. Someone's here."

"Oh, to the shop? To buy something? Finally—"

She hung up and spun to find her Uncle Norman, rushing in.

"What the heck are you doing? You're going to break my window and give me a heart attack."

"I told you," her uncle began to huff and puff, "I had to tell you face-to-face and I just couldn't hold it in anymore, so here I am, fast as I could."

"What is it? What is so important that you had to break down my door?"

"The old man is dead."

Jamie was glad for the broom to hold onto. The old man was dead? He was a such a nice man, the nicest, had forgiven her the rent when she couldn't make it, many a time. He would say to her, "I'll trade you rent for one of these sexy knick-knacks." She gave him many beautiful tapestries and intricately carved sculptures of women with pendulous breasts or young men frolicking in the nude. He would assure her that it was more than enough, laughing as she filled his arms. He had been there when she and her mother had come up with the idea for this store and he had believed in them. He had been there when her mother died and had forgiven her the rent that month as well—wouldn't hear of her paying, pushed the money away as she tried to hand it to him. Now he was dead.

There was a time when she hadn't considered that all the people in her life could one day just disappear, die. But now it seemed death was flanking her.

"What do you mean dead," was the first thing she said.

"Last week. My district manager told me earlier, before I called you. That's why I called you. I started having all these thoughts about mortality and how close to mine I was and I panicked."

"I can't believe it," Jamie said, not registering her uncle's complaints. She moved over to the counter to find the stool. She had to sit down.

She rested the broom against one of the gum bins and took a seat. In the background her uncle went on about how he was next, just you watch.

"How did it happen?"

"Oh, that. It was a heart attack, poor thing. Now, hear this, his grandson inherits all of *Shire Mall* and I hear he's going to lease it all out, with the exception of my store, to a local company."

Out of instinct Jamie grabbed another piece of gum, this one peanut. Ugh.

She gulped hard.

"I'm so sorry, honey. We all love your shop."

Before she could process the news any further, she noticed a small group of red-shirted workers waving from the Bulleye's side-door, drawing hearts in front of their torsos.

Uncle Norman, catching Jamie's gaze, looked back furiously. He waved his cane and shouted, "Get back to work! This isn't break time, you layabouts!" Apparently even behind the closed door, they got the message. They dispersed. "You've got to crack the whip, dear, or they get sentimental and stop working. Can't let them take advantage—" here he banged the cane repeatedly for emphasis "—Not. For. A. Second."

"So, they all know about it too."

"Bad news travels fast. Sorry, honey." Uncle Norman leaned in closer as he spoke, "Apparently the kid wanted to renegotiate the contract. And that was a to-do, let me tell you. Lawyers have been asking to see all my records since. But they wouldn't tell me why at first. Anyway, I'm subsumed by paperwork! Paper cuts galore! Look at my hands. Look!" Jamie noticed that three of his fingertips were covered in Band-Aids. "You should get a call soon, I suspect."

Jamie wasn't sure what to say. So, she didn't. She just blew bubbles and then pulled them back into her mouth.

He reached out a hand and patted her wrist. "It'll all be OK, dear. Don't fret. You'll bounce back. You're full of talents."

She stopped blowing bubbles and spoke. "Oh yeah? Like what?" She heard a venom in her voice that surprised her.

"Oh, honey. You're young. You can do anything."

The store's phone rang, that tinny metallic sound marking the hour of her demise. She watched as the light beside L1 blinked.

CHAPTER TWO

The girl at the front desk grimaced as Luke Garrett walked in with his backpack. She must've been just a year older than him and every time he'd come here, she had been, to be polite, confused. The first time they met last week, she sat Luke in a conference room and forgot to tell his lawyer that he was waiting. They couldn't meet after that because the lawyer was booked all day. The second time, a few days later, she informed the wrong lawyer of his arrival and Luke had to wait an extra half an hour to be seen. He did not think this third time was the charm and he wondered what she had in store for him today.

Her grimace told him that she did not want to speak to him, but he didn't take it personally. He had seen her with other clients, and he knew she would've been just as displeased no matter who walked through that door. He imagined for a moment what it would mean to go to work every day as a receptionist and dread the part when you encounter another person.

He hoped nothing quite like that was in his future.

As he walked in, he tried smiling because he wanted to seem friendly. He had resolved to seem friendly, not just with her but also with the lawyer he was about to meet: Frederick R. Harris.

Frederick R. Harris, Esq. had served Luke's grandfather for countless decades and, consequently, seemed to feel ownership over the man's affairs. Were things to follow logically, Attorney Harris, would now serve Luke as legacy to Zachariah Garrett—also known as Pop-pop. Beyond that, one might've presumed that the attorney would want to maintain a client who had just inherited a considerable real estate portfolio. But, so far, Luke and Attorney Harris seemed to have different ideas of what service should look like. Luke would have appreciated some direction in carrying out his own ideas about what to do with the small empire his grandfather had bequeathed him. But Attorney Harris had other plans for at least one of the properties, a dead mall on the outskirts of the small city of Pittsfield. The lawyer claimed that Pop-pop (or as he called him, Zach) planned to sell the property to the state as the site of a new prison. And every time Luke had spoken to the man, he had sat through all the reasons Luke's ideas were wrong and they should sell the mall to the state.

Before he dealt with the attorney, however, he would have to survive the young lady at reception, Brenda.

"Good morning, Brenda," Luke said, "How are you?"

Brenda looked up from her desk lazily, as if she'd been awoken from a nap. "Can I help you?"

"I'm here to see Fred Harris."

"I got it. Attorney Harris. Hold on," she said, holding up a finger. She consulted a flow chart on the wall. First, she typed something on the computer. He could hear the sound of an email going *whoosh!* Then she consulted the chart again and looked up at him. "You can take a seat," she said and thrust her arm out mechanically. She swiveled right around to the chart again to carry out the rest of her duties. Well, that was easy, he thought. He didn't have to do anything. Apparently, the firm had fixed the problem of the bad receptionist with a flow chart... brilliant.

He still felt uneasy though. He stood up part way to see the receptionist behind the high desk. "You did call Fred and not Jean, right?" he asked, citing the last visit.

"Attorney Harris will be ready in a minute," she said.

It was like she had been reprogrammed, he thought and tried to relax. When it was time, she sent Luke into the office.

"Thank you," he said, looking at her warily.

The office was a mess. None of the decorations had been set up. They all were put in boxes: picture frames, clocks, knick-knacks. And the boxes lined the wall, beneath where their contents should have been hung.

Luke took a seat, moving a stack of files onto the desk in the process.

"How are you, Fred?"

"Attorney Harris."

"I'm not calling you that."

"You've become rather sure of yourself quickly, haven't you?"

A STICKY SITUATION

Luke simply smiled.

"You need to get this girl out of the mall," said the lawyer.

"You mean, Ms. Parry? My tenant?"

"You need to get her out of this mall as soon as possible. We're going to evict her. Quite simple. If we have to, we pay her. No big deal. Problem solved. Bing bang boom."

"No. I don't think that's the best thing to do. I have another plan that—"

"Listen, Luke. I knew your grandfather. I knew what he had planned for this property. I know what he wanted. And he left you all this property, not so you can manage it, but so you can live a comfortable life, you and your mother, and not have to worry about money. Either of you. With this deal with the state, you don't work anymore. It's simple."

Luke took a deep breath. It was going to be hard to talk about this with the man, he wasn't open minded, and he was a bulldozing sort of man, just kept talking until he flattened you good.

"I do not believe that selling the property is what my grandfather wanted for me—"

"Kid, you're eighteen. You don't know what he wanted for you. I knew the man decades. He would want his daughter and grandson taken care of."

Luke continued, undeterred, "He always talked to me about what it meant to be a landlord. I know that he would've loved my idea if I had just presented it to him."

"Why did you not?"

"Not what?"

"Why did you not present it to him? If it was such a good idea, why didn't you tell him about it when he was alive?"

Fred knew what kind of man Pop-pop had been and knew very well why Luke had not presented the idea to him. Pop-pop had not been an easy man to talk to. He never responded to questions he was asked. He only spoke when he felt like and could never be persuaded of anything. Luke saw Pop-pop every Saturday morning at seven AM since he was twelve, when he was picked up and taken around to the properties to collect rents. He would spend the morning knocking on doors asking people for money just as the sun was rising on what was mostly people's day off. Most of the time he got yelled at, but eventually people got to know him and forgave him for the early hour. Others weren't as forgiving and yelled at him or shut the door in his face. But his instructions were simple: don't leave until some money was in hand. One day, on one of these excursions, Pop-pop had promised that he would buy Luke a new car if he got straight As until twelfth grade. In eleventh grade, the final semester, the calculus test had been especially difficult and, try as he might, Luke had earned a B plus, which brought down his average slightly. Sheila, Luke's mother, had pleaded with her father that he give Luke the prize—that he had earned it, that an A- was an A. The old man had even put the money in escrow for the day that was fated to never arrive. But the old man refused to be reasoned with. Luke never made a peep, except to tell his mother to quit it. He had said this one Saturday, in front of her father. She had cornered her father when they were to go collect rents and Luke had practically whispered, but she quieted down to listen to him, and he told her point blank to stop asking for the car. He had lost. He had tried hard, but he had lost the bet, and he had not earned the car. Luke thought he saw Pop-pop smile that day, though it was fast enough that Luke barely perceived it.

But now as he sat in front of Attorney Harris, he knew that he must not give in to this man. Luke and his Pop-pop hadn't had many conversations, but it seemed to him that his grandfather might agree with his view that a man needs to be brave enough to take chances and make a way for himself: win or lose. So, he was going to do things according to his convictions. He spoke up now, answering the attorney, everything inside of him trembling with nerves.

"He was a man of few words. But one of the times he did have something to say he put it in writing and signed his name beneath it. It was his will that I inherit his real estate portfolio and that I have the power to govern it. And that's what I intend to do. I'm going to take the meeting with Shire Roots and see if they want to partner with me to carry out my plan."

The lawyer seemed to grow red and inflated. But he didn't say anything for a while in which his eyes roved the ceiling like a giant toad looking for an unlucky fly. "You will want to get rid of the girl either way. I can help you there."

"Let me speak to her. I'll see what her situation is and maybe we can come up with a plan."

"Plan? What plan? You have to evict her. This is a liability issue. In order to do what you want, you need to empty the mall of every business but the

A Sticky Situation

Bullseye store, and, if you don't and something happens, it'll shut down the whole project and get you sued for as much as you're worth. She'd have a claim, you know."

"I'm taking the meeting with Shire Roots and nothing will go forward before that anyway."

"Ugh. Weed. This is your plan? Your grandfather would be ashamed."

Would the old man be ashamed? Luke wasn't sure. Pop-pop had barely expressed any thought at all. Luke couldn't imagine where the man would have landed on almost any topic. Since he had no idea what Pop-pop thought about weed, he decided he wouldn't worry about it. But he still wanted the lawyer to help him if he could, so he tried not to be blunt. He felt that he had gone a bit too far already earlier. "I will make sure there is no liability issue. I understand what you're saying."

"I really don't think you should be taking big meetings without me present. You need some guidance. I'm sure their lawyers will be present."

"Maybe. But I don't need one. Before I sign anything, you'll have a good look at it, not to worry."

The lawyer harrumphed and stood up. He looked even larger now as he stood. He was looming. "I'm not agreeing to this idea of you going alone. You are eighteen years old, still in high school. What makes you think you can handle this type of business deal? Your idea will not work. I already looked it over. It will be better to sell. A sure thing. You already have a buyer and can make ten million. You could live off the interest alone. You hear what I'm saying to you? With that kind of money, a man could do anything he wanted."

Luke sat quietly a moment. With ten million a man could do almost anything he wanted. Fred was right about that. But there was one thing he wanted to do that ten million couldn't make possible for him. His plan had the potential of revitalizing not only the mall, but also the region itself. It had stuck in his mind as something akin to destiny to pull off this feat and the only thing that could stand in his way, he believed, was himself... if he sold that property. If he kept it and got it going again, he had the potential of making his property worth more than ten million and would bring in more traffic to the area.

"Thank you for your advice," Luke said finally.

Fred smiled. "I'm glad you are seeing things my way."

"But I'm going through with my plan," Luke continued. "I know that I will need help—" Here the lawyer went to interrupt, but Luke held up a hand. "We'll talk soon. After the meeting with Shire Roots."

The lawyer shouted for another few minutes about this "golden opportunity," but Luke just listened and then excused himself.

CHAPTER THREE

This was it. The phone call that told her she was done for. When Jamie and her mother had come up with the idea of this place, she never imagined this, that little more than a year later her mother would be dead. And now the old man...

She reached into her pocket for gum, mindlessly. She unwrapped it while staring at the phone. As it rang, she slowly put the gum into her mouth.

"Wake up, darling!" shouted her uncle.

Jamie startled. "Oh. Yeah."

She picked up the phone and put her ear to the receiver. She waited, the line silent.

Then a voice came from the other end. "Hello?"

"Oh yes, hello," said Jamie, recognizing the voice as Mrs. Piedmont. "Mrs. Piedmont? You're calling about your order?"

"I thought you had picked up the line, but I didn't hear anything. It was a bit eerie."

"I agree, Mrs. Piedmont. It was eerie. But it's just a bad connection. Would you like to come in today to pick up your print?"

Jamie's customer would be in shortly to pick up a special order. As she hung up the phone, her Uncle Norman watched her.

"Honey, you can't just fall apart."

"I'm not falling apart."

"You could barely answer the phone."

"Well, you threw a lot at me at once. I just need a moment to recover."

They stayed silent a moment and then Uncle Norman went to a shelf and found a mini huaco to play with. The figurine was wooden and carved, a little Incan wearing a barrel. When he pushed the barrel down, a phallus almost as big as the whole figurine popped out. Jamie listened as her uncle laughed.

"That never gets old."

"This whole time I thought I'd convince you to travel for me. But now it won't matter. Not if I'm going to be shut down."

"Oh, darling. It's sweet that you thought you could change my mind. Cute. Really adorable. But no, I'm going on this last trip to Peru because I really want to go, but I'm not going to go around sourcing your wares anymore. You have to be a big girl and face your fears."

"What are you talking about? I'm going to be closed down. There's no point in getting on a plane. I'll have no need. No shop to shop for."

Her uncle smiled sheepishly. He decided the Bullseye couldn't continue the morning without its manager, so he dismissed himself and went back to work through the side door leading from the mall into his store. The door usually stayed locked, to avoid theft, but it made a quick shortcut to visit Jamie. Otherwise, he'd have to exit the Bullseye and walk across the parking lot to the mall's main entrance. This was a small journey Jamie had trouble getting people to make. Few people visited her store.

Apart from her fan club, as she called them, almost no one came into her store. That's why she had been so grateful for the old man. He had always been forgiving with her, but he knew that her store didn't get much traffic. He asked her once about the peculiar "theme" of the shop. That's what he had called it. Why would a young brilliant girl like her want to run a store like this in a small town of small-minded people? Her answer had never satisfied him, she was sure. What she didn't know was why he had taken pity on her, but he had. And that meant that she didn't have to face the enormous reality that she was now running the store alone. Not worrying about a mounting debt is part of what helped her survive this year. For that the old man had a piece of her heart. It had never occurred to her that her mother could die. Not really. She had had, of course, the knowledge that her mother grew older and that the ultimate role of a human was in death. But it hadn't seemed real to her...

She would miss the old man, the way he always had a warm smile for her. He was a rather quiet old man, but if you got him talking about the mall, the way it used to be, he would go on non-stop. He seemed to love this mall and was happy that she wanted to rent a space in it. She had keys to the whole place. At first, when she had just opened, Jamie would leave her mother at the store and

A STICKY SITUATION

explore the empty mall, the only light streaming through the glass panes in the ceiling. Peering into the dark storefronts, she thought, should seem creepy, the eeriness of a desolate privacy in a public space, but they just seemed sad to her. She wished for neighbors for her store.

She wiped the tears that had appeared as she thought of the old man. She knew already what to expect, she felt herself steeling in the knowledge. She would never see the old man again, never hear him speak. The respective thought had knocked the wind out of her almost daily for months when her mother had gone. But this time it wouldn't do the same to her. She was safe. Whatever that thing was that hurt inside her was too busy with her first loss to really feel this one. She thought so at least. She hoped so.

She had to prepare for Mrs. Piedmont. She grabbed a clear bag from behind the counter and started to fill it with gum, picking out anything that wasn't fruit flavored. Mrs. Piedmont was not adventurous in her gum choices. Her choices in art, however, were quite scandalous. Scandalous to most, but not Jamie. Jamie had been fascinated a long time with the subject, had even written her cornerstone essay for her BA in cultural studies on what she called "cultural erotica." Today Mrs. Piedmont was picking up a print by a Peruvian painter who makes images of lesbian sex. The figures were extremely stylized and slightly abstract, soft long brushstrokes of browns and pastels formed the limbs and torsos. The painted women lay on their sides in dirt, each performing oral sex on the other in an unbroken circle—a sexual symbol of eternity. Jamie filled the bag of gum and placed it on the counter. From the back room she brought out a wrapped package two-feet long and wide and placed it on the counter.

Jamie's fan club consisted of a group of women, mostly elders, all with adventurous tastes. Through the contacts her mother had made when she was alive and even some of the one's her uncle had made in his travels, Jamie supplied the women regularly with art work for their homes. The sales weren't frequent, but they were steady, at least one or two a month from the group of ten. She was grateful for them. They were her loyal customers.

She heard Mrs. Piedmont's heels clacking out in the mall entrance. And there she was, a middle-aged lawyer that loved to shock her in-laws with sexually explicit artwork. They were visiting for the weekend and she wanted to hang the painting above the guest bed. Jamie didn't judge, she just supplied.

"Good morning, Mrs. Piedmont," she called out as the woman walked into the store.

"Nothing good about this morning. I told you the in-laws are coming. They'll be here today. 'Oh, Patricia, still no children?' That's his mother. Asks me every time. I tell you," she said while putting her purse on the counter. Jamie could smell her perfume. Something intensely floral and musky. "The woman must be blind. I'm almost fifty. If I haven't had kids yet, what makes you think I'm suddenly going to pop one out? Anyway, how are you?"

Jamie chuckled. "I'm OK. Actually, no I had some bad news. Mr. Garrett, the owner of this mall, died last week."

"Oh yes," said Mrs. Piedmont. "I heard."

Had her Uncle Norman called everyone in the county with the news? How did everyone already know?

Mrs. Piedmont continued, "The grandson inherits. He's going to sell this place to the state. They've wanted this site for their new prison for years. I guess they'll finally get their claws into it. Oh, I'm sorry. That means you'll have to close up. I'm sorry. I didn't mean to be insensitive. Oh no, how am I going to shock my idiot in-laws without you? You always do the trick. What am I going to do?" Mrs. Piedmont started digging in her purse.

Jamie started to blow bubbles again, then sucking them back into her mouth. It was like a person tossing a ball up in the air and catching it, a repetitive movement that distracted her from stress. The thought of losing the store made her want to start crying and then all the other sad thoughts she kept at bay started clamoring to be heard.

Mrs. Piedmont pulled out a tissue. That was sweet, Jamie thought. Jamie moved closer from behind the register to reach for it when Mrs. Piedmont swiped at her face, snatching the gum right out of her mouth.

"Ugh. You were driving me nuts with that stuff," Mrs. Piedmont said as she balled up the tissue and put it on the counter.

Jamie was so caught by surprise she didn't really react. She just kept mouthing, "um, um, um..."

"You got a lease on this place, right?"

Jamie nodded.

"He can't just kick you out. He'll have to sweeten the pot somehow. Maybe

A Sticky Situation

you'll get enough to open a new storefront. You know this isn't really a good location," she said looking around herself. Then she met Jamie's eyes and waited for a response.

"Thanks for the advice." She smiled and then picked up the wrapped print. "Should we take a peek?"

"No, you saw it, right?"

"Yes, I wrapped it."

"OK, that's good with me." Mrs. Piedmont stared at Jamie again. It was slightly uncomfortable to have her face studied so openly.

"What—" started Jamie.

"—call me if you need me. OK?"

"Thanks, Mrs. Piedmont. That's really kind." Thanks for giving Jamie something to look forward to. It was becoming obvious; she was going to lose her shop, one way or another.

"Keep me updated. I want to know what you end up deciding to do."

"Promise." Jamie smiled.

Mrs. Piedmont paid and thanked her for the bag of gum. "You maybe, take a little break," she said brandishing the bag over her head. "You're going to get a cavity."

Luke stood at the front door of his house. He didn't know what was waiting for him in there. His mother had been unpredictable for years, moods plunging then soaring, and the past week, worse. Sometimes she drank in the early morning and ended up passed out on the couch before the soaps were on.

His worries, though, were ill-founded. When he opened the door, he was welcomed by his mother's voice, singing. Sheila had wanted to be a singer as a child, even convincing her father to pay for lessons. Her singing still had flashes of real beauty, especially when she was meant to sound sad. She loved to sing old country songs about heartbreak. Apart from that, singing was auspicious. Singing meant good moods, brushed hair and teeth, pancakes, smiles.

And there it was: the smell of blueberry pancakes wafting into his face, enveloping him in a warm sweetness as he entered the house.

"Ma?"

"Daaaaaaaarliiiiing," she sang. She stood in the kitchen by the stove, running her fingers through her jet black and silver hair, which was teased up into a light confection. "Hope you're hungry. With the way you rushed out this morning, I know you must not have eaten a thing."

"You're right, Ma. I didn't eat a thing," he said and gave her a kiss on the cheek.

She giggled at his touch and then put a plate in front of him as he sat at the table. "Thanks," he said, as she lay a fresh pancake straight from the pan on top of the stack. The pancakes were perfect, golden, hot, fluffy, buttery, sweet.

Luke loved days like this.

Sheila closed her robe tighter as she sat down across from her son, arms crossed. "You left here so quick, I didn't even get to say good morning to you."

"Had a meeting to get to. Sorry."

"I know you had a meeting. Don't be smart."

Luke sighed. Maybe he had let down his guard too easily.

"I should've been there with you," Sheila continued.

"Ma. You were there for the first meeting. This one was just about the properties and my next step. You didn't have to be there for that."

"I'm just your mother. Who am I to be included in important matters? My father dies, leaves you everything and me nothing. And you think that's right?"

"I don't know, Ma. I'm not the one who made the decision."

"I don't like your idea. I don't see the point in giving up this deal with the state, that Harris was talking about. It's sure money."

Luke stood up calmly.

He looked at the table as he spoke. "I don't want to keep fighting over this."

Sheila watched him a moment. "Sit down," she said. "Eat."

Luke looked at her as he took his seat, wary. He ate while his mother drank coffee and talked about his curriculum. He had decided that in order to run a business, he'd have to quit school and finish the year homeschooling. Luke had always been organized and most of his core requirements had been fulfilled. Three of his classes this year were electives, time he would now mostly use for work. A meeting like today would've been a nightmare had he been in school; his absences alone would make it impossible for him to graduate. Also, it was a good idea because his mother was brilliant and could teach him for free. She lived off a trust her father had set up that covered the bare minimum expenses and they lived in one of her father's properties. Whatever other needs she

A Sticky Situation

had, she supplemented by working from home packaging cheap jewelry for a Greek immigrant with an online business. But now as Luke learned advanced calculus, no one was a better teacher than his mother. Had she not had so much trouble with depression, who knows what Sheila might've accomplished. But she was notoriously unreliable, especially with money. Luke had made sure the past few years that the bills were paid on time and that they would not be in arrears. His grandfather had paid him for his work every Saturday too, so he had always been able to feed himself with that money whenever his mother forgot about him, which was often. It was no wonder to him when the lawyer had called them both in to inform them that Pop-pop had left Luke the entire estate. Sheila would've burned through those assets within the year; Luke was certain. His grandfather had trusted him. That's what this inheritance meant. Trust. He would take care of his mother, he would grow his legacy, he would succeed in making his grandfather proud. He told himself this, all while ignoring the needling thoughts that he was too young, too inexperienced, too ignorant.

"I do think that no matter what you do, you have to get that tenant out of there. It's a liability issue." She took a sip of coffee.

Luke put down his fork and swallowed. "I don't think Pop-pop would've evicted her like that. He never did things like that. He always talked to the person and tried to work something out."

"You can't have a construction crew in there with that person there."

"I know that, Ma."

"I want to see you make your vision come true. I hope you know that. I'm trying to help you."

"I want to evaluate her business. If I play it right, then she might want to come back when we reopen."

"I see. Clever. But Shire Roots is going to want to know that there are no tenancy issues before they agree to partner with you. You already have lots of things stacked against you. You don't need something else that isn't in your favor."

"I understand. I think there's something I can do to make sure this doesn't become a big problem."

"Just make sure you don't get too technical. Don't forget you're very left brained. You don't want her to think that you don't think of her as a person."

Luke smiled and ate his pancakes. He was getting it from all sides today. He thought of his grandfather. He could picture the man, but it didn't make him sad. He wasn't sure what that said about him that he didn't cry at the death of his grandfather. Surely it meant he was a cold heartless monster, he thought. Though, he did remind himself that despite spending years of Saturday mornings with the man, he didn't have much of an emotional attachment to him. Pop-pop hadn't really cultivated it. Besides commanding he be addressed as Pop-pop, Zachariah Garrett had not showed any affection or inspired it. But respect—that he had cultivated in Luke. As Luke imagined the man, he felt immediately the pressure to succeed in his plan, to prove himself worthy of this great burden of inheritance.

That's also how he thought of it, very privately. A burden.

He knew his mother was hurt that she was not trusted with it all. But she couldn't have run the place even if she had been. She was smart enough, but no one who knew her would let her manage a dollar. He didn't really know how to address it. The decision wasn't his to make, but he was going to run with it and trust his instincts. Clearly his grandfather had trusted him.

After pancakes they sat and did derivatives. He tried to milk Sheila for all she was worth when she was in a mood like this, able to walk and hold conversation. They did that for a couple hours before he went upstairs to study US History.

The bell rang later that night. It interrupted the stupor Luke's textbook had cast over him, a famous advanced mathematics text simply named, *Analysis*. He yawned and dabbed his chin. Then Luke bound down the stairs to answer the door. When he reached it, his mother had just begun to stir, a lit cigarette hung from her lips, and she moaned. Luke let out a soft sibilance and outstretched his arm to signal his mother stay relaxed.

He opened the door.

"Here he is, local big shot real estate mogul, Luke Garrett! And the fans go *hahhhhhhh*." His friend Ricky was on the doorstep, knees bent as he oscillated, hands around his mouth, mimicking the hiss of a stadium audience.

Luke moved out of the doorway. "C'mon in, buddy." They hugged tightly until Luke patted Ricky's back and they let go.

"Hey, Ms. Sheila," Ricky said and waved at Luke's mother. Sheila managed to

A STICKY SITUATION

raise her eyebrows before clumsily ashing her cigarette next to the tray.

"I think that's all you'll get out of her tonight," Luke whispered. He took the stairs two at a time and Ricky followed. Once they got into the room, Ricky immediately started to tidy.

"Do you know you have three glasses of water up here? All half-drunk." Ricky sniffed at one of the glasses and made a face, scrutinizing.

"I'm trying to stay hydrated," said Luke and turned to look out the window. The moon was near full and had a dark yellow tint.

"Well, you have to drink for it to work," said Ricky behind him.

A memory from at least ten years back came to him, how on a night very much like tonight, he had looked up at a moon blazing this brightly and wondered if the world had any supernatural creatures; witches and ghosts and werewolves were the ghouls then, but now what haunted him was more concrete yet just as shadowy—the specters of marketing, business plans, construction costs, permits, taxes, the welfare of hundreds of tenants loomed in his mind and threatened to scare him so deeply that the moon itself seemed sinister.

"You know, dust bunnies can easily be avoided with a broom. You're seriously neglecting the under part of your bed. You're raising a colony under here. Oh, look at this one chase the other one."

Luke turned to find Ricky with half his body under the bed. He went and pulled at Ricky's feet, just a gentle tug. "What are you doing under there? I swept a few days ago. There are no bunnies. Let me see." Then Luke was beside Ricky, half underneath the bed, on his belly, peering into darkness. "There's nothing here," he said, finding little dust to speak of.

Ricky laughed. "I just wanted to see if I could get you under here," he said. "Turns out you're susceptible to a little lark."

Luke laughed and carefully turned on to his back. Now they were both under the bed. "Where did you hear that word?"

"Lark? We were studying John Milnhouse for English and the teacher explained it."

"You mean Milton?"

"Millhouse, Milton, who cares?"

Ricky and Luke looked at each other beneath the frame of Luke's bed and laughed. They squiggled out from under and sat up on the floor.

"WDC4?"

"WDC4."

Luke stood up to start his video game system. They killed zombies for a little while. Then Luke caught Ricky looking at him repeatedly. "What's up?"

"No, nothing," said Ricky, refocusing on the screen.

"What is it?"

"Just…" Ricky squirmed where he played on the floor.

Luke smiled suspiciously. "What is it?"

"Just proud of you, that's all."

"Oh yeah?"

"You said you would take over this real estate business thing and do school from home and you're really doing it. You're already a big businessman and you haven't even finished high school. You're like an adult."

Luke couldn't help but feel his stomach tighten slightly. Ricky wasn't wrong, but Luke felt like he had been "an adult" for even longer. Taking care of his addled mother, making sure she didn't burn down the house with an errant cigarette had made him grow up a long time ago. He had also done without the guidance of a father, his own making a disappearance act before Luke was even born. But he took the compliment. It was true that he was facing a big challenge head on and so he let himself feel proud too, just for a moment.

"Can I tell you a secret?"

Ricky put down the controller and his character was immediately overrun by zombies, but he turned and looked at his friend. "Please do," he said and folded his hands on his crossed legs.

Luke's brow furrowed; his eyes narrowed. "I'm—" Luke wasn't sure he wanted to say this out loud, but Ricky looked at him expectantly. "I'm… afraid."

"I knew it."

Luke jolted his head up.

Ricky looked shocked at himself a moment and then recovered. "I mean—it's totally natural, right? You're taking on a bunch of new things you've never done before."

"It's the people," Luke said, looking at the screen as it announced GAME OVER in a blood-like font. "There are so many people who now rely on me to make sure they have a good place to live, a safe place. Hundreds."

A Sticky Situation

"Hundreds?" Ricky's eyes widened.

"Hundreds." Luke took a breath. "If this doesn't work out, I might be forced to sell to make up for my losses. And then where will all these people be? At the mercy of some developer maybe or some slum lord? If I'm not careful...my grandfather's work just..." he mimed a plane heading down in a nosedive and made a whistling sound.

"It's serious business."

"Absolutely. Serious for sure."

"And that's why you'll succeed."

Luke cocked his head sideways and thought about that a moment. "I don't get it."

"That's why you'll succeed. Because it's too serious not to. You always succeed. I've never seen you fail at anything. All the way back to first grade, you never falter."

"Falter. Good one."

"SAT prep!"

"I think I kinda get what you're saying. I have no choice but to make sure this all works out."

Ricky grinned.

CHAPTER FOUR

When Jamie walked into the kitchen through the back door of the bar, she heard, "You can't say you don't like it if you leave your ass open all the time."

She ignored that.

It was a game the cooks and busboys played, whereby they spanked each other's butts. "Hello, guys," she said as she walked in and everyone looked up to greet her.

She saw Steve trying to spank Billy, who covered himself with a spatula. "Not in front of the ladies. That's the rule."

Jamie didn't really need a reminder of why she didn't eat the food at the bar, but here was a good one. She walked through the swinging doors into the front.

It was only six o'clock, but the bar was already mostly full. The first thing she did was greet the bartender and ask if she needed anything. Leah was on this shift. She smiled brightly at Jamie, who smiled back.

"Jamie! So glad you're here. It's a bit nuts in here already. The busboys are late and Dean is stuck in his office doing god knows what. He said he wouldn't be out much all night. So, it's just us."

Dean was the owner of the bar.

"You need me to take these racks?" Jamie asked while pointing at a couple full racks of glasses. Jamie spent the next fifteen or so minutes clearing all the dishware from behind the bar, even bussing plates and glasses from the tables. The waitresses smiled at her. "Thank God, you're here," they said to Jamie as she spun around the place lightening the load for everyone.

When she was done, she also brought out the clean glasses and cutlery, set it all in its bins for the waitresses to set their tables. That's when busboys arrived, grinning. "Sorry," said one of them to her as she wrapped cutlery in napkins. The other said, "Thanks."

A STICKY SITUATION

Released from bus boy duties, she went to the back of the kitchen to fill an ice bucket. She could hear slapping and the cooks laughing it up. She navigated the kitchen, yelling, "Behind. Behind!" Then she refilled the ice behind the bar. As Jamie bent to put down the ice bucket, Leah hugged her from behind. "You're the best," she said. They stood up, Jamie slightly embarrassed. She could really use some gum right about now, but she wasn't allowed to chew gum at the bar. There had been too many instances of her popping bubbles in front of customers...and over their drinks and food. Leah was always extremely nice to her, which on its own made her uncomfortable, but she was also the sister of Jamie's ex, Ben. So looking at her was always a reminder of him, of the countless hours she'd spent at their family's house, hanging with both of them. They also had gone to high school together, Leah and Jamie, two years apart and in different circles, but that had given them enough time to be around each other. Jamie liked her enough. They were never great friends, though Jamie was sure Leah would disagree. Leah always expressed affection openly and confidently. Even now she held Jamie's hand and asked her what she was doing on the weekend.

Jamie pulled her hand away, smiling, and started to fill a glass with ice. "I think he wants another gin and tonic," Jamie said to Leah, nodding her head at the other end of the bar.

"You've got to have some plans," Leah pressed.

Jamie started to feel her jaw make a chewing motion though there was nothing in her mouth. If she told Leah she had no plans, she might get invited somewhere. The last thing she wanted was to hang out with her ex's sister and have everything reported back to him. But luckily, she had the store, which opened every day, and she was going to ask to work Saturday. It had occurred to her that the old man's grandson would probably require rent, so she needed the hours.

"Nope, no plans. I might have to work Saturday. And I have the store."

"I thought you might say that. You're always working."

"Got to pay the bills," she said. "I'm going to go outside for a sec." It took a lot not to run outside. She had too much on her mind to have to worry about Leah, who was nice, but who obviously didn't see Jamie's point of view. Jamie did not want to hang out with her ex's sister. She thought that might be obvious, but, apparently, not to Leah. She dashed into the kitchen, where they were all laughing and calling each other "homos for keeping their asses open." Outside, she stuffed her hand into her pocket. She unwrapped the gum and threw it in her mouth without even looking at the wrapper. Banana. There was a crash behind the dumpster that startled her. She looked up, the gum popping rapidly against her teeth.

A raccoon scurried out from behind one of the dumpsters and disappeared behind the other. She relaxed. Raccoons were nothing to worry about.

She added more gum to her mouth. Cherry. Not a classic combination, but still good.

Did she have a problem, she wondered? Yes, she told herself. She had a problem. A gum problem. She shook her head. Had she ever heard anything as pathetic? An addiction to gum—gum breaks, gum gobbling. She'd always been a fan, but it wasn't until a few months after her mother died that (and so many little things could be traced back to that) she had allowed herself to just have as much as she pleased. It was soothing immediately not to limit herself, to just, in this one little thing, let herself be sincere, let herself chew as much as she wanted. And it was the chewing that she liked, even more than the flavor. She wanted to be able to blow all the gum, pop them all too. Not all gums were good for both things. But she could, with precision and care, make every gum blow or pop. It was a strange private little boast of hers. She knew that this was a distraction, but it was harmless, she told herself. Apart from the occasional but intense soreness she'd developed in her jaw and the spasms near her ears, there wasn't much downside to calming herself with oral gum gymnastics. It was better than drugs she told herself...or resulting to spanking her coworkers just to keep her head on straight.

By the time the bigger rush came in, Jamie had made sure everything ran like a well-oiled machine. She made the busboys hustle. Dirty plates did not linger, dishwashing kept up a steady supply of clean ones, nothing piled up, cutlery, glasses and ice were always in supply. She knew how every part of the bar worked and anticipated needs before anyone else did. She was good at this, managing systems, making them run better. But she couldn't seem to figure out the same thing with her shop. It had bothered her immensely that her customers were so few. But she had some sort of mental blockage. No practical

A STICKY SITUATION

marketing idea popped in her head. And if by some lucky circumstance, one was presented to her, she might feel an increase in ambition, she might even have thoughts begin to whisper encouragement, but all efforts would fail. Her mother's memory, her ideas, her spirit were so connected to the place that to give it up, to change it even, meant Jamie had to loosen her grasp on the memory of her mother.

But why was she running this weird little shop? It no longer made sense, not now that she was alone in it. It had been *their* project, not hers. It had even been mostly her mother's idea, orchestrated by her. It was a long story, but her mother had taken Jamie's academic interests in cultural representations of erotica throughout the globe and tried to monetize them for her. Jamie had strong suspicions that her mother was trying "to set her up in life." She often used that phrase to refer to the money she had won, a few hundred thousand dollars on a slot bet, which she had used mostly to travel. And, voila!, their interests aligned. Her mother would do the traveling and Jamie would tell her what pieces to get through video chat while she finished her last semester of school. They had done exactly that. Her mother traveling to thirty countries in sixty days. From there her mother explored the markets and, together, through Zoom, they curated the shop with the wares of artisans making erotica. It was a fun project and a wacky idea. Neither quality strange to her mother. Her mother always had zany ideas. Jamie had kept it running, this last dream of her mother, through sheer willpower. But now with her uncle no longer agreeing to travel and source her stock, Jamie wouldn't be able to keep happy the few customers she did have. And there was no way she was getting on a plane. After the incident, she hadn't gotten on a plane or a train or a bus. She hadn't even driven farther than ten miles out of the little rural city she lived in and then only to go to work in the bar, which was in the neighboring town.

She had a lease. And like Mrs. Piedmont had said, she couldn't just be forced out empty handed. So maybe she should just relax, let her shop close down and move on. She could do something totally different. The bar job was supporting her, not with a high-class lifestyle, but it was supporting her house and her bills. She could hold onto the bar job and think.

When the crowd in the bar started to die down, Jamie started to do some sidework for her coworkers. During the weekdays, she was basically a floater.

She helped with everything and more than justified her small hourly rate. It was on alternating Saturdays that she bartended and stayed the whole night. Tonight she'd go home a little before everyone else, but first she had to go speak with Dean because she wanted to make sure she worked Saturday night. If she was going to keep the store, she was going to need more money. But Saturdays were a competitive shift, so it was fifty-fifty whether he had room for her.

"Where have you been all night?" she asked as she entered *The Dean's Office*, as she had dubbed it. The name hadn't really caught on with anyone else but her.

Dean was lying on the dilapidated couch, a slit in the fabric spilling out stuffing near where his head lay. He seemed groggy, which was unusual for him. He was usually out getting in the way behind the bar or in the kitchen. He didn't answer.

"You feeling all right, Dean?"

Dean stirred again, sitting straight up. "Sorry," he said. "I was asleep."

"You know you sleep with your eyes open? I thought you were looking at me this whole time."

"Oh." He laughed. "I've been told that once or twice, yes. Don't come any closer," he said.

Jamie stopped near his feet.

"I might be coming down with something," he said. "I feel a little run down. But I'm glad you came in here. I wanted to talk to you. Let's go outside, get some fresh air. I don't want to be contagious." He got up with a big groan and went to his desk. He ducked behind it, looking in the drawers, then popped up, producing a mask. "Let's go," he said covering his mouth and nose.

They went out back and Dean stood by the dumpsters, while she stood against the wall.

"That's at least six feet," he said to her.

She nodded.

Lowering his mask, he sighed and pulled out a pack of cigarettes.

"Those are shaving years off your life."

"Yeah. You tell me every time."

"Sorry," she said, grinning. She pulled out some gum and started popping bubbles immediately.

"I would say the same thing about you with that gum," he said. "You're

A STICKY SITUATION

gonna rot your teeth."

"I wanted to ask you about Saturday," she said, ignoring the subject. "Think you could use me?"

"I could always use you," he said. "I already have someone behind the bar with me. So I could really use your help floating, if you want. I'd ask you to bartend, but Trent's already got alternating Saturdays with you and I can't just cut him out. He's reliable."

"No, I wouldn't want that," she said, turning suddenly to her left at the sound of something moving nearby. She stepped closer to the parking lot. "I saw a raccoon here earlier. Something is crawling around out there."

They both looked to the woods.

"I wanted to talk to you about your hours though." Dean pulled on the cigarette butt, the paper crinkling loudly as it burned. "I'm going to be helping my wife open a hair salon."

"Cynthia's going on her own?" Here Jamie perked up. Cynthia was a nice lady and if anyone deserved their own salon, it was her. Jamie pulled at her own hair and examined her ends. They were split, but she just hadn't had the time to get it taken care of.

"Yes. She's going to be over by the liquor store on Dalton. A good spot. Lots of eyes. But that means I'm going to have to help her at the desk. I won't be able to be here as much. So, I thought of you."

"What you want me to help her at the salon instead?"

"No," he said, inhaling smoke again. "Here. I need you here. If you want, as a manager?"

This surprised Jamie. "Manager?"

"Yes, you run the place. But, I'd have to teach you a whole lot about what I do here in the day before I even open. Purchasing and all that. You know some of it already."

She nodded. In the daytime... So she'd have to give up the shop. What a weird coincidence, she thought. In the same day she learned she might lose the shop, Dean asked her this. Maybe it was a sign. But no sooner had the thought appeared, when she felt a painful tug at her heart. Close the store... It suddenly felt more real, more immediate, more final. Could she say goodbye to her and her mother's venture?

He looked at her, searching her face for some response. He had asked her before about her store, how she had ended up running a place that was so unusual. She had told him some cursory details and he hadn't asked for more. But she knew that he knew this meant the end of *The Cuckoo Cl*ck*.

"I'll need to think about that," she said.

He nodded. "I thought you'd say that," he said. "Take a few weeks. Think about it. It comes with a significant pay increase, of course. But I just want you to know, you're the only person I trust to do this for me. There's no one else I think could handle it."

Jamie tried to smile but it came out awkwardly. There was too much on her mind for her to react solely out of happiness. There was some happiness at this news though, which also surprised her. She liked that she was so highly valued.

"I'll let you know soon," she said and they parted ways.

The day had been long, so she went home to shower and to think. There was so much she needed to think about.

Jamie went straight for the couch when she got home. The day had been exhausting. But that was better than being free and fretting all day, so she didn't complain. She was glad for the distraction of work. Work was her best friend now-a-days.

As she watched Pat Sajak simper on the screen next to a bored looking contestant, she reached beside her where she kept a bowl of gum. She began to chew. While the work had indeed helped her not to crumble, she now felt the worries press in. Chewing helped slightly.

But soon it wasn't enough, and she changed the channel to music and began to clean. It seemed her anxiety had not exhausted as she had, so she was now at its whim. She began with dusting and then started to sweep. The piles for the first floor were infinitesimal. Her house was already spotless, due to her regular cleaning schedule.

Through the Madonna track on her 80s playlist, she heard her cell phone chirp. She had a text.

It was Ben.

She had dodged Leah's invites all this evening so that she didn't have to encounter Ben. And here he was, defying her intentions. She stood grasping the

A STICKY SITUATION

broom and opened the message. It read: *I hope you're doing well.*

Why wouldn't she be well? She laughed at that. There were plenty of reasons. But then she figured maybe Ben had heard about the old man too. She wrote back despite her desire to just ignore the message. This was the first message from him in the months since they had broken up. What was he looking for?

She typed back, still balancing herself on her broom, the bristles splaying outward. When she noticed the bristles bending, she leaned the broom against a nearby wall. Her message read: *Doing OK. What's up?*

She sent it. Then she kicked herself mentally right after. Why, oh why, had she responded, "what's up?" That just invited more conversation, which she wanted less of, not more. But she had been polite, unsure how to respond to him. Now she set the phone down and dreaded his reply. What would come of this, she wondered.

She walked over to the TV, dazed, and watch the printed name of the artist and the track flash over the screen, always in a different corner. She didn't want to have to think about Ben now too, on top of everything else—the old man, the store, the bar, her mother…

I heard about your landlord. Just made me think of you.

Was he trying to console her? Did he worry about her business? No, he didn't worry about that. He had always wanted her to close the shop, she couldn't imagine that now he would encourage anything other than that outcome. So, what was he after? She didn't know and she didn't want to know. She went to the kitchen and got herself a glass of water, then she started to nibble on some crackers. Her stomach started to settle when she heard the chirp again.

I've been thinking about you a lot lately.

The feeling that followed reading the text confused her. On the one hand, she smiled, nostalgically, for the affection that had once been hers. She thought that if she just gave the word, he'd be over to console her right away. She imagined it, his arm around her shoulders and it gave her a warm feeling. But her stomach also sank as she thought of all the things he had said when he broke up with her because, on the other hand, he had hurt her and those memories, while no longer fresh, still ached. He had left her by herself when her mother died, more concerned, she thought, with controlling her life and her grief than with actually helping her through it. She had loved him for years. They'd dated since high school, but she had made a decision that she would not let anyone control her feelings, no matter how well intentioned.

    She did not fail to remind herself that she had *moved on*. He was a thing of the past, not something she should be spending much of her energy on. She thought about these things as she put away the crackers and started to search for some more gum. Near the door, on a buffet table, she found a piece of vanilla cream gum in a crystal dish. She wondered briefly what her mother might say if she knew there was gum in deposits all around the house. Meanwhile, Ben's voice crept into her head and she remembered him whispering "I love you" one night in his car after they kissed. She could feel his warmth, see his stubble, his eyes shining with the lone streetlamp's light. That had been the last time he had said that to her. It ached that she wouldn't hear the words again, that she had lost something that, at least then, she had considered precious. What did she consider it now? She wasn't sure, but she didn't want to encourage him any further or confuse him in anyway. She had moved forward, moved on, whatever one called it, she had done it. She typed back her message and then hit send.

    I'm OK. Thank you. Night.

    That was a clear boundary. *Night*. It said the conversation was over. The message acknowledged him and thanked him, but it didn't encourage. She supposed she had answered in the best way possible, but still she felt this discomfort in her stomach. She didn't want to hurt him and if he was reaching out then he was making himself vulnerable. Now she felt regret, wondering if she had hurt him with those five little words. But she shook her head clear. If he was expecting something from her, then he had gotten there on his own. He had certainly not gotten any encouragement from her. So, she tried to soothe herself with that thought. Any bad feelings were in his head, she told herself. They were not her doing.

CHAPTER FIVE

Luke stood at his window before the sun had yet come up, a dim lamp in the corner of the room. He was showered, groomed, dressed. Even his shoes were tied. He saw himself reflected in the glass. He looked away. Today really mattered. Pop-pop had always handled conversations with tenants, conversations that consisted mostly of Pop-pop listening. He would listen carefully to someone's story, let them cry it out, fret until they were relaxed. Then he'd make a judgment. More often than not he left the tenant's home with a payment plan in place and at least some money in his hands. One of the few things he said to Luke was that people should have a safe place to live, the landlord shouldn't be an enemy, the landlord is a public servant.

Luke had read very few books about business before he figured out that his Pop-pop was in the minority. For most people, being a landlord was simply business. Luke wanted to keep his grandfather's legacy. Today, he hoped that Ms. Jamie Parry, the tenant he was meeting this morning might want to partner with him in his venture. Rather than let the mall die, Luke wanted to revitalize it, bring in local cannabis vendors with their own farms as the draw. Dispensaries in the area were extremely popular, making tens of thousands easily in a weekend. But it was the traffic he coveted. If he could get people to go to the mall for weed, which was a sure thing, he could make it so that they had to at least pass the other stores before they left. Foot traffic—the lifeblood of any mall. It was a simple idea and, he thought, brilliant. Foolproof.

He just needed to make sure that his tenant didn't pose a problem...and that he kept his Pop-pop's legacy alive...

The question of how to accomplish this had kept him from sleeping most of the night. He woke every hour, recognizing that he'd been thinking through the problem in his dreams; though, when he examined them, they were a jumbled mess of anxious images.

His eyes ached. He was tired. But he stood there and watched the sun rise down the street. He had breakfast with his mother, who lectured him about how it would just be easier if he evicted the tenant. That way he could start construction the moment the cannabis dispensers said, "Yes." He evaded her as much as possible and ate his pancakes. He took it as a good omen that it was a pancake day. He and his mother agreed that after the meeting they would rendezvous back at the house to debrief and study for the next exam. When Luke left the house, his mother spun around the kitchen with tears in her eyes singing Patsy Cline's "I Fall to Pieces."

The drive to the mall in his beat up 2001 Honda Civic was full of potholes. It felt like a personal attack on his kidneys. A woman swerved in front of him at one point, making him hit his brakes, but nothing seemed to rattle him. He was calm and prepared. He was ready for success.

As he entered the mall, he wondered how his tenant attracted any customers. The lights in the main entrance were not on, and to get to her store he had to walk through an abandoned food court, across a tile floor that echoed the clack of his shoes. In his opinion, it was creepy.

He had been here to collect rents years before when the mall was still popular enough to warrant being open. But the mall had closed its last department store years before—excepting the Bullseye, which seemed immune to the problems of the *Shire Mall*—and, with that, the whole thing had shut its doors. Luke had not even realized that anyone was renting in the mall until a week ago, when Attorney Harris told him about the tenant. Apparently, she ran a store selling, according to Attorney Harris, "sex toys."

When his grandfather had gotten sick last month and the doctors gave him and Sheila such a fatal prognosis, Luke had proactively started to plan what he would do when he had the reins. He had been terrified. Terrified was not a strong enough word to describe the sense of existential doom he felt, knowing that the last responsible adult in his life would soon die. He resolved he would not even think about relying on his mother, and he didn't want to be caught unawares and make any mistakes he would regret. Although his Pop-pop would be dead, he couldn't shake the idea that somehow his grandfather would know if he made a mess of things.

A STICKY SITUATION

He could see a woman through the plate glass storefront. That must've been her, Ms. Parry. She looked younger than he had imagined. For some reason he had expected that this type of store would be run by an older woman, someone with too many cats and not enough friends.

He stood at the entrance of the store, giving everything a once-over. He looked over his head at the amulets clanging together. "Hello," he said.

"Hi," she smiled. "Welcome to *The Cuckoo Cl*ck*. I'm Jamie." She blew a small bubble and then popped it in her mouth.

"My name is Luke Garrett. I'm your landlord's grandson. Well, the landlord... now."

"Nice to meet you." She stood up then from her stool, but it was an almost imperceptible movement as she didn't gain any height by standing.

"You don't seem surprised to see me."

He was nervous. He hadn't expected her to be so beautiful—her gorgeous chestnut curls, her bright green eyes, her warm smile, those buckteeth that surprised and charmed him with butterflies in his belly. This had never happened to him before. He had had women answer the door naked when he was collecting rents and it had left him unfazed. When his grandfather was in the car waiting, there was no time or energy to think about anything besides the task at hand. It flashed in his mind, this spark of danger he hadn't anticipated: he was alone, with no one to report to, no one to please but himself. And the first time he went out on his own, he was what—smitten? What a complete idiot, he scolded himself internally as he stood at the door of the store trying to keep from showing any of these thoughts and feelings.

He took a step closer. Awkwardly. He seemed unsure if he was stepping into danger. The bubble Jamie was blowing popped.

"I was sorry to hear of the ol— of your grandfather," she said. "He was a kind man. I'll miss him."

Luke nodded and took another step closer.

"You can come in," she said.

He nodded and chuckled. He stepped to the other side of the counter. Jamie held out a hand in front of him. Then she opened it to reveal a few pieces of individually wrapped gum. "Have one," she said. "They always calm my nerves."

He took one and nodded. "Thanks," he said. He held onto the gum but didn't chew it. "I was hoping that you might help me learn more about your store."

When he stepped closer, he could smell her, that warm scent that settled in his belly like a burning brandy, something like berries and cream and fire. He felt silly and dazed and, oddly, hungry. That was one part of him, a primordial part of him. Another part thought, "Don't let her trick you with her considerable powers of attraction." He knew that was wrong. He knew that this feeling wasn't a trick on her part. It was just one of those things, one of those animal things. He hadn't experienced it before, but he recognized it from movies, from books. But he knew that he had to remain professional and that meant he couldn't act any differently than if she'd been anyone else. Bitterly, he thought that this might all be easier if she had been a gorgon. Then, at least, he wouldn't have to look at her and they'd both know why.

"I inherited this property," he continued explaining. "I know most of the tenants. But you are a surprise to me. I didn't know Pop-pop, uh—my grandfather had been renting this space out to anyone."

"Well, he was the best. He was always so nice to me and my mother. This was the ninth and last location we found. If it weren't for him, I wouldn't be here."

Luke couldn't help but look around the store again. He wasn't shocked to hear that no one else wanted to lease a space to them. The store was ill-conceived. That was obvious. An erotic art store in the Berkshires? The location was totally wrong. For one, her ideal clientele would be one that had large amounts of discretionary income and was open to being educated on the work; it was more of a gallery than a store. And this city had suffered too much economically to be home to more than a handful of people fitting that description. Add to those barriers of sale, the fact that the store was poorly decorated, had no music, had an unappealing and poorly strategized store design, bland lighting, and was in a dead mall, and you had a recipe for failure. It made sense that she couldn't pay her rent. He had noticed that his grandfather had forgiven her many months of rent. He had taken something unspecified in exchange each time; something from the store, Luke imagined. It seemed bizarre to him: Pop-pop walking out of the store with something phallic...

"Are you OK?" Jamie asked. Luke had spaced out a few moments, simply staring at her. "You looked like you went someplace else," she said mimicking a plane in flight. She reached into her pocket for gum.

A STICKY SITUATION

"Sorry. I am a little distracted," he said. "I didn't get much sleep last night."
Jamie made a pitying sound and then started to pop her gum softly.
She really loved gum, he thought. A little strange but not criminal. He realized suddenly that she probably thought he was in mourning over his grandfather. The idea made him both want to laugh and cry.
"So, what can I do for you?"
"I thought maybe you could give me a tour, tell me about your shop."
"Sure," she said. She smiled radiantly.
She took him to the shelves, which were arranged in broken concentric circles, reminiscent of Dante's circles. And, in the center of them all stood a four-foot red carving of an Incan, a huaco, with a phallus almost as large as its body. He glanced at it warily when she wasn't looking. She explained to him that she had organized the store by country. The shelves were also arranged particularly. The top shelves had minor trinkets. Ceramic salt and pepper shakers that were in the shape of a penis or a pair of breasts. Pencil sharpeners in the form of a butt. Shot glasses with drawings or photos of naked men and women revealed as one drinks, coffee mugs doing the same. It was surprising to him how similar these things were across cultures. All the countries represented seemed to have these sorts of items. They were a bit crude and obvious. The next shelves down, however, had items that were a little more artisanal. There were figurines—ceramic, wooden, stone—of naked young men and women, most of them, respectively, in the midst of athletic activity or in an angle of repose. Here were the huacos and typical goddess statues. Then, if the shelf was bare enough, there were prints of paintings, most of them beautiful, all of them explicit. And the bottom shelves all contained books, erotica in both literary and comic form.
As she explained all this to him, the history of the items, their origins, their purposes, she seemed to light up. Americans, she claimed, seemed mostly to create erotic art that was in response to over-developed senses of propriety and it was only done when it had some sense of purpose, mostly practical like sex toys. Peruvians seemed to make these figures, such as the huaco, out of both humor and respect for the process of life—a confrontation of both the absurdity and the comedy of sex. It seemed the whole world felt the need to express itself through erotica, and he'd never known. The longer she spoke, the more comfortable he felt in the store. "All art is symbolic for the buyer,"

she told him. "You make associations and art can only make you feel what is already inside of you, in your head and heart. The trick is to buy something that makes you feel a way that you like. If you buy the right piece you might have the chance to walk by something every day that resonates with you in a positive way. But you can't force it. The power is there or it's not." He wondered if there was something in this store for him.

She was a great advocate for her store and its vision. That surprised him. He had, frankly, expected her to be incompetent.

She did seem nervous too. She kept blowing bubbles and then popping them inside her mouth. He didn't mind the gum, but he did glance repeatedly at the four-foot huaco in the center of the room. It was obvious she had spent many years cultivating a nonchalance when it came to her work's subject.

"You seem really...passionate," he finally said. "How did you get interested in this stuff?"

This stuff, he thought. She'd probably heard that before. She probably figured he thought her store was pretty strange.

"I didn't mean—"

She waved it away and told him the story: that she had been undecided in her major and took an anthropology course centered around erotica of primitive peoples. It had interested her that, unlike what she had experienced growing up in the area, most people saw erotic art as an expression of life, and she found that commonality comforting, that most people had this one interest in common and expressed it in similar ways. But she kept any mention of her mother silent. That was a can of worms she didn't want to touch.

She finished the tour by showing him the tapestries she had acquired and hung on the backs of the shelves, large beautiful ones with saturated colors and images of sex acts and naked people.

He kept wondering how the store could open within his vision of the mall. It certainly couldn't in its current state. But he couldn't help but find her sincerity, her knowledge, her (possibly maladapted) courage in opening such a store in such a location, sexy. This woman was smart, she was funny, she made penis sculptures seem like the epitome of humanity's self-expression, but none of that had translated to sales, none of that made *The Cuckoo Cl*ck* viable...not to mention that name...it wasn't good.

A Sticky Situation

He had asked her the only human, non-technical question he could think of, like his mother had told him to. All that filled his mind were technical questions about her business, how much she grossed, who her customer was. But he could infer most of that for himself. What was important is that he stay on task and not react to her the way his Pop-pop had. Nothing was getting in the way of his goal. She was beautiful. But so was his vision for this mall. He turned around and looked out at the empty food court. It hurt him to see it this way, a place he'd been to as a child, a fixture of the area. Now it was a skeleton, some macabre reminder of how Pop-pop couldn't answer the challenge of the times. He was going to answer the challenge. Nothing was going to stand in his way. Nothing and no one.

He found a print of a copycat painting of *The Dream of the Fisherman's Wife*. "I see these prints would catch a hefty price. Do you sell a lot of these?" He suspected the answer was no.

"I do have a regular group of customers. One of them purchased one of these actually." She added fresh gum into her mouth.

"How often does that happen?"

"Well...once a month...maybe."

He doubted that. "Sell anything else in a month?"

"Yes."

Luke noticed her smile had faded. She was getting angry.

"What are you getting at?" she asked. She waited for his answer.

Luke was confused. How had his Pop-pop done this? Talking to tenants always seemed to go uneventfully for him. Luke had listened carefully, just like Pop-pop. He had listened to much more than he felt was necessary. Listening to her had been such a pleasure that Luke had lost sight more than once of why he was here. That couldn't be the problem. His Pop-pop had been decisive too. Pop-pop had made a decision and seemed to rule, like a judge. He was not forceful, but confident and quietly commanding. Could Luke do that? He could try.

"Your business model is pretty poor."

OK. That *was* judgment...

"Did you come here to grade me?"

"No. Sorry. I just mean that in order to be a viable store for the mall you'd need to make some changes." He hadn't even told her his plan for the mall yet.

That probably should've been one of the first things he did. She had no context for what he was saying. Maybe he should've practiced more with his mother, he thought.

"You mean this mall with no one else in it? Sorry I didn't know people were clamoring to lease your spaces."

"Technically you don't have a valid lease here," he said, looking around the store again. "I'm sorry that's not important. Just let me tell you my plans, so you understand. I think this mall—"

Luke stopped talking because Jamie had walked away. She disappeared behind the counter.

"Ms. Parry?" He stepped closer, wary of her behavior.

She popped out from behind the counter. "Got it," she said, waving around a packet of papers. "See this here?" she asked and smiled. She still looked beautiful, he thought. He couldn't stop noticing that, but she was no longer friendly. In fact, her voice seemed to get stronger, throatier. "This is a lease," she said and started to flip the pages roughly as she held them up in the air. "This," she said pointing to a page, "is the old man's signature. Zachariah Garrett. Tell me again about this technicality, young man."

Young man? He nodded softly. This was getting out of hand. Somehow, he had made her do a one-eighty. "Yes, you do have a lease."

"OK, so why are you here again?"

"I just meant that you haven't paid your rent on time. Technically you have broken the lease."

"Is that a threat?"

She disappeared behind the counter for a moment and then popped up again. This time she held a pack of smaller papers in her hand. "These are receipts," she said as she slammed them on the counter. "Each month I've been here is accounted for."

He took the opportunity to flip through them.

"See. That's your grandfather's signature. Isn't it?"

It was. Pop-pop had signed receipts for months that Luke knew, from his records, she hadn't paid. According to Pop-pop's signature, she had no debt to pay, and she hadn't defaulted on the lease. She was now popping her gum rapidly again. It sounded to him like fireworks, the kind that pop excitedly

A Sticky Situation

across the ground.

He had no idea what to say. This is what his mother had warned him about: he didn't want her to think that he didn't see her as a person, as opposed to a set of problems to correct. Not to mention she was terrifying him.

"I just meant that you don't make a lot of sales, your customer base is too small to support this store, you can't pay your rent, and I can help you change all that. We can work on your store and change it so it works."

She shook her head. When she spoke, she did so quietly, but she was so tense that the words came out with a tight, careful air.

"I have a lease for eight months. I will pay you your rent. You have no need to come back here without written notice. I think you should leave now."

"Ms. Parry," he started.

"No. You need to leave." She didn't care right now what his vision was. That was obvious. She started popping her gum rapidly.

"Ms. Parry, I just want to help you."

She turned away slightly and stared at a tapestry of a satyr surrounded by nymphs. Luke said something else, but she didn't seem to hear it. She just waited silently until he exited the store.

He crossed paths with the mailman at the door of the shop.

"Morning, Jamie," the man said, giving Luke a once-over.

Luke stood at the door and looked back. The mailman went straight for the gum.

"You have the craziest flavors," he told her. "I swear, once, I got one that tasted like earwax."

Luke left.

Jamie smiled at the mailman. When he left, she was still shaking. She felt like she couldn't read, but one of the letters had an official looking seal she hadn't seen before. She opened it. It was a summons. Luke Garrett, represented by Attorney Frederick R. Harris, was suing her, Jamie Parry. She had a bench trial in a week, where her eviction would be considered.

She blew a big bubble and held its shape. She startled slightly when it popped, the sound echoing through the store.

CHAPTER SIX

When he had decided on homeschool, Luke asked the principal if it were possible for him to continue to be part of the drama club. To his and his friend Ricky's excitement, the principal agreed.

Luke greeted his friends as he walked into the high school's auditorium. He had become an oddity, so they flocked to him to ask questions. What did he do with his time? Did he play video games? Did he skip class? What did he do for lunch? Almost no one knew about his grandfather's death, and Luke had told only Ricky about what it meant for him, all the responsibility of a large real estate portfolio. Ricky had been awed at the prospect of his best friend being some powerful real estate mogul.

At the moment, Ms. Debby, the drama teacher, had set he and Ricky up in a corner of the backstage with some cans of paint for one of the sets, which was the facade of a small country house. "Can't tell you again how happy I am you're still here. Florinda made the right choice letting you stay in drama club. She certainly did. You're my best painter," she said to Luke, who felt she might pinch his cheeks at any moment. "Anyway, paint the whole thing in this eggshell. We'll do the trim separately after. I just want it to have a very homey, wholesome feel, you know...," she continued. Meanwhile, behind her, Ricky played peek-a-boo with his Naruto backpack. Luke nodded at Ms. Debby, stone-faced, willing himself not to laugh. Then she left them alone to give instructions to others.

"How's life as a billionaire?" asked Ricky, beaming.

"I'm not a billionaire," Luke whispered as he looked over his shoulders for any stray listeners.

"Close enough, I bet." Ricky put his face inches from Luke's and stared intensely into his eyes while he whispered hoarsely. "Why won't you tell me how much money it is?"

A STICKY SITUATION

"There is no money," Luke said through gritted teeth. He pushed Ricky's face away. "It's just the properties."

"No money. Yeah. Right. Anyway: *properties*. That's plural. I did some investigating on a real estate app and it estimated what just one of those multi-family buildings is worth. Times that by two or more and you're a millionaire. I'm guessing you own more than two plus the mall, so, yeah, you're loaded now. You can't hide it from me, Lukey Poo. I'm your best friend in the whole stinking world. Ricky knows all things," he hissed.

"I don't want to talk about that part of it. It's not anywhere near as cool as you think it is. It's just pressure beating on your head like a hammer." Luke rolled his eyes. He didn't want to make his friend feel bad. And he did want to talk about it, but after the morning he'd had with Jamie, he couldn't imagine bringing up his failure without crying. And he wasn't going to do that, especially on stage within earshot of the rest of the drama club. In fact, he could hear another group of set designers working somewhere nearby, discussing whether Wendy's, McDonald's or Don's Burgers had the best fries in the area. Apparently, this particular McDonald's was a flop.

Luke changed the subject and Ricky let him.

"Asked that guy Devon out yet?"

Now Ricky looked nervously over his shoulders.

"Shush. No one needs to know about Devon. He's not even out."

"Oh, sorry," Luke said as he cut the brush along the edge of the trim.

"But no, I haven't said anything to him."

"Why? You're not getting any younger."

"Because I don't even know if he likes me yet. He just told me his secret. That's all. That doesn't mean he has to like me."

"I think you're full of it. What kind of person kisses someone they don't like? I mean, he did kiss you, didn't he?"

Ricky kept looking over his shoulder. "Yeah."

Luke laughed. "Sounds like you didn't like it."

"I liked it," said Ricky, suddenly focused on carefully brushing along with the wood grain. "I just don't want him to be confused. He's not even out yet. What if he only did it because I'm the only gay guy he knows and he just wants to experiment? Have you thought about that, Mr. Gigolo? I don't want to be some guy's first try. I want more than that."

Luke understood. He wanted his first time to matter too. He hadn't even kissed someone. He wanted to tell Ricky about Jamie. He was plenty confused. She had made him feel teeny-weeny and he had failed spectacularly at what he had intended with her, but he couldn't get her out of his head. She seemed to radiate in there like some golden bucktoothed idol.

Luke let Ricky tell him about the latest anime he was watching, one in which the protagonist had been summoned to a new world as one of the heroes who might save it, but he couldn't fight. Instead, his special power was instant inter-dimensional Amazon delivery.

Luke and Ricky painted the whole facade and moved on to help others. When they were done, they headed down to the gym. Luke had promised Ricky he'd be his workout buddy. There was no one else in there after drama club. They got out pretty late, the sun already set. They started with lightweight squats, warming themselves up. Ricky liked to pick up the two and half pound weights and spin them around, miming the discus throw.

"You're going to accidentally let go of one of those and break something."

"Not to worry," Ricky said. "I'm a professional."

Luke continued his warm-up, shaking his head. Now that they were alone, he could tell Ricky about Jamie. Luke told him about this morning's meeting, not only how he had tried to explain to her his vision for the mall and how she could be part of it, but also how he had failed spectacularly and been unceremoniously chucked from the store like trash. He also told him that his mother and lawyer wanted him to evict her as soon as possible.

"She can't get in the way of *Shire Mall 2.0*, brah. I don't care if she's pretty," said Ricky. Luke detected a slightly bitter tone. Ricky had told Luke that it was all over and done with, his feelings for Luke. Luke thought it best to let the moment pass without comment.

"She can't. If I had to, we'd strong arm her. Buy her out of her lease. If I had to. Not that I know where'd I get the money."

"I really don't get it," said Ricky as he spun around with his hands low to the ground. "Are you rich or not?"

Luke ignored the question. "The point is not to do that though. If I start off the way they want me to, I'll never be worthy of what my grandfather left me.

A STICKY SITUATION

I know he left it to me because I was his only hope. I want to know that I didn't waste this chance. I don't want to just win and be ruthless. I want to be like him and help people. I think he'd want that."

"I thought you guys weren't close."

Luke reset the bar and walked toward the little subterranean window letting in indirect light. He could see a small patch of sky. They weren't close, he and Pop-pop. But this wasn't about that. This was about rising to the challenges of life. His grandfather had had a lot of faults, Luke was sure, but one thing he did respect about Pop-pop was his integrity. His grandfather always allowed people some dignity in their honesty. Luke had learned at least that much from the man and he wanted that quality for himself. Though, this morning had been a pitiful showing.

"I mean. She was smart. Really smart. She knew like everything about sex art." He walked back to the bar. Ricky hadn't done his set.

"Sex art?"

"Cultural erotica, actually," Luke said as he started squatting.

"Ooh. Sounds hot."

"It kinda is. And it's more than that. It's art. It doesn't just turn you on in the usual way, man. It turns on like your chakras, every energetic portal into your body starts whirling awake. She's amazing. She made me want this stuff. She made me think I needed it to like energize or something, every day."

Ricky had stopped spinning his so-called discus. He was sitting on the floor now, looking intently at Luke and frowning.

"Did you say chakras? What the hell are you talking about?"

"Nothing, man, forget it." Luke reset the bar with a clang.

"No no." Ricky stood up now. "You said mana orbs were coming out of you. So now I just have to figure out: have you lost your mind or are you in love with this girl."

"What? No," Luke said and sat on a nearby bench, the fabric beneath hanging loosely behind his ankles. "She made me weak. I lost all sense of what I was supposed to be doing and got all robotic and pissed her the hell off. I don't know why. I just became an idiot."

"Yeah. You're in love with her."

"Stop saying I'm in love with her."

"OK. I won't say you're in love with her. Chill."

Luke could feel his shoulders were tense. Ricky started spinning again. Why had he gotten so angry just now? Luke took a deep breath and held it. He tried to slow down his breathing. He had a vivid flashback to Jamie calling him "young man," and it made him feel small.

But he considered what Ricky was saying. What if he were in love with her? How would that work? Could he still work with her? Could he evict her? If there's one thing he knew, it was that no one and no thing was standing in the way of his goal. So, yes, he could evict her, if she stood in the way of greater things. Yes, he could, and he would, he told himself. But first, he'd see what she'd do with a chance to save herself.

CHAPTER SEVEN

At the bar the next Friday night, Jamie couldn't walk from the kitchen door to the bar, she was forced to push her way through the crowd. Blondie played loudly over the speakers. Above the bar played various sports. She didn't even greet the bartenders. She just grabbed the rack of glasses and head back to the kitchen. Dean stopped her on the way with a hand against her shoulder. "I'm glad you're here," he said in her ear over the music and laughter. "I was going to ask you to bar-back. But I see you're on it."

In the hot kitchen, the music was also blasting Metallica. Jamie dropped the rack at the dish station and headed for the back door, reaching in her pockets for gum. Ephraim, the dishwasher, shouted through a cloud of steam, "que te pasa?" She turned around, hands still in her pockets. He was smiling at her. Ephraim was always kind to her and taught her Spanish. She bit back the rage and heartbreak. "It's just something with my store, but I can't talk now. It's so crazy hot in here," she shouted back. She turned around and pushed bodily into the back screen door. She could hear the dish rack crashing into the washer and sanitizer behind her. She pulled out two fistfuls of gum as she leaned against the wall, facing the dumpster. She brought both fists to her nose and sniffed. That calmed her, that moment of breathing, and she squatted down, her apron making a small table between her spread knees. She dropped the gum onto it and started to sift through the pile, picking the right one.

The screen door opened again and Ephraim came out. "You've got a serious problem," he said, crossing his arms.

"The only problem I have," she said without looking up, "is that I can't chew in there." She selected a piece and unwrapped it. She relished it, holding it above her upturned mouth like a cartoon cat finally eating a pet goldfish out of the bowl. Tamarind. The perfect amount of sour for a night like this.

"What is wrong with you?" Ephraim said and nudged her with his foot.

"Stop it. I'm fine."

"Ay nena, tu no estas bien."

She didn't understand that phrase and gave him a bewildered look. "Just eat your gum," he said and sat down next to her, with his back to the wall, his knees forming a triangle. They sat quietly for a few minutes. Jamie looked up at the stars. It was nice. Then he got up to check the rack and Jamie spit out her gum and went inside too.

She spent the whole night restocking the bar with heavy barrels of ice and cases of beer, clearing dishware and glasses from all the tables, spurring the busboys to work faster, sweeping up broken glass, pushing through the sweaty crowd and into the steamy kitchen, Metallica and back to the bar, and back to the tables, and back to the kitchen, back and forth and back again. She never said "hello" to anyone and worked silently, relentlessly with breaks here and there to chew gum. At one point, while she was filling the ice Leah said, "It's wild tonight in here. Look." Jamie looked up and looked at Leah. She was wearing a little tube top over tight jeans and she had glittered her lipstick. She was pointing out two very drunk men dancing together, one making the other twirl under his arm. But this didn't really reach Jamie. She gave a cursory smirk and took the barrels back to the kitchen where they were now blasting Megadeth.

Outside she chewed whichever flavor she picked at random. Sesame. It tasted like food, but it was elastic and let her grow big bubbles which she then sucked back into her mouth repeatedly like she was pulling taffy. She made it pop between her teeth a few times, loud like a gunshot from afar. She didn't understand. Luke had said he didn't want to evict her. He had said he wanted to work with her. But then why had he hired a lawyer to evict her? Had he come in to trick her?

If he had, it was a lousy trick.

She saw this boy coming from far far away. She had thought that he looked dangerous. And he definitely had a fang or two, but she didn't fear him. He simply made her angry. Angrier than she had remembered being for a long time. He had insulted her, her mother's work and dream, the shop Jamie and she had worked on together, the very one Jamie had spent a year running without support, the one that she loved and hated because it reminded her

A Sticky Situation

of her mother. Jamie knew this. She knew how her feelings were complex and that maybe something good could come of it. But she couldn't see how, and this thought was soon subsumed by the wave of anger crashing inside her. He had insulted her. He had challenged her. He had threatened her. He had made a grave mistake. She wasn't going down easy. She popped her gum so loudly that Ephraim came out to check what it was, all wide-eyed.

"You scared the hell out of me," he said blinking, and then he went back inside, shaking his head.

The next morning, she woke up a bit before the sun. She showered slowly, just letting the hot water soak her.

When she was done, wrapped in a towel and still dripping on to the bathroom rug, she heard the phone ring. It was early, so she assumed it was her Uncle Norman. "Good morning," she said.

"Hey, Jamie."

She knew who it was instantly. She reached for gum in her pockets, forgetting she wore a towel. "Ben," she said. "Oh, hi. I thought you were uncle Norm."

Ben chuckled softly. If anyone was a fan of her uncle, it was Ben. He laughed at everything the man said. "How's my Uncle Norm?" he asked.

It still bothered her that he said that. But it was petty, so she didn't address it. "He's happy as a banana. Going to Peru soon."

"Wow. He's still helping you."

"No, this is his last trip for me," she said.

"I'm sorry to hear that. Is that what has you so down?"

"How would you know if I'm down?"

"I can hear it in your voice."

She wanted to let it comfort her, his voice, his attention. It beckoned her like a warm bed she loathed to leave in the morning.

"Your sister has a big mouth. I'll make sure to tell her when I see her."

"She's just worried about you. That's all."

"And so are you, I guess."

"Is that surprising? I've held you while you slept."

Jamie swallowed. There was the call of that warm bed, the imprint of her own body waiting to envelop her again, but there was also something else, something familiar and a bit sticky—a tinge of guilt. "Your sister is a sweetheart. I'll just make sure to tell her not to gossip about me to her brother."

"How is everything?"

She gave in. Slightly. "My store..." She waited for him to say something to her about it, how she was wasting time on the store, how it was bleeding her dry, like he'd said when they broke up months before. But he didn't say anything to that effect and that relaxed her defenses a bit more. "The landlord died and his grandson wants to kick me out." Instantly she felt she'd spoken too much. "It'll be fine," she said, trying to close the flood gates.

"Well, let me help you. You know Todd is a lawyer. He could help you out. I'll ask him for you."

Todd, a lawyer. Those words together seemed laughable. She'd seen Todd perform many a keg stand and she had even tutored him in English, when he was a senior and she was a freshman. How he made it through law school she would never know. But he was wily and often talked himself out of trouble. Still, she wouldn't trust him with anything.

"Thanks, but I've got it covered," she said.

"OK," he told her. "Just know I'm still here for you. If you need me." His voice had this tremendously warm quality. It made her want to cry a bit, like it was pulling the tears out of her. A part of her begged her to invite him over and let him hold her in his muscular arms, but she no longer trusted that part of her. The two of them were good friends and after some time they might be again, but they definitely needed to grow apart, without each other's influence. She had too much to figure out, too much to work through to have to figure out a relationship as well. Not with him, not with anyone.

"Thank you, Ben," she said. "I do know that." She did. If she called, she knew he would answer. They had dated for years. In some ways, he felt like her best friend. But, as hard as it was, she resisted his comforts. She didn't want to go back. She needed all of herself to move forward, to overcome this obstacle that stood in her way.

They said goodbye.

A few days later, Jamie had the day off at the bar, so she called her friend Amanda when *The Cuckoo Cl*ck* closed. She just said "Drinking?" into the phone and

A STICKY SITUATION

hung up after she heard Amanda's "yes."

Her Uncle Norman came by to wish her luck in court the next day. "Hey," he said, "If the judge is hot, give him a little wink for me."

When she locked up for the night, she taped up a sign that read,

Closed for the day.
Back tomorrow
-The Cuckoo Cl*ck

Then she met Amanda at Jamie's house, where her friend picked her up. They went to Amanda's apartment.

It wasn't until her second sangria that Jamie finally told her friend what was going on. She sat on Amanda's pink velvet couch and told her about Luke and how he had threatened eviction. Jamie explained that Luke had tried to make it seem like he wanted to work with her, but then she got the notice he was suing her. "What a sneaky little thing," Amanda said with her mouth hanging open. "The nerve. And was he cute on top of it?"

This stumped Jamie for a moment. Sure, she had thought so at first. He had a mysterious, almost devilish look, but it had proved too close to being accurate. So, no, he was not cute on top of it. She told her friend so, while sucking hard on her straw.

"Well, you don't seem hot and bothered by him at all."

Jamie noted the sarcasm. She stood up and went into the kitchen. "I need another one," she said and Amanda followed her. "OK. Fine," Jamie said loudly so her friend could hear. "The outside of him is...interesting."

"Ooh. Interesting." Amanda laughed.

"Why are you trying to make this a sex thing?"

Amanda gasped and fake fainted against the wall. "A sex thing? Get your mind out of the gutter. I'm talking about love."

"Love? With that punk. Thinks he can kick me out of my own shop. When I have a lease. I'm not going anywhere. He's the enemy, Amanda."

"OK. I hear you. But you're so fiery and alive. I haven't seen you like this in a whole big while, so I'm just saying I like it. I miss this Jamie. Kick-ass Jamie."

Jamie couldn't help but feel a little bad about this. She had been trying her best all this time, ever since her mother died. She hated that her struggle was so obvious.

"Thanks," she said and took another sip.

"OK. I can see you're worried, but you have a lease, right? He can't just evict you for no reason."

"Well, he might have cause. He can say I didn't pay my rent...more than once. But, honestly, I can't talk about this anymore. It has me so angry. Can we change the subject?"

"That's no problem." Amanda held up a finger and hurried to the kitchen for her second refill too. Meanwhile, Jamie thought about court the next morning. She knew what she was going to say—the truth. And she hoped that it went in her favor, but there was not much else she could do. She couldn't afford a lawyer. She did, however, think she made a good argument for her lease being valid.

When Amanda came back, Jamie started on a new topic. "Anyway, get this. Ben called."

Amanda threw herself into the sofa and kicked her feet up. She yipped like a cowboy. "Yip yip," she said. "A horse always goes back to its rider." Jamie laughed at this too.

Amanda asked why they didn't work out again. "I always liked Ben. It helped," said Amanda, "that he was hot hot hot."

"Hotter than a turd on a shingle!"

Now it was Amanda's time to laugh. "That's not the saying!"

"I heard that from my uncle," Jamie confessed. "But no, you remember how he was after my mother died." They sipped more sangria.

Amanda nodded. She did remember. It was a confusing business. In Ben's desire to be there for Jamie in her time of need, he had overplayed his hand, demanding she spend less time at the store, which wasn't succeeding. He had made all the pertinent arguments. The place was being supported by her income from the bar for one thing, instead of supporting itself. After her mother died, Jamie would no longer travel, so the store was at the mercy of another. She spent all of her time there, alone, with almost no customers and he told her it made him sad to think of her like that—lonely and feeling abandoned.

Jamie reminded Amanda of all this and they talked mess about Ben for a while, moving onto a fourth sangria, and then the conversation ended up going back to Luke. Amanda had asked Jamie to describe him.

Jamie stood up and reached far above her head with her hand. "He's like this

A STICKY SITUATION

tall," she said, giving a little hop. "He's a broom."

"Ooooh. Yes already."

"Actually... well—he's not skinny but he's not big either. He looks kind of strong maybe. He was wearing long sleeves so I didn't get a good look at the arms.

"I can work with that. What else? Tell mama."

"OK. Mama," said Jamie crumpling back on the couch and sipping her drink. "He has all these scars on his face. Like from really bad acne. And it makes him look kind of rough, kind of wild. I might like it if he wasn't such a turd muffin." Amanda whooped. For a moment Jamie was having fun, but then the memory of him became too vivid and she was angry again. "You know what he said to me, 'Your business model is pretty poor.'" She tried to say it like him, like a man, and lowered her voice.

Amanda choked on this one. "What did you say to that?"

"I called him 'young man' and kicked him out."

Now they both doubled over laughing while holding their drinks up from spilling. It was eleven PM and Jamie decided it was time to head home. She did have court in the morning. But now she was not so nervous. She was too drunk to be nervous. Luckily an Uber was available at that time and it was not long before she had stripped, brushed her teeth, and fallen asleep in bed.

CHAPTER EIGHT

The same night that Jamie went to Amanda's, Luke was practicing for a meeting he had at the end of the week. His goal was to convince a local cannabis company to expand their business into production, using his mall as their exclusive site for a number of years. This would drive traffic to the mall, and after some clever diverting tactics, that traffic would return the mall to its former identity as a bustling marketplace.

Sheila was helping him. Her hair looked teased into a storm, with silver rays jutting out at unflattering angles. Today had been a drinking day for her, but she was still sharp.

He began his presentation for the twelfth time. "Gentleman, I believe you should expand your production—"

"No no no," she said. "No pussyfooting around, Luke. God damn it. We've gone through this already. No one cares what you believe. No one is going to sit through a presentation of you talking like a little mouse. You have to tell them what their problem is and how you're going to fix it. Be rough if you have to be. But be honest. And stop being timid."

"Gentleman!" he started again, speaking louder. "I want to help you—"

"You're doing this to piss me off, I think," Sheila said. She poured another shot of whiskey into her glass and used her finger to stir it. This she said tired, defeated. "No one gives a damn what you want, Luke. No one. Stop telling them your personal business. Tell them *their* personal business. Do you understand what I'm telling you?"

"Yes, Ma." They had been at it an hour by now and nothing he did pleased Sheila. He knew that if he showed a weakness, she'd catch it. And she caught a very many of them like gnats between her fingertips. But he didn't feel any more confident. His mother was right, yet the more she yelled at him, the less

A STICKY SITUATION

he seemed to be able to come up with creative solutions. "I need a break," he told her.

He got up, shoulders heavy, and started to leave the kitchen.

"I haven't dismissed you yet," she said.

"Ma, I'm done for the night. I'm not going to argue with you about this again."

She stared at him as she swirled her drink around in her hand. He could tell that she held back some ferocity. He wasn't getting anywhere with her, except for building a long list of "don'ts." So, he stared right back until she scowled at him and spat, "Go to your room. And if you fail, well that's on you and my father. I'm not going to worry about it any damn more."

He went to his room and threw himself on the bed.

His cellphone rang. Luke groaned. It was Attorney Harris. This day would just not end.

"Hello, Fred."

"Luke? This is Attorney Harris. I'm calling to let you know you've got to be in court at 10 tomorrow. Bench trial. Don't be late."

Luke sat up. "What? I have to go to trial? For what?"

"Be at the court before 10. I'll talk to you tomorrow."

"Wait. What is this about?"

"Your eviction matter."

"What eviction matter? Are you talking about Jamie Parry? I told you that I would handle that."

"Listen, kid. I have had a long day and I'm going to bed. I'll talk to you tomorrow." Attorney Harris hung up.

WHAT THE F#&*!!!!!!!!!!!!!!!

Luke's breath suddenly came fast and heavy. He could scream, but the last thing he wanted was to alert his mother. He breathed so hard it seemed he might rocket off his bed through the wall, until he got lightheaded and woozy, and his muscles relaxed, and, disoriented, he fell asleep.

Jamie had just finished brushing her teeth and sat in the chair by the window in her mother's room. She had a handful of gum and was chewing away vigorously while she watched one of her neighbors leave his front door back first. He was trying to close his dogs inside the house behind himself so he could head to work.

Jamie had imposed a rule: no gum at court. She knew herself and she knew that if she got nervous, she might blow a bubble right in front of the judge. She couldn't risk that. But she was so nervous. She hated that she had to go talk to a judge in front of whoever decided to waltz into court that day and discuss her private matters. She started a steady rhythm of blowing bubbles and then popping them in her mouth. She spit the gum into a tissue and tried a new one. This one was less elastic and she used it to make loud popping noises. It calmed her, this little ritual, and she did this for a while before getting dressed and drinking coffee.

When she left the house, her nerves were slightly less fried. Her stomach was grumbling with hunger, but she ignored it. She didn't want to add any more elements to the mix this morning. She'd eat after. In celebration. When she won.

She told herself that and it relaxed her a bit more.

At the court she didn't find parking along the whole street and needed to park a couple blocks away and walk. The morning air was chilly, but the sun was shining and warming the back side of her. She was glad for the little jacket she'd found in her mother's closet, which helped keep her warm too. It felt like a good luck charm, like she wasn't alone. She looked around for Luke, not wanting to bump into him unwittingly. But she was the only one on the street.

When she reached the entrance, the court officer at the door said, "Get in and keep in the heat. It's like Siberia out there." Jamie smiled at him weakly. He was clearly trying to be funny, but her anxious mood was unmovable. He told her to put her belongings in a bucket, which would then go through an X-ray machine. She nodded and put her wallet in the bin and, beside it, on the belt conveyor, an old briefcase she found in her basement.

As she looked through the metal detector, she saw Luke at the end of the hall. He saw her too. To her surprise she felt confusion rather than anger at the sight of him. Luke was pointing at her and a fat, squat, very red man with piercing blue eyes and a cheap tan suit scanned her up and down. The man pulled Luke down by the arm and talked rapidly into his ear. Then the man pulled Luke through a doorway to the right and out of sight. She felt less nervous when she couldn't see him.

"Come through," said the officer, who smiled at her. She walked through and nothing beeped. When she had her things, she asked where to go for a bench

A STICKY SITUATION

trial. "Go down the hall and turn left," he said. "Then go down to the end and check in at the clerk. After that wait in the courtroom."

"Thank you."

The ladies at the clerk's office directed her too. One of them was someone she went to high school with but never really spoke to. She looked directly at Jamie but did not react like she recognized her.

The courtroom was packed, and it was loud, voices echoing. The room was split in two. On one side the murmuring audience, on the other were the judge, a clear booth to the side containing a man in an orange jumpsuit, and before the judge a bunch of lawyers sitting on benches. One of them, in the center, loudly recited a litany of crimes. Jamie looked for an open seat and noticed Luke in the back corner, his lawyer red-faced and still whispering in his ear.

She found a seat near the front, squeezed between two large men. It was only 9:45. She waited, watching the lawyers move back and forth, entering and leaving the courtroom. Someone who looked like a cop, burly and bald, called out a name in a hoarse whisper, people passed her back and forth. The judge—Judge Barlow she heard someone call her—was stern and impatient this morning. She corrected the lawyers before her. Through her eyes, anyone could see they were slow and unprepared. Barlow snapped at one lawyer who tried to approach the bench. A court officer stepped forward. The lawyer apologized and stepped back, muttering to himself and making faces as he turned around. People behind Jamie whispered and some laughed quietly.

This woman would listen to her case. She was tough, but Jamie thought that she might listen to reason. Jamie would just tell things as they happened and tell why they happened and Barlow would either understand...or not. Jamie told herself that she had done nothing wrong. Barlow would see that. She would win this case. Jamie had a legal lease still. That's all that mattered in the end. She hoped. She wished she could be chewing gum right now. Instead, she dug her nails into the briefcase on her lap.

Her name was called by someone near Barlow. This was it. She stood up. Her face grew hot and suddenly seemed engorged. She stepped past the people in the front row, avoiding a nude foot in flip flops. Wasn't it too cold for that? A court officer directed her to a podium with a microphone. Everything—the officer's badge, the lights overhead, the microphone on the podium—suddenly seemed so bright. Her mind went blank and she felt lightheaded. Barlow caught her eye and nodded at her in acknowledgment. Jamie nodded back.

This close Jamie could see the judge's long curls. She was beautiful. Somehow that made her more terrifying.

Jamie breathed and the scene started to swirl into focus again. Jamie saw, out of the corner of her eye, diagonally to the right, the red-faced toad-like man stepping up to the other podium, Luke beside him. She tried not to look at them. It was strange, just last night she was so filled with anger she could fuel a jet engine. But now, she was intimidated, she was nervous. She wanted to cry. This courthouse was so big and all the voices echoed and everyone behind her was listening and would soon hear Luke accuse her of not paying her bills. Everyone would hear how she couldn't hack it on her own, how she fell apart without her mother. And they'd hear how weak she was because even a year later she still couldn't bear the thought of her dead mother and that made her an ineffective shop owner, a failure. She could feel the tears welling up behind her eyes, building pressure behind her nose.

She breathed...

Her mind cleared.

"Ma'am!" They had been trying to get her attention. "Oh, sorry," she replied, folding one hand over the other's cold fingertips. She nodded. "Your right hand please," said the clerk, raising his own sternly. His palm was pink. She raised her right hand. "Do you swear to tell the truth, the whole truth, and nothing but the truth?" She nodded again.

Barlow spoke, attorney Harris spoke. Jamie shook her head. She was having a hard time focusing. She took another deep breath and forced herself to listen to Luke's lawyer.

"...the property, your honor, is most likely going to be sold in a deal with the state's department of corrections. This has been in process since before Mr. Garrett's grandfather died. Even the other tenant, Bullseye Corp., is willing to make arrangements to leave the site. We just need assurances of the same from Ms. Parry. Mr. Garrett is only eighteen your honor. He is still in high school and has no experience running a real estate portfolio of this magnitude. He would not be an effective landlord for Ms. Parry and considering her inability to pay rent in January, February, March, April, May, September, and October of last

A STICKY SITUATION

year and February and March of this year, she would not be able to meet the conditions of tenancy. In the interest of making the transition a bit smoother, we would like to offer Ms. Parry ten thousand dollars for vacating the premises within the month after the termination of her lease."

Jamie had not expected this. Ten thousand dollars was more than a year's worth of her expenses, almost two, not including the store. She could work at the bar. She could be the manager there and live quite comfortably with this little nest egg. Also, Luke was eighteen. That was a surprise.

But what this lawyer was saying was not exactly true. He was making it sound like she was a deadbeat and that's not how things happened. Jamie glanced over at Luke and the lawyer was shushing him now.

Barlow looked at her. "What do you have to tell me, Ms. Parry?"

Unsure what to say, Jamie just opened her mouth and started speaking. "He's right that sometimes I couldn't pay the rent. But after my mother died and I had to run it by myself, sometimes I didn't sell enough. I would've closed then, a year ago, but Mr. Garrett, his grandfather, told me that he wouldn't hear of it. He told me to stay and that he would take some items from my store in exchange. Mostly it was gum. He was a big fan of my gum selection. I did not decide not to pay. I just couldn't. I paid when I could and he insisted that I stay until I could get the store selling more."

"Thank you," said the judge when Jamie stopped talking. "Do you have questions counselor?"

The red-faced attorney Harris turned to face Jamie. His eyes roved all over her, like he was homing in on a juicy fly. "Ms. Parry. Good morning."

Jamie nodded.

"Do you admit that you didn't pay rent for the nine months mentioned?"

She knew the answer to that. She sighed. This is what she had prepared for, this question. She steadied herself before speaking. "No. Mr. Garrett took things in exchange for rent and gave me a receipt each time. Technically, I paid my rent."

The lawyer sneered. Barlow looked at Jamie. She could feel the woman scrutinizing her too.

"Do you have these receipts?"

Jamie lifted her briefcase and put it on the podium, where it landed with a thump. She heard people whispering behind her. "Sorry," she said. "I have them here. I also showed them to Luke when he came to my store recently." She opened the briefcase. Barlow made a gesture to hand it over. Jamie looked to the security officer. "Here's the lease too and a card he wrote to me with his signature as samples."

Barlow nodded and lowered the glasses on her head. She held the documents up and scanned them in the air.

"Have you had a chance to see these, Mr. Garrett?"

Luke said, "Yes," and Jamie noticed the lawyer swing his hand into Luke's shoulder.

"It appears to me that the late Mr. Garrett considered the months in question paid in full."

"I have a few more questions, your honor," said the lawyer.

Barlow nodded and folded her hands over each other.

"Ms. Parry," said the lawyer and Jamie looked at him. "How would you characterize your relationship with Mr. Garrett?"

That was a weird question. "What do you mean? He was my landlord."

"Why would he forgive you debts so often?" Here the man's mouth spread wide into a shiny indecent smile.

He was trying to trick her to admit guilt. She breathed steadily. "Again. I don't have any debts."

The lawyer stared at her annoyed. "You do think it was unusual that he would take gum in exchange for rent?"

His questions were so tortuous she couldn't help but parse them out carefully and when she did, the questions proved to be rather simple traps. "That's a leading question if I ever heard one. I don't know if it's unusual. I don't tend to ask people if they can pay their rent. Seems pretty personal."

The lawyer was getting more and more worked up, a vein across his forehead growing turgid. "What did you do to convince Mr. Garrett that this was a fair exchange?"

"OK. Are you trying to imply something? You could just spit it out. I'll tell you if it's true or not." She felt much more in focus now. She had feared this guy a moment ago, but now she could see he was full of hot air.

The lawyer looked desperate now, blustering and red-faced. "You do admit

A STICKY SITUATION

you find it unusual that he'd take gum in exchange for rent."

"Attorney Harris. Asked and answered," said Barlow.

Luke spoke up then. "Your honor."

"Sir?"

Jamie could hear the lawyer whispering harshly, "Don't say anything."

Luke looked at the man and then turned to Barlow. "Your honor, I don't think attorney Harris is representing me accurately."

Attorney Harris whipped his fat head around at Luke. Jamie could see his hand clenching.

Barlow told them she'd address his concerns with representation in a moment and then asked Luke what his concerns were regarding the trial.

"Your honor. I do not want to evict my tenant, Ms. Parry," said Luke. He looked at Jamie. She caught his gaze. He looked sincere. "I told Attorney Harris this many times before, but he is convinced that he knows better than me what I should be doing with my inheritance. I have every intention of honoring Ms. Parry's lease or coming to some mutually beneficial arrangement. I never wanted her integrity questioned and I certainly don't want to use the court to remove her by force." And now he turned to Jamie and spoke to her directly, "I'm sorry about this confusion. But I really don't want to do anything to hurt you."

Barlow frowned. "Mr. Garrett, you will address me, not Ms. Parry. I won't have any crosstalk in my court."

"Yes, your honor," said Luke. He crossed his hands behind his back.

This is what he had said at the store. But she hadn't listened to him. She had let herself get angry and then wouldn't listen to reason. She'd always been a bit of a hot head when she felt she wasn't listened to, but lately it had come out of her with everyone, even Amanda and Uncle Norman. Maybe she had been wrong about him. She looked over at him and remembered what he said to her. *Your business model is pretty poor.* It made the fury light up inside her again. But she tried to respond differently now. She would have to at least listen to him, especially after what he was saying. It was the reasonable thing to do and also the furthest from what she wanted to do, so she knew it had a high probability of being the right course of action.

Barlow asked both Luke and Jamie if they could come to some agreement on their own? They both nodded. She told them she was sure they could find a solution and dismissed them from the court room. She then spoke up to attorney Harris.

"Attorney Harris, I don't like these types of miscommunications in my courtroom. I'd like you to confer with your client outside of here and get on the same page, especially before you come back into a courtroom. Could you agree to that, both of you?"

"Yes, your honor," they both said.

With that Jamie stepped out of the courtroom and quickly made her way outside of the courthouse and into the sunshine. She was at a small plaza and found a bench. The sun was beating down and warming her so much her jacket was beginning to be too hot.

She took some more breaths. She had done it. It was a great surprise to her that she had been so nervous this morning. More than once she had felt faint. She had expected that she would be angry at the sight of Luke but was surprised how overwhelming her nerves had been that she felt no anger. She'd have to talk to him again and settle all this mess, but at least she couldn't be pushed around anymore. What was his strategy that day they met anyway? To piss her off? It didn't make sense really. Every time she thought of him, she heard him saying, *Your business model is pretty poor.* And, poof!, she was pissed off. What the hell was the guy's deal? Was he like some arrogant boy genius or something? Too smart to function like a decent human being? But now the judge was involved, maybe they could reach some accord now.

Just then she saw Luke exiting the courthouse with his lawyer right behind him. They were arguing. She could hear the lawyer's voice from here. Luke stopped talking and then he started walking her way. The lawyer walked away in a huff another way. Were she and Luke going to talk now? She didn't want to do that now. What if she simply started walking? Yes, she got up and started walking over by the other courthouse, towards the library. Soon she'd be out of sight. "Ms. Parry!"

She was caught. She turned around. "Yes," she said rather gruffly. She felt herself frown despite her best efforts to seem nonchalant. She really didn't want to do this now. A few more moments of peace after a morning like this were not too much to ask. At least, that's how it should've been. But it wasn't. She waited to see how he'd start this.

A STICKY SITUATION

"I meant what I said in there. I'm not trying to get rid of you." He waited a moment for her to respond. She swallowed. She was stumped. He looked into her eyes and seemed satisfied with what he found there because he started talking again. "I have a plan for the mall and I thought maybe you could be a part of it. There'd be more traffic, more money to be made. Can we just meet up to talk about it and I can explain? It doesn't have to be now. I bet you want to go home and rest. Especially after a morning like this."

He was saying all the right things, except for one. Go home and rest? On her fainting couch, surely. This guy had no idea who he was talking to. Still, it was a complete reversal of the first time they met. Whether he intended to or not, he'd been an ass that first meeting, but they might be able to work out something now, especially if he was going to approach her in this way.

"Give me your number," she said. Luke chuckled nervously. He was nervous. That was a good sign in her book.

She told him to expect a call in the next few days about where and when to meet. He nodded. She examined his scars a little more closely, but only for a moment. Their texture was so intricate, they almost looked like embroidery. She walked away scowling. She couldn't help it. He bugged her.

In her car, she let out a moan. It was 10:20. That whole ordeal had taken only about thirty minutes. She couldn't believe it. It was over. She had won. She would keep her mother's store.

So she'd say no to Dean about the bar?

She wasn't sure. She had figured, rather naively she now noted, that the court's decision would answer her greater question of what to do next. It was a question of destiny and she knew that the courts didn't have opinions there. But it surprised her just how much she could make herself forget or believe in order to make sense of things.

She went to the store and met a customer, who was looking for a gift to give her father-in-law for his retirement party. She bought a Palad khik from Thailand. Jamie had explained that it was an amulet that was incantated over to call forth deities and their powers. But that it didn't have to be, it could simply function as a powerful symbol of fertility. It was common in Thailand and even hung over the doors of shops like here at *The Cuckoo Cl*ck* for luck. The customer giggled as she left the store. There were times like this when she really loved the store. She liked teaching people.

Also, this was her first sale since Mrs. Piedmont's specially ordered print. Jamie was feeling much better than she had at court. She didn't know what would come of her talk with Luke or what exactly he wanted, but if he thought they might be able to work things out, she had some hope too that they could. She looked around at her store. It made her heart hurt. She saw her mother everywhere. Could she say goodbye to this place? It wasn't doing well financially and sometimes she had the thought that she should let the place go. But these thoughts lived beneath the surface. Right now, she wanted to make the store work more than she wanted to let it go. She didn't want her mother's idea to die. It deserved at least one good attempt, she thought.

CHAPTER NINE

Ricky and Luke jogged around the school's track after drama club. Sitting on the bleachers were a group of girls talking and laughing. Ricky looked out of the corner of his eye when they whooped the second time. It was a group of sophomores and he just tried to ignore it and kept jogging.

"Do you think I'll be in shape by summer?"

"I think if you're gonna get close this is the way to do it."

"What a pageant answer," Ricky said bitterly.

"Exercising this much is going to pay off. Then you can get the quarterback of the football team."

"Not too loud," whispered Ricky as they passed the group of girls again. This time the girls sniffed the air and giggled as they passed.

"You're back in the closet?"

"No, but I don't need everyone knowing I have a crush on the quartersnack."

"Everyone wants a bite of him. Not to worry. Even I see the appeal." Luke poked at Ricky's belly and then sprinted away.

"Hey! Hey! That's not fair," said Ricky running after Luke. "Don't run so fast!"

When they were done, they were both covered in sweat. They threw themselves to the lawn surrounding the track, Luke removing his shirt. He was pale still and his skin shone bright white in the sunlight like the underside of a fish.

"You're blinding me."

"I can't help it if I'm not Puerto Rican and my skin doesn't look like coffee splashed with milk."

"That's right. Even Edward didn't choose to be a pale one."

"My lot in life," he said rubbing his torso dry with his shirt.

It occurred to Luke that Ricky might be watching him and wondered if he should put his shirt back on, but he couldn't quite see the harm. If Ricky took a peek, no one would combust. The running had made the skin against his abs even tighter. His mind whispered that he looked pretty good. He wondered if Jamie might think so. But the thought was fleeting and highly unusual, it didn't stay, as swiftly as it came it went.

He told Ricky about the court and how awfully it had gone.

"Did you fire that guy? He deserves it."

"No, it's not that easy."

"What's hard? He went behind your back and tried to force you to do what he wanted. He sounds like a bully."

"But I don't know what I'm doing when it comes to the details. I don't want to make a mistake and sign away my whole inheritance.

"Dude, that's not how that works. You'd notice if you were selling it all. One, it'd be obvious. Two, you're not a complete idiot."

"I don't want to mess this up."

"Who you need to worry about too is that girl. Cuckoo girl. She's a problem."

"You know everyone keeps saying that, but for some reason I just don't think she is. She's a sweet person."

"Where are you getting sweet from? As far as I can tell she's done nothing but kick you out of her store and terrify you."

"I'm not terrified."

"Every man stands in awe of the you-know-what. Even us gay guys owe our lives to it."

"I'm more worried about my first business meeting tomorrow."

Luke told Ricky all about the cannabis company he was going to approach the next morning and talk to about expanding at the Shire Mall. He went over the whole plan for the mall again and, also, over his fears that he won't be listened to because he's so young. But Ricky reminded Luke that he is officially a man and that they all better watch out because he's coming for them. Luke nodded, his nerves telling him that Ricky was a liar.

That night, he avoided his mother by slipping by her as she was passed out on her recliner. He went to sleep, but it was disturbed. He found himself waking up in the middle of struggling to answer difficult questions. But each time he shook his head and went back to sleep.

In the morning, his mother was quiet, which was not a good sign. Luke went

A STICKY SITUATION

downstairs warily, but he didn't see her. He snuck down so quietly, he must've passed her while she was still in bed, and neither noticed. He slipped out the front door with his backpack, happy to avoid her in such a dangerous mood.

Luke stood outside the cannabis dispensary, trying not to puke. He had decided to wear the blue suit that he'd bought for his grandfather's funeral. He had no other suits. But he swapped the shirt and tie underneath for a clay red sweater. He decided that he didn't want to seem too stuffy with his shoes on, so he wore a pair of navy-striped brown leather sneakers he'd found at a yard sale last summer.

The sign on the front door read,

> Ring bell
> Show ID

He was only eighteen, would he even be able to get through the door to make his pitch? They hadn't warned him about this in the email.

He rang the bell and showed his ID. "I'm Luke Garrett, I'm here for a meeting with the owners." He waited what felt like an eternity for the buzzer to sound, but it never did. Instead, someone came out. A bald man with a Ramones hoodie came out of the door and smiled. "Sorry, man. I can't let you in through this door. It's the law because you're too young. Could you go out back? That's the only door you can come in. I'd take you, but I can't leave my post, man. Someone will meet you there."

Luke nodded. He went around the building where there were vans parked alongside. The building was an enormous rectangle and he had to walk almost a quarter mile to reach the back of it. It would've been nice if they'd sent an escort. But Luke tried not to take it personally. In fact, there was so much about this interaction that he had no concept for. It was all new to him and what made that nerve wracking most of all was that he wouldn't be able to read social cues. He'd had trouble doing that with everyone, except with Ricky. For the most part, they were straight forward with each other, so there wasn't much guessing to do. But what would he do here? They might be able to insult him to his face without him even knowing it. Were there games to be played, a hazing to expect? He knew he was in the professional world, but these were still people and they were men. But it was a different field entirely, how much would carry over? For instance, now, was this a slight, that he hadn't been led to the back door? Or would it have been insulting with an escort, as if he needed to be guided delicately like a child? He decided that these questions were good ones, but he couldn't possibly answer them. Only the people he was meeting could and he certainly was not going to ask them about it. He knew that much. So, he'd have to just play the game without knowing the rules. He did have his mother's advice. So he wasn't going in empty-handed. While she presented it poorly, her advice made lots of sense. He needed to make sure that he let them know why they needed him and not the other way around. That was a powerful weapon right there.

He finally reached the end and turned to see how far he'd come. The sun was beating on his head, but as he turned the corner, the shade cooled him. There was a security door just a few yards away. It opened as he neared it and a voice said, "Hello."

Luke reached the door and stepped on the other side of it. A man of medium height and build was standing behind. He had on a sports jacket with a t-shirt underneath. Instantly, Luke felt himself relax. For two reasons. One, the t-shirt. Two, even though the man was two steps above ground, he and Luke met at eye level. He had dreamt all night that the man he'd meet would be as tall as him. He wasn't used to that and every time he imagined it, he sensed his confidence diminish. He knew how to be a tall person among not so tall, he knew the jokes that would be made, the questions that might get asked, the way it so easily allowed for icebreaking. But now there was nothing to worry about. This was an auspicious start.

Luke smiled and introduced himself. It turned out the man was not the owner but the manager. His name was Tisdale, Daniel, but he like to be called Dan. He also had a habit of rubbing the edge of his front teeth with the pad of his right index finger whenever he stopped talking, not every time but often. Dan brought him through a small hallway lined with shelves filled high with boxes of little plastic containers for selling weed. So the owner, Alex Gibbons, might be a tall man after all.

They went through another security door. Here the weed was kept in buckets that were jerry rigged with tubes to automatically control for humidity. He could hear whooshing noises coming from about seven of them as the flowers inside them cured in their little nests. Dan told him that they had set up this curing station recently when the farm space had become overcrowded. He had done his

A STICKY SITUATION

research. They cured about five pounds in each bucket. They had fifteen. With a three-week curing schedule, that meant they were selling enough to support ninety pounds every three weeks. Taking into account tier pricing, they made, thirty-three thousand dollars a week. Luke had estimated just that amount. He was extremely proud of himself for guessing so well.

Now that he saw the operation for himself, he thought he could definitely convince them to expand at his mall. They benefited from avoiding a huge initial investment, instead they could simply improve the infrastructure of their space at the mall. And the space was unlimited. Even with them and a host of stores at the mall, more than half of the place would remain vacant. It had huge growth potential. But Shire Roots was just one piece of the puzzle. He planned on convincing two other small places running a small grow to join as well. They would be in direct competition these three places, but the mall could support that easily and their expansion into farming would ultimately lower their costs. The competition among the three of them would be part of the appeal, to see how they tried to outdo each other with the best bud. Almost instantly the three dispensaries and farms would be competing with the top dispensaries in the area. And he would lease the space to them for thirty years. That was the other perk—they didn't have to worry about moving for a very long time. That's if he could get Alex to listen. Luke hoped against hope that the man wasn't tall. If he was tall, all bets were off.

They peeked into a room where weed was being weighed carefully and put in containers. There was also someone filling joints by hand. People smiled and talked excitedly when Dan told them Luke was here to discuss a new site at the *Shire Mall*. If they were any indication of his reception by the owner, things were going to continue going well.

In one room they produced resins and concentrates. Their operation was small and cramped. Luke imagined these machines multiplied at the mall, a whole factory of weed. His plan included expansion as a supplier to other dispensaries. He had already spoken to a few within a 50-mile radius who would be interested in locally grown cannabis and were at least willing to try the weed and visit the facilities when they were finished.

The tour was fantastic, but he was getting antsy. "Dan, when will I meet Mr. Gibbons?"

Dan chuckled.

"We're headed to Alex's office right now," he said. They walked to the end of another hall. The office there was a small windowless space the size of a small galley kitchen. Tiny and cramped with filing cabinets. Luke guessed those drawers couldn't be opened while someone sat at the desk.

At the desk was a small woman with dark blonde hair tied into a long ponytail. She was wearing a t-shirt with a blue wave print on it and jeans. She looked up, "Hi, you Luke?" She stood up and scratched her cheekbone with the side of her hand. "You the one who wrote me that email?"

Luke nodded. So, Alex was a woman and he had called her Mr. Gibbons. No wonder Dan had chuckled.

"Well, you're a bright kid. I had to meet you either way." She stuck her hand out to shake his. He grasped her hand. She had a firm handshake.

Luke felt himself get hot and red-faced. She had made him feel proud and embarrassed at the same time somehow.

"I like your operation," Luke said. "It's got a lot of potential for growth. And just guessing at your sales numbers, I can tell that you can handle an expansion no problem. I'm willing to bet you're actually under-supplied every month, and you could grow more if only you had the space."

She looked behind Luke and smiled. Luke turned and looked at Dan who was smiling too and nodding his head. "Just hold your horses there, Luke. I want to hear all you have to say, but first let's go somewhere more comfortable." They walked out of the office and he followed her into a small room off the dispensary. He could see through a slim window in the door that people were lining up outside to make their purchases. "They can't see in here by the way," she said. Luke nodded. "OK," she told him. "Shoot."

He grabbed a folder out of his backpack. He showed her some papers. He listened to his mother and didn't start with what he believed he could offer. Instead, he asked her how she felt about expansion. It turned out his instincts were right. She needed to expand both at the dispensary and the farm. Demand was outpacing supply and the only thing that kept them going was supply from other growers. The estimates he'd made at building were correct and he pointed out that if they improved the site at the mall, they could start their grow operation for a fraction of the cost of building. She was easy to engage in

A STICKY SITUATION

conversation and he was able to show her how she could grow at the mall. She listened to him and asked questions. They were difficult ones concerning what would happen if one of the dispensaries totally outperformed the others. The possibility existed. He could promise that he would provide space for expansion, but he could not make promises about consumer spending habits. He expected the three business would grow together—a rising tide lifts all boats. He explained that he would have auxiliary draws: glass shops and smoking clubs and food that catered to working families. It would be a one-stop shop all driven by the industry that already existed.

"I've already spoken to the dispensaries in the tri-state area. They are more than happy to buy supply. As you know, there's a shortage in the area. The three of you could expand beyond your own stores. And if you worked together, you could even start a brand together, or a special line. The possibilities are good."

"Who else are you planning to approach?"

He told her the other two dispensaries he had meetings with. She whistled.

"You are just hitting up all my friends. You know I think this could work. Hold on. Let me give them a call."

Luke almost jumped out of his skin. He had set up meetings with them already, but maybe he could close this deal in one day.

Alex called one of the other owners, "Todd," she said, "it's Alex." She made him hold for a three-way call. Luke assumed they must be very good friends because they both waited patiently to be connected. "I've got this brilliant kid with me. Luke. He's telling me a plan for the *Shire Mall*. You have to listen to this. Go on, Luke. Tell them your plan."

Luke told them how he had the idea of saving the mall by driving traffic with dispensaries and farms. He told them about how they could expand and what leasing perks he offered. At the end, Alex excused herself and picked up the receiver. They had a conversation in front of him. "That's what I thought," said Alex. "Yes, absolutely. I know I'm needing it."

When they were done, Alex sat back in her chair and pushed the conference button. She whistled again. "You sure do have a big brain in that head of yours. How old are you again?"

"I'm eighteen," he said. The other callers seemed impressed too. They were all interested in doing business once he explained his plan, but one of the owners,

Todd, had raised a question. "What about Jamie," said Alex.

For the second time, Luke felt he might jump out of his skin. How did they know about Jamie?

"Jamie is a really smart person and I think her shop could be perfect for the new vibe for the mall. She and I will be coming to an arrangement that works for both of us. I'm looking forward to working with her."

They seemed appeased, pleased even. But before they wrote contracts, they needed assurances that he was capable of what he claimed and needed a development plan ready within the month and concrete news about the arrangement with Jamie. Luke assured them that he would be ready within the month with all they asked.

After he stepped outside through the back door, he hurried around the corner to the long wall on the side of the building. He jumped up and yipped. He jumped in place over and over, punching the air. He mouthed a scream. He had done it! He had made the whole arrangement in one meeting. There was just one obstacle. Jamie Parry. But she was open to talking now.

He imagined her again.

Those soft curls falling around her face…

Those sparkling green eyes…

He shook his head. Now more than ever he needed to master his feelings. Their first conversation had gone totally off the rails that first time because he'd lost his head. He wouldn't do that again. His plan for the *Shire Mall* was in the balance, he had only one month to figure it all out, and nothing could get in his way, especially not some pretty bucktoothed girl.

CHAPTER TEN

The bar wasn't crowded the night after court, but there was some sort of convention in town because an ever-increasing group hollered whenever new patrons came in. They all seemed to know each other and all wore green t-shirts with a stylized yellow hornet on the front, the caption reading, John Quincy for the win.

The boys in the kitchen were in prime form, spanking each other so hard you could hear their yowls in the front of the house. Jamie head back there now, just as the door swung open and the group hollered again.

"Boys!" She said into the kitchen, her voice piercing through the din of play. "Apart from how unsanitary it is for you all to be touching each other's butts while you handle food, no one wants to hear you yelling 'homo' like a bunch of middle-schoolers. At least I don't want the customers hearing it shouted before your silly snickering. So why don't you all go wash your hands and find a game that doesn't require slapping or slurs? Don't give me that look, Robert. Or are you telling me you've reached the full capacity of your creativity?"

The cooks looked at her, blinking. One raised his hand.

"Yes, Robert."

"It's Rob actually. That's all I wanted to say. Sorry. Thanks."

"OK, Rob. Why don't you help the other boys find a more appropriate game to play tonight?" She said this in a calm voice.

The cooks all looked at each other and then nodded their heads together.

"Good," Jamie said and left the kitchen.

Leah was on too. Since Jamie was on a roll, she decided to approach the topic that had been on her mind tonight. She was careful to make sure she kept herself calm and collected. "Leah," she said, when they had a quiet moment and Leah was dusting a shelf. "I got a call from your brother the other day."

"Oh? That's good. You guys are talking again."

"Actually, he wanted to talk to me because you'd told him that maybe I looked like I needed someone to talk to."

"Oh. That."

"Yeah. Do me a favor. Please don't tell your brother stuff about me. I need a bit more privacy than that. And I don't want to have to worry that you're going to talk to him about me."

Leah looked shocked, hurt, and apologetic all at the same time. "I'm sorry. You're right. I will be careful not to say things to him about you."

"Thanks so much. Thanks for listening to me."

Jamie figured that had stung a little, but, overall, the conversation about boundaries had gone over well. She was glad to put it behind her because she didn't have much energy to give it. She had a whole bar to wait on and bus and a phone call to make. She had decided that she would meet Luke at Lucky Pat's. There were always tons of people there, so at least if it went bad she could avoid a scene. Or create a better one, she joked to herself.

She went out to the front of the bar where the reception was best. Luke answered after one ring.

"I knew you'd call."

She wasn't sure what to think of that. Other than it seemed a bit silly, but still she smiled despite herself. "I told you I would," she said. "No guesswork involved."

"And I trusted and believed you. I have good judgment."

Jamie popped some gum into her mouth. She chewed it up before answering. "Are you trying to banter with me right now?"

"Yes. I think I'm doing well."

She paused again and he laughed nervously.

"We're not at a bantering stage. This is business."

"You're absolutely, right. And you're very serious."

"Yes, I am serious." She popped her gum.

"Yes. You are. Is that gum you're chewing, seriously, no doubt?"

"OK. I'm hanging up now. Meet me at Lucky Pat's at 6:30 tomorrow."

"You've got it."

She hung up. That was oddly chipper of him, she thought. She felt a bit heady.

A STICKY SITUATION

The blood had risen to her head and she could feel that she was red in the cheeks.

Jamie walked in through the doors of Lucky Pat's at six thirty sharp.

"I'm meeting someone," she said to the hostess.

The hostess made a face, an oh-lucky-you face. A sincere one. Pathetic, Jamie thought.

"He's over here," said the hostess and walked off to the back of the restaurant. Jamie followed to a three-quarter booth in the corner. Jamie was certain the employees must call this table the kissing booth or something. It had a small opening to enter and was shaped like one of the seats on a spinning tea-cup ride at Six Flags. She felt like he might turn the table at any second and spin the whole booth right round. Could they have sat them at a more awkward table?

"Hi," he said, trying to jump up then but banging a knee painfully on the table. "Ouch!" He laughed. "Come sit down, please," he said smiling excitedly.

She caught the annoyed look the hostess was giving her and thought *ok, sheesh, I'll sit.*

Jamie maneuvered her way into the booth and Luke sat along with her. He smelled like pine trees, like pine trees warmed up in a pie, warm spicy pine trees.

Jamie frowned. He smelled sexy. Why the hell did he smell sexy to her? He was eighteen for god's sake and, so far, fifty percent jerkwad.

The hostess wished them a good time and then gazed at Luke as she walked away. He did look cute, she guessed. But he wasn't exactly drool worthy. Jamie rolled her eyes.

"I asked them for a quiet corner," he said and shrugged.

The nearest couple was three tables away. The bar was behind a wall and so they were truly in a quiet corner. Even the music seemed faint here.

"She liked you," Jamie said.

Luke laughed. "No."

"She couldn't keep her eyes off of you."

"Let's talk about your shop," he said.

"Shy, huh?"

"I wanted to tell you my plan. It would really work for your store, I think."

"OK, what is it?"

He explained to her that he had three cannabis dispensaries with different business models to form a sort of consortium at the *Shire Mall*. They would compete, but it wouldn't be direct. They each had different specialties. Then he would make sure that traffic was funneled out through an array of stores, one of which could be *The Cuckoo Cl*ck*, if she wanted it to be.

"That is a clever plan."

"That's what people have been telling me," said Luke, grinning.

"Don't let it go to your head."

"I won't," he said sincerely. "I just want it all to work out."

She could tell that he was excited. That touched her, to see him so sincere, so innocently proud. But she wasn't quite sure she wanted him sticking his nose in her business. He had already caused havoc. Did she really have tolerance for more?

"We just need to change your business model a bit. So that you can be ready for all the traffic you're going to get."

"Change my business model? I don't trust you."

"You don't know me yet."

"You've taken me to court. That tells me a lot."

"I'm sorry. My lawyer jumped the gun. He seems to be taking all of this personally, but trust me, I gave him a piece of my mind. We never should've been in court. I wanted to talk to you and help you, not threaten you. All I want is for your store to be ready for the big time. Things could be different for you."

"Let's pretend these aren't veiled threats for a moment. When will all this happen?"

Then the waitress arrived with a plate of curly fries.

"I hope you like these," he said.

But Jamie had already reached for them. She nodded and grinned through her mouth full of potato.

"Veiled threats? There are no threats."

"So? When?"

"When what?"

"When does all this need to happen by?

"We need to get out of the way of the contractor in a month," he thought back to the owners of the dispensaries. He had promised them he'd handle this

A Sticky Situation

situation by then. "The plans are being drawn up now. That means we have a whole month to test some changes at your store and see how it goes."

"We? Meaning you? I don't think that's a good idea. Look, I thought maybe I could hear you out, but I'm not really looking for a partner in my shop." Even as she said this her heart ached for her mother. She definitely did want her original partner back, but she wasn't ready for a new one.

"Don't think of me that way. More of a consultant. Let's just brainstorm some ideas. I can help you implement them. I really want a thriving mall and the more good stores I have, the better."

Luke reached out to grab some fries, but Jamie swatted his hand away. "No, no," she said. "Tell me more about the other good stores you have."

He told her that he had approached a few glass stores and a few of his grandfather's old tenants. He had some bites among them. As far as the fries, though, they were almost done, Jamie's fingers and lips covered in salt.

"Can I just come by and brainstorm with you? That's all I ask."

The waitress asked them how everything was.

"Delicious," said Jamie and started to get up. "I think he's ready for the check," she said.

"Where are you going?" asked Luke.

"Time for me to go. Thanks for the fries," she said. "Let's meet tomorrow at my store. Nine? You can brainstorm with me."

Luke nodded, unsure what to say.

"Next time get them with the chili and cheese," she said and walked out.

Uncle Norman lived in a storybook cottage by the side of the road in Holyoke. It was a squat house on the edge of a ravine, the house built with large river stones and surrounded by maples and pines. The little round windows always had candles burning in them and as the day darkened, the cottage appeared almost magical. Deer often treaded nearby in their search for young brush and a couple times she had seen an owl or two hiding in the branches. She knocked on the arch wooden door and listened for the pitter patter of her uncle's feet.

"Mercy, back. Back," she heard him say and then the door opened, the aroma of something sweet and spiced wafted out. "My favorite niece! What a lovely surprise."

"I'm your only niece," she said entering the house straight into his warm embrace. The warmth of his hug and the house instantly relaxed her. Her defenses faltered under the influence of exhaustion and kindness. She could feel the tears creep up again as Mercy, the calico, wove among their feet.

"Come in, Jamie. Let me close out the cold."

She heard the door close heavily and she removed her sneakers. As she stepped from the landing into the sitting room she was overcome with the house's comforts. A roaring fire played its shadows against the golden wood beams and the silver blue mason work of the walls. A gigantic and tasseled oriental rug with an unusually high pile covered the floor and the furnishings were green velvet and leather with wool throws and fluffy pillows. She jumped onto the couch and stretched out. Uncle Norman grabbed a throw and covered her with it and she snuggled against a soft suede throw pillow, Mercy jumping up silently onto the arm of the couch and then up to its back to curl up.

She heard her uncle fumbling with something in the kitchen as she luxuriated, letting the fire and the soft purring of Mercy melt away as much tension as it could. By the time he returned with a tray, set it on the stone coffee table, and settled himself into an armchair, her eyelids had grown heavy. "Oh, dear," she heard her uncle say and then she fell asleep.

When she next opened her eyes, her uncle was shaking her awake.

"Dear. Dear. Wake. It's a nightmare."

Mercy hissed and jumped off the couch as Jamie sat up, wondering where she was.

"What is it? What has got you so upset?"

"That obvious?"

"Well, you were thrashing about and when you came in looking mopey, I knew something was wrong, yes."

Jamie brought her feet up to the sofa and hugged her knees. She didn't know how to start. But she started talking, letting out her fears. She explained about Luke and his veiled threats, about his stupid cheeks, and his unearned power. But the problem hadn't started there. Not really. The problem was with her business, she knew. Its lack of customers. The mall's lack of traffic. Location location location. Her location was a bust. Maybe it was not even the mall itself, she realized, but the small rural city where she lived. Barely 80,000 people live

A STICKY SITUATION

in it and much of them struggled to survive the past two decades since the local plant shut down. There were businesses that thrived in the area, but they all had something in common that her little shop lacked. Value, necessity. No one wanted what she had to offer, no one respected it. She was a laughingstock. Even at the bar, where she picked up some shifts a week, they confused her interest in erotica with an interest in prostitution. She had to set more than one man straight on the subject. So where to start, what to do? She could blame Luke, her uncle told her, but that wouldn't fix anything.

"My little niece. I hate to see you so lost."

Jamie sniffled as Mercy hopped up on the opposite end of the sofa and glared at her. The sweet smell had intensified and she smelled cinnamon.

"Well, my dear, resurrecting a failing business can be a challenge, but it's not impossible. Just like in matters of the heart, it takes time, effort, and a little bit of luck. You must take a deep breath and assess the situation with an objective eye."

Heart? Who had said anything about the heart, she thought?

"Start by identifying what has gone wrong and take responsibility for it. Have a heart-to-heart with yourself and get to the root of the problem. You need to make some changes, whether it's revamping your marketing strategy or considering new products, new services, or even a new target market. But most of all, be patient and be kind. Business like matters of the heart require faith and a positive outlook."

The heart again? "Why do you keep talking about the heart and feeling?"

"Well, the way you described the young man. With such vivid detail. You told me all about his face. I just assumed he sparked interest."

"Interest. You're joking. He's a foul little cretin with too big a piece of the pie." Luke had something up his sleeve, she thought, something he wasn't saying. It was just a matter of time before she figured it out.

Her uncle smiled warmly and, to her fury, with a knowing wink. "Speaking of pie," he said, standing up. "I've made your favorite. Blueberry and apple cinnamon."

This news made her soften. "Thank you, Uncle Norman," she said as he walked into the kitchen.

What a ridiculous notion—that she would like Luke. First of all, he was eighteen and still in high school. There was no planet where she would even look his way with anything other than mild curiosity for his strange way of being. That awkward directness of his... Her uncle was losing his marbles.

But all these thoughts melted away easily when Uncle Norman returned with a large slice of warm pie, a giant glob of whip cream melting on top. Mmmm, heaven. Heaven was blueberries and cinnamon. She thought. Uncle Norman, and Luke, were right about one thing, though. Her shop. She was going to have to revamp. Recreate. Reinvent.

"Now, shall we talk about Peru?"

"You won't give up on this will you?"

"Absolutely not. I can't travel and bring you things for your shop forever. I'm old and I'm tired. And you're young, you should see the world and have adventures."

"But the planes."

"Yes, the planes. They don't often fall out of the sky."

"Uncle Norman! Don't say 'planes' and 'fall out of the sky' in the same sentence."

Uncle Norman laughed heartily. "You'll have to face your fears soon enough," he said. "But excuse me, I didn't mean...But yes, small steps. First, the shop."

"Yes," Jamie said. "First the shop." She could feel the flipping in her stomach stop as she thought of her shop, on the ground, nowhere near a plane.

CHAPTER ELEVEN

After that day she'd gone to court, she had had only one customer. Since then, it had been quiet on the store front. But that didn't interrupt her morning ritual. She dusted, carefully, every single object in the store, every shelf, the edge of every book, the shaft of countless huacos and salt and pepper shakers. This was how she'd gotten through the death of her mother, by painting a steady stream of mindless labor. She did well at the bar for the same reason—she could focus on tasks, on not stopping, on not thinking. This had also created her troubles. Not thinking did nothing to soothe her pains because she hadn't made any real moves toward a future and that made her feel stuck. She was in the same house, at the same store, doing the same thing, watching everything crumble around her. Her uncle had forced her to face it by refusing to go source her wares. If the old man hadn't died, she wondered, would she have already given up this store? Would she have said yes to Dean and currently be managing the bar? She wasn't sure. If the old man hadn't died, if Luke hadn't pissed her off, if she hadn't felt attacked, would she have even spent any energy in saving *The Cuckoo Cl*ck*?

Anger had woken her up. She was grateful for it. The last time life had thrown huge change at her, she had just stood there. Those changes had subsumed her. But not this time. If she gave up the store, it would be on her terms. Not Luke's, not the old man's, not Dean's, not the courts', not her uncle's or anyone else's.

Luke would arrive any moment. She popped her gum in her mouth, feeling the bubbles burst rapidly against her tongue. She finished dusting and went to retrieve the broom to sweep next.

Now she thought about a strange encounter she'd had earlier this morning. It started yesterday when Jamie bumped into her Uncle Norman in the parking lot. He was all aflutter with preparing documents for his district manager and squealed maniacally when he saw her. "Honey," he said. "Would you believe they're still drowning me in paperwork? Heathens. But now that I have you here: I called my friend Gregory after what you told me the other night because he went through something similar to you. It's not that uncommon really that people have trouble running a shop. He told me that he had some advice for you if you'd stop by his place in the morning. He could help you, dear. Go see him tomorrow. That's an order—in case you weren't sure."

Gregory ran the store beside the museum. He sold souvenirs based on the museum's collection. Luckily, he opened at eight, so she would still be able to open her shop in time.

Jamie stepped into the store nervously, peeking her head around the door. There was no one around. "Hello," she called out softly.

"Oh, hello. I'm back here," a voice came from the back of the shop.

Everywhere she looked were prints of the local museum's collection, replicas of the artwork, fancy frames, jewelry, and reproduction furniture. She stepped through to the back and approached the older shop owner who greeted her with a warm smile. He finished clamping together a large frame.

"Pass me that hammer, would you?"

Jamie found an array of hammers on a nearby table. "Uh—"

"The big one."

She handed him the hammer and he went to work, the sound hammering Jamie's ear.

"So, Jamie, my girl! What's got you looking so glum?" the older man asked over the banging.

Jamie figured it didn't make sense to be coy. "I'm just struggling to keep my shop afloat," she replied.

"I'm sorry. What? Can't hear you over the banging."

"My shop is struggling," she said again, louder this time.

The older shop owner nodded knowingly. "Ah, yes," he shouted. "Running a business can be tough. But let me tell you a little secret, my friend. The key to success is to never give up."

Jamie looked at the older man. Was he joking? She reached into her pockets for gum, but she'd left it in the car. She asked, "Really? That's it?"

Gregory chuckled as he put down the hammer and then lifted the frame to examine his work. "No, of course not, my girl. That's just the beginning.

A STICKY SITUATION

You need to be creative, innovative, and always think one step ahead of the competition. Let me give you an example."

Gregory walked over to a dusty corner and pulled out a large, antique hat. "Now, this hat has been sitting here for months. No one has shown any interest in it. But watch this." He put on the hat and walked around the shop, striking dramatic poses and reciting Shakespearean soliloquies.

Jamie couldn't help but laugh. "What are you doing?"

"I'm creating an experience, my girl. I'm making this hat come alive. And now, watch this." He took off the hat and put a price tag on it that was twice the original price. "Now, that hat is no longer just a forgotten dust collector. It's a one-of-a-kind, theatrical piece that people will want to buy. As long as I give a performance that is."

Jamie looked at the sad hat, amazed that he was serious. "Brilliant," she said.

The older shop owner nodded. "It's all about presentation, my girl. You need to find ways to make your products stand out and give people a reason to buy them."

Jamie nodded.

"I can see you're not convinced."

Jamie smiled as politely as she could. "I've never thought of myself as theatrical. I'm not sure I can do that."

Gregory looked at her a moment, long enough to make Jamie feel uncomfortable.

"What is it?" she asked.

He went back to hammering. Jamie was unsure what to say next. She looked around the back of the shop and saw many large prints. She sifted through them carefully and discovered a print of Peter Paul Rubens's "Leda and the Swan." She stared at it intently, not even noticing that Gregory had finished hammering again and was looking over her shoulder.

"Do you think he pecked her with the beak?"

Jamie busted out laughing. "Of course," she said, "the question is, 'what did he peck first?'" They giggled together. "It really is a beautiful piece." Gregory nodded. "Did you know," Jamie asked, "Rubens started painting at fourteen? At fourteen I was just learning to ride a bicycle."

They both chuckled. "That's what I'm talking about. Character. Add a little character to your presentation." Jamie turned to face Gregory, who had a look of care on his face. "Look, your shop is all about human sexuality, one of the messiest parts of human life. You can't be shy. Sex draws them in. But only you can explain to them the significance of the work. Make them believe that the work you sell is not a novelty."

"OK," Jamie said, but she really was just thinking about rushing out to the car to get some gum. Her patience was wearing thin. "I think I get it."

Gregory gave her a look of suspicion.

"I do. I do. I need to find a way to engage with people. Or have them engage with my shop."

"Yes! Theater! Bring them a bit of theater. I'm telling you. They won't forget it and they'll want to buy something for your efforts. Here's another secret. And if you tell anyone I said this I'll deny it to my grave. The customer often has no idea what she wants. You have to tell her. You are the commodity."

She had left the store thinking that the man was obviously a whacko, but he had gotten her thinking. Now as she swept, she thought about what it could mean for her to be the commodity. How could she sell herself?

Just then she heard the penis amulets banging against each other as her door opened.

Luke.

She turned to see him smiling nervously. He was so tall it almost looked ridiculous to her. It didn't help that he seemed to hunch whenever he was nervous.

"Hello," he said and waved a bag around over his head. "I brought donuts," he said.

"They better be frosted," Jamie muttered.

"Um...glazed?"

Jamie walked over and snatched the bag out of his hand. His eyes widened. She took the bag over to the counter. Inside were two donuts, a cruller and a bear claw and a handful of napkins. She took a napkin and spit out her gum. "What are you having?" she asked.

Luke looked confused. She bit into the cruller, moaning at its tenderness. She hadn't eaten breakfast. Of the sundry tasks she set herself, breakfast often wasn't one.

A STICKY SITUATION

"No, of course," he said. "You have that. I had pancakes this morning."

She put the cruller back in the bag and then bit the bear claw. "Thank you," she said.

"No problem. Seems like you need it more than me." Luke walked over to the shelves and picked out a book to look through. "So, what would you like to change about the store," he asked without looking at her. He was trying—and failing—to be nonchalant. She supposed this was better than unabashedly abrupt and overly frank.

She still wasn't sure what he had to offer her. It felt patronizing the way he was trying to help her. Had he ever run a business? What authority did he have? She felt herself getting angry. A repeat of last time is something she wanted to avoid, however, so she decided that instead she should just ask him about what she was thinking. She took a deep breath.

"Have you ever run a business?" she asked the back of his head.

"No," he said as he flipped through pages.

"Then why do you think you can help me?"

"I've read a lot of books about it," he said.

Books weren't enough to tell him what she'd gone through. Books wouldn't explain that she'd lost her mother, that this shop was their last connection, and, yet, that the shop was a burden, that she didn't know if this was something she wanted or if it was something she grieved over—an altar. It ticked her off that he thought he could come in here and just change things without considering the delicate complexes that constructed them.

"I don't think books can explain what this store means to me, just the way it is."

Luke turned around and looked at her. "Ms. Parry..." He paused. "What they can tell me is how to run a business. And they also tell me a lot about your business and how you run it based on certain factors."

Arrogant. "What do you know about my store, you're a high school student?" She took a deep breath. That was hardly a good argument, she thought. She wouldn't let anger get the best of her again. She took another deep breath.

"I don't want to offend you again."

"Don't worry," she said and grabbed the bag of donuts again. "I'll munch on this—" she pulled out the bitten bear claw "—and you talk. I promise. While

I'm eating this bear claw, you'll be completely safe from my wrath."

Luke chuckled. "OK," he said incredulously, but he didn't hold back. "I know that your store struggles to make even one or two sales a month. The people who buy from you are a small dedicated pool, but they're not numerous enough to support your overhead. You were able to cover rent in June, July, November, and December. So, I figure you must make a few more sales in the summer and during the holidays, but it's still not enough to pay your overhead costs for more than a month. I know that your store lacks visual appeal. You can get away with that when the product is extremely cheap and a staple. But a store like this with expensive and unusual stock could only do well if it appealed to the appropriate demographic: middle-aged people with money. That crowd visits from New York, but they stay in south county and have enough antique stores down there to keep them busy. Besides that, they only respond to sophisticated, cool, and pretentious packaging, something your store lacks. You're selling a product no one in the area needs or wants, you charge way too much, and you are in a terrible location. In order to save your store, you need to sell something people want, move somewhere better, and charge more appropriately. Luckily, I can help you with the 'somewhere better.' This mall will be bustling once again. But in order for your store to really shine in it, you'll have to rethink the store, possibly completely."

Jamie watched him a while, long enough for him to start to nervously hunch and mindlessly chew at the inside of his cheek. "You're right," she told him. She put the half-eaten bear claw in the bag and then put the bag onto the counter. She stood up. "Come here," she said.

He closed the book he was skimming onto his finger to mark the page and he walked over to the other side of the counter. She looked into his dark eyes and at the lines and divots in his face. It surprised her still that his rugged complexion gave him not only a sense of danger, but also of vulnerability. His expression was nervous and curious, but it seemed to betray implacability. Something soft about him, she thought. It seemed funny to her how often that word seemed to apply to people who were unquestionably intelligent.

"What do you suggest we do first?"

Luke's eyes lit up like a kid's being offered a huge cone of cotton candy. "First we run some tests. Focus on a small selection of items to sell. We hang the

A STICKY SITUATION

tapestries so people can see them. And we arrange it more like a gallery. Then we see what people respond to most."

"Why fewer items? Doesn't that just mean we have fewer chances to entice people?"

"If you curate the items, they look more significant. Also, people often need to be told what to look at and what to want. They want to make sure they make good choices, especially when those choices have a learning curve like art does. If there are a million options, at best, they'll just be confused and buy nothing. At worst, they'll decide that what you have to sell doesn't have value."

"How are you so sure about that?"

"It's just marketing."

"They teach marketing in high school now?"

"I'm allowed to read extracurricularly."

Jamie nodded. "Yes, you are," she said. He was smart and, possibly, nice. So, they'd do what he said. But who would they test it on, she wondered? "We can invite people for a party, like an opening? And I can talk about the art."

"Yeah, that's a great idea!" Luke sounded excited.

"Hmm, I could write up little cards to explain the art when I'm not around." She was starting to feel excited now too.

"Yes, now you're cooking with gas."

"That's a really old expression."

"My mother says that all the time," he said and smiled.

Jamie thought of a problem. "Where do I put all the stuff that's not out on the floor?"

Luke grinned. His eyes sparkled. "Luckily," he said, "you know the landlord of this joint." He pulled out a large set of keys and jangled them. "We can just put it all in the space next door."

They spent the next hours trying to choose what they'd sell. Jamie had a hard time choosing between sculptures made in the Greek style or those made in Thailand. "Well, if you pick these," he said picking up a sculpture of a young muscular man reclining over a rock, "You get three options. If you pick the Thai ones you only get one." The Roman statues were in two other poses. Eventually she chose the Romans and they carried over the sculptures they hadn't chosen to the empty Hot Topic space next door. They tried carrying the shelves, but they were too heavy, so they made moving pads out of paper towels and slid the empty shelves out of the shop.

At one point it looked like Luke was afraid to touch some Palad khik, the large penis amulets. "They don't squirt," she said. "You can grab them." Luke reached out slowly. When his hand was almost around one of the magical shafts, Jamie yelled, "Boo," and made Luke practically jump out of his skin. "They're made of wood, Luke. Relax."

"I know," he said and tucked a bunch of them into the crook of his arm and took them next door. Jamie laughed as she watched him.

When they had narrowed down their choices to the ten objects, they started to hang the tapestries. "Good thing you had all these tools in the back," Luke said walking out of the storage closet with a toolbox in one hand and a long ladder in the other. "These are really beautiful," he said, stretching out one of the tapestries. "How are we going to hang these without making holes in them?"

"They have little heavy-duty laundry clamps next door," she said, referring to the Bullseye store. There had been no customers and while Jamie loathed to close early, she locked up the store with a sign promising to be right back in twenty minutes. They went together next door and ended up in the toy aisle. "I loved these when I was a kid," he said, pointing at an erector set. "You were born to be a little real estate mogul," said Jamie kidding him. She noticed he turned red, but this didn't make her want to tease him further. He seemed too self-conscious for there to be much joy in making fun. "C'mon," she said, tapping the back of his shoulder, "let's go find the clamps."

In the aisle with the clamps Luke disappeared, leaving her alone. When she walked to the end of the aisle, she found him wrapped in a shower curtain, clamped at the waist and the neck. "Don't I look great?" he asked. Jamie checked around for onlookers, but she couldn't help but laugh. "You look stunning, girl!" "There's a reason men don't wear dresses..." he said, camping it up, batting his eyelashes. "You ladies don't need this competition."

"When you're right, you're right," she told him.

Back at *The Cuckoo Cl*ck* they began to hang laundry lines and then the tapestries. Almost instantly the store started to look richer and more interesting, gone were the beige walls under the ugly green fluorescents. Now rich

A STICKY SITUATION

colors marked the walls, scenes of nudity and passion. Luke took a moment to absorb the power of that one wall they covered. He stood akimbo, nodding. "We did a good job," he said. "This laundry clip idea really worked."

They covered the rest of the walls and then set up the ten objects they'd chosen to sell along the walls, so that the center of the room was open. When they were done, the place certainly had visual appeal. Due to the tapestries, it seemed like the walls themselves were moving, men and women expressing their most sexual natures. His favorite was a Rubenesque figure reclined on a bed, a sheet covering his genitalia. The figure was a man, languid and beautiful. Luke didn't think he'd ever looked that comfortable and relaxed. He wondered if he could do it too, relax in his bed like that, without a care in the world, soaking in the pools of sunlight seeping past the opening of a velvet curtain.

"That your favorite?" Jamie asked, breathing heavily after placing a bunch of sculptures on a shelf. She pointed at the Rubenesque man. "That was made by some lady in Santa Fe. I told her I loved her work on Instagram and she just sent me this to sell for her. Sadly, I've had it for a year and no biters."

"Someone will see it and want him now," he said.

"Poor guy, probably feels pretty rejected so far."

"He's strong. He'll be just fine," Luke said.

They both admired their work, both nodding. Throughout the day, Jamie had had moments of noticing the surreal when she would look at Luke, surprised by the fact that they had gone from fighting in court to working together. It felt good to work on the store together, after so long alone. She felt happy and excited.

Unfortunately, Jamie didn't have the night off from the bar, so she had little time to prepare for the opening. So Jamie decided it must be put on the following night. She went through a list of things she still needed to do: make flyers, choose music, get food and drinks. She asked, "Should we serve wine?" Luke nodded. "You won't be able to have any," she said.

Luke stuck his tongue out at her. They both laughed.

"I've been here a lot longer than I thought I would," he said to her. "I should go. I have to study and do some homework."

"I really can't believe you're still in high school."

"Well, homeschool."

"Your liar lied about everything. Sheesh."

"Liar?"

"Sorry your *lawyer*."

Luke nodded. "Yeah. I'm not sure what to do about him. I know I need some help and he's a shark, but I'm not sure I trust him."

They said goodbye. In an awkward moment, he seemed to go in for a hug, but Jamie extended her hand. "Thank you," she said, "for all your help." He nodded and smiled and then left.

Jamie watched him disappear through the mall's large entry hall to the front door. She looked around her store and admired their work. She hoped this taught her something about what to do. She refilled the gum bins next to her register. Then she closed up the shop and went home to design flyers before her shift at the bar.

CHAPTER TWELVE

When she'd woken up from her nap, all she wanted to do was lie back down again. But she supposed she should get her night started, so she got up and started to fill the tub with hot water. She went over to the mirror and found a clip on the hand towel. She used it to put up her hair. She wasn't washing it tonight and she didn't want to get it wet.

It burned her cold feet when she set them in the water, but she gritted her teeth through the discomfort and soon had settled her body into the warm tub. She lay there, water to her shoulders, and thought about her store and Luke. She fumbled through her phone, playing a game mindlessly against her bent knee popping out of the water.

He had been so helpful the day before. It was nice of him. He was, in fact, it turned out, much nicer than she had first thought. But what really troubled her was a memory of Luke's face when they'd shut off one of the lights last night. His features were half hidden in darkness. The space had hideous lighting—fluorescents. What she really needed was some mood lighting, something with a warmer personal touch. She could borrow all the lamps from her house, but, disregarding one Tiffany-style lamp that she loathed to see broken, she only had three. She called her friend Amanda to ask to borrow some lamps, but she received no answer. She texted. Still nothing. The only times Amanda didn't answer a text right away was when she had company, so Jamie assumed that her friend was with a man on a date. She'd have to think of someone else.

She called her uncle. He said he had one standing lamp she could borrow, but even then she figured she needed many more.

She thought of Dean, but then thought of his wife working so hard to open the salon and decided she didn't want to bother them.

She tried to think of who wouldn't see the request as a burden and Leah popped into her mind. Leah then Ben. Of course, the universe was sending her towards Ben. "Because the universe likes drama," she shouted to herself, her voice echoing off the tile.

Leah's and Ben's family had an antique business on the side. If anyone had extra lamps hanging in their basement, it was them. In fact, she seemed to remember seeing some when she was last down there. Though that had been quite a while back. If anything, they might have some at the store downtown. But could she really call up Ben and ask a favor? Leah was less complicated, but after the last conversation they had had, Jamie felt weird about talking so casually to her. She didn't want to prod Leah's already hurt feelings.

Jamie wasn't quite a schemer, but she tried to imagine what might happen if she went down to Ben's house and knocked on the door. Leah, she thought, was at the bar tonight. So there wasn't much chance of encountering her. And even if his parents were home, there was nothing to worry about. She could just ask them for the favor. They'd be happy to help her. She was sure of it.

Ben might not even be there.

But what if he were…

What if he answered the door?!

Well, she thought, maybe nothing much. In the stupefaction of seeing her, Ben would dumbly comply with her request, and, considering he would most likely be in the midst of making dinner as he was wont to do, she could just insist on grabbing the lamps herself. Then she could run out of there without seeing another soul. Bim bam boom! She would be free and clear.

No.

She dipped to her neck in the water and shook her head. No. Of one thing she was certain, if she encountered Ben, the night would be anything but bim bam boom.

And he wouldn't let her off that easily anyway. She knew that. It would be: stay for dinner, talk to the family, tell us what's going on in your life. She wouldn't get out of there with less than a pound of pasta in her belly.

She looked at her bank account…

Yeah. No. there was no chance of just buying the lamps herself. It occurred to her that if she had a credit card, she could purchase them, use them one night, and then return them. She started to berate herself for not taking her credit

A Sticky Situation

more seriously the past few years. What twenty-two-year-old didn't have a credit card? But then she let it go when she had the thought: what about the bulbs? She'd have to buy those too. And she couldn't return used bulbs. That'd be wrong. Wouldn't it? So, the plan was a no-go, even if she had a credit card. The only thing that made sense was to borrow lamps... and bulbs.

So that was settled. She was going to Ben's.

She stepped out of the tub and let the water drench the bath rug.

Her outfit was quick. T-shirt, jeans, a baseball cap.

Before she knew it, she was parked in front of an immaculate Craftsman on the east end of town at the crest of one of its rolling hills. Many memories came flooding back. That gave her pause. Were a few lamps really worth seeing Ben again and opening that can of confusion? Her store depended on it. Her mother's legacy deserved a shot at least. She had to go through with her and Luke's plans. She had known it wouldn't be easy. To be fair, she hadn't quite expected this, the necessity of seeing Ben when she had made those plans with Luke.

But she was jumping the gun, assuming too much. It was entirely possible that Ben was at one of his baseball games. A small league, just two teams, played at the local field a few times a month.

Or he might be at a friend's house.

Yes, there was no guarantee he was there at all. She shouldn't predict catastrophes.

She decided it was a good idea not to bring gum. She didn't want them to notice that she was nervous. So, even though it killed her to do it, she emptied her pockets. Then she walked up to the house and she knocked. It was a tiny knock, imperceptible almost. But to her surprise a voice called out something she couldn't quite make out and then the door was being opened. She could hear the little mechanism in the lock as it turned.

"Jamie?"

She felt every part of her body relax, even her buttocks.

"Mr. Centelli," she said, when she saw Ben's father, Jack. "How nice to see you."

She heard Ben's mother, Lisa, call out, "who is it?" Then she appeared behind Ben's father. Jamie felt like she wanted to jump up and down. Maybe this would go as she had hoped—easy.

"Jamie?" asked Lisa. "Jamie! Come in. Oh my gosh!"

They both stepped out of the way and Jamie stepped up into their foyer, which displayed a large Norman Rockwell print.

Lisa grabbed her into a tight squeeze and patted her head. "Oh, Jamie, honey. I thought we'd never see you again. I couldn't bear it." Then Lisa grabbed her shoulders and pushed her back to get a better glimpse of Jamie's face. Lisa's mascara was starting to loosen, and her eyes blinked, trying to express the tears from her sight.

"But I said," began Jack from behind her, his big belly and beard moving up and down as he spoke, "there's no way she won't come over here and see us again. She'll have to. She'll miss us too much."

Lisa practically cried, "What took you so long, huh?"

Jamie cleared her throat and swallowed. She looked at both of the Centellis, their eager waiting expressions. She'd have to tell the truth, because if Mrs. Centelli sensed anything polite but untrue, she'd call it out. "I just—" Jamie swallowed again. "I just thought maybe it would be uncomfortable after what happened between Ben and me."

"What?" Lisa shrieked. "Why would it be uncomfortable? It's just us."

Jamie reached for her pocket and then remembered there was no gum there. She laughed nervously. "Well, I thought I might see Ben, and we needed a break."

"Well, yes, honey, of course." Lisa let go of Jamie's shoulders and turned to stand beside her, a hand on the small of Jamie's back. "Come sit. Come," she said and began to lead her into the living room.

"I'll make coffee," said Jack, happily. This was the routine. She'd come over and let them dote on her. Asking for the lamps would be no sweat. "Jamie, you want some donuts?"

Man, that sounded good, but that also meant she might have to stay longer. She remained polite, let out an excited, "yes, thank you!"

Jamie scanned the living room for sight of Ben. There was none. She assumed if he were here, he would've shown himself by now. So things were going according to her wishes. But she still worried that he might come through that door behind her.

"Sit, sit," said Lisa, guiding Jamie beside her on the love seat.

They sat, Jamie holding her knees tightly together, hands on her lap. She

A Sticky Situation

was nervous. She didn't want to do anything that felt manipulative. She simply wanted to ask people who cared about her for help... without having to see Ben.

"Tell me. How's the store?"

They got there quick. But Jamie didn't want to ask for a favor right off the bat. That would be in poor taste. "Actually, it might get shut down by the landlord."

"What? Oh, no. Did you hear that, Jack? They might be closing down the store."

Jack called out, "What did you say? I can't hear ya."

Lisa turned and spoke even louder, "I said, 'they're closing down the store!'"

"Oh, no. Who's closing the store? Jamie?"

"No, the landlord. He's closing her store. Keep up." She turned to face Jamie. "It's so sad," she said and shook her head.

"The landlord? But he's dead," Jack answered.

Lisa rolled her eyes. "Men," she said and smiled at Jamie. "So, tell me what do you got to do? That store is already the wackiest place I've ever been in, not sure how you can avoid that?"

Jamie laughed. "You're right. My store is a lot to take in. Well, I am actually cutting down on what I sell, so it's easier to... digest. The landlord and I have been working on it together. He has this whole big plan, and he's really hands-on. I hope this works is all. I have the reopening in two days." Jamie shook her head.

"Are we welcome to this 'reopening?'"

"Yes, absolutely, of course you are. I need everyone I know to come out and support me."

Jack appeared with a tray of coffee and donuts. "You look like you're starving, Jamie. Here's some treats for ya. You're too thin, my dear," he said smiling. He set the tray down on the table and then sat across from them in a club chair. "What's this that you're getting evicted?"

Jamie startled at the word.

"Oh, Jack. Don't say evicted. Can't you see she's worried?"

"I'm sorry, honey. Sometimes I don't think." Jack waved both his hands.

"It's OK. I just need to change a few things. I don't know about getting evicted, not yet at least. We'll see what happens. Everything depends on how the re-opening goes. So, you're able to come? In two nights?"

"Yes, we can come. We'd love to," said Lisa.

"Have a donut," said Jack, pushing the plate slightly with his big hand. "They're from Cece's."

Jamie grabbed a donut. It might mean staying longer and risking seeing Ben, but she figured there was no point in wasting a good donut. The jelly was delicious. She had just noticed some jelly drop on her chin, Lisa was reaching out with a napkin to dab at it, when the door started to open. Jamie went rigid.

"What's wrong, dear?" asked Lisa as the door opened.

Jack turned to look at the door. "Who's that?" he said.

Leah appeared from behind the door, pulling out her key. "It's just me. I forgot my name tag. Can you believe Dean sent me back home to get it? As if everyone who comes in doesn't already know my name." She was shaking her head and then she looked up. "Oh! Jamie!"

Jamie broke into a wide smile. She waved. "Hi!" At least it wasn't Ben, she thought.

Leah walked over, leaving the door open. "What are you doing here?"

Before Jamie could speak, Lisa said, "She came to invite us to her reopening. It's in two nights. Apparently, lots of surprises await us. But that's to be expected. It is the *Cuckoo Land*."

Jamie smiled. "*The Cuckoo Cl*ck*," she said, softly.

"Sorry, dear, it's *clock*. I got it."

Leah made a pouty face. "That's too bad. I'm working that night. You know what, I have something to show you. Can you come upstairs while I come find my name tag?"

Jamie looked at Lisa and Jack. They nodded. Lisa said, "yes, go, go."

Jamie navigated past Lisa's legs and followed Leah upstairs to her room, hoping as she went up the stairs that Ben wouldn't show up.

Once Leah opened the door, she spun and pulled Jamie in by the arm. Leah closed the door behind her, checking to make sure they weren't followed. She whispered loudly, "You know they're going to bring Ben, right?"

Oh my god. In all the worry to avoid Ben and the worry of getting these lamps, she had not even considered this possibility. Of course they would tell him about her visit and tell him about the store. She had defacto invited Ben to her re-opening without even thinking. Leah smirked and started to search for her tag.

A Sticky Situation

Jamie sighed. "I didn't even think of that. I just came here to see if I could borrow some lamps for my re-opening. I didn't mean to—"

"You really should know better. You've known them a while," she said, digging in her hamper.

"But I couldn't not invite your parents, especially since I'm basically inviting the whole town." Jamie looked around the room. It still looked the same as it always did. She still had a banner across the top of a wall that said: Prom Queen.

"I guess you're right," Leah said. Then she shouted, "got it!" She turned to face Jamie. "I feel for you, girl. Good luck. But I got to run. By the way. There are a bunch of lamps in the basement. I'm sure you can borrow them no problem."

They went downstairs together, Leah practically running down the steps. "Mom," she yelled at the door. "Jamie needs to borrow some lamps. Let her have the ones in the basement."

Then Leah was out with a smile and a wave, Lisa, calling out, "You're leaving already?" to a closed door.

Lisa stood beside Jamie at the front door. Jack had stood up and was looking at them. "What's this, you need some lamps?" Lisa asked.

Jamie nodded. "Yes, I almost forgot to ask," she said, trying not to seem too eager. She could practically hear the door to the Centellis closing safely behind her with no sign of Ben. "I do need some floor lamps."

"Well, you've come to the right place," said Jack, lumbering closer. "We've got a whole bunch in the basement."

He wouldn't hear of her following down there. "The steps are too narrow, honey, and the ceiling has nails jutting out all over the place. You stay up there and visit. I'll bring you what you need. How many do you need?"

"Five or six would work," said Jamie, disappointed she couldn't go down to help. Instead, she sat down at the kitchen table with Lisa, who began to ask her questions about her eating habits.

"I assure you, I'm eating," said Jamie. "Not to worry."

"I don't know. The way you ate that donut, you seemed hungry."

Jamie laughed. "I always eat like that, Lisa. I love donuts."

"Can't argue with that," said Lisa. "But listen. How are you doing? With your mom."

Jamie should've anticipated the question, but it still hit her like a bag of bricks in the belly. Lisa caught her expression. "Oh, honey," she said and reached a hand and placed it on Jamie's wrist. "I'm sorry. It's still so fresh."

Jamie felt pressure build up behind her nose. But she pushed back the tears. "It's OK," she said. "I just have a hard time talking about her still. But you didn't do anything wrong. Don't worry."

"You're such a little trooper," she said. "When I lost my mother, I was a huge mess for months. It passes. It doesn't get easier, but it hurts less often."

Jamie nodded politely. This conversation was worse even than seeing Ben, she decided. She tried to change the subject. "So, how's the law office?" Lisa worked as a paralegal for a local attorney.

That did the trick and soon Lisa was complaining about her boss. That topic was inexhaustible, Jamie knew from experience, having heard about him countless times. Twenty minutes passed, Jamie slyly watching the clock, waiting to hear Jack come up the stairs. After what felt like an eternity, his heavy step came up the stairs. He had five lamps in his arms.

"This work for ya?" he asked with a big smile behind his large grey beard.

Jamie jumped out of the seat and practically clapped. "That's perfect! Thank you so much. You have no idea how much you're saving me."

Jack wouldn't let Jamie help carry the lamps. He just followed her out to her car and loaded them in her trunk.

"I left the bulbs in them," he said. "In case you need them."

Jamie gave Jack a great big hug. "Thank you."

Jack chuckled and patted Jamie's back.

Lisa didn't let her leave just yet, however. She came out of the house and insisted Jamie come back in while she pack her some food to take home. Jamie was soon given two tote bags full of leftovers, even a full lasagna from the freezer and a loaf of Italian bread. Jamie thanked them and hugged them. Lisa began to cry as she said goodbye. "You're like a daughter to me," she said. "You know that. We're here for you no matter what."

Jamie was taken by surprise again. She hadn't expected to feel so much gratitude or love. But here they were, the Centellis letting her know that she was loved. She felt energized now. She could do this, she could save her shop, she thought. She thought of Luke and how much he was trying to help her. She really was lucky.

A STICKY SITUATION

The drive home with the lamps and the food settled her nerves. Amidst her thoughts about how grateful she was for the Centellis's hospitality and generosity, she even forgot about Ben. She popped some gum in her mouth as she drove home.

CHAPTER THIRTEEN

The next day she went to the print shop and requested a couple hundred more copies of the flyer.

The boys doing her printing giggled in the back of the store. She could hear them *shushing* each other and then she noticed them stealing looks in her direction.

When the machine stopped whirring, the clerk wearing a puka shell necklace dropped the stack on the counter. "Two hundred copies, miss," he said. "Hot off the press."

The other clerk stood further back in the shop, leaning against a doorway, looking at his feet, obviously holding in his laughter.

"Yeah, we just banged these ones out."

Now the clerk in the back relented and let out a high wheeze of a laugh.

This wasn't the first time she'd encountered this. She pursed her lips, thinking. "You're curious about my little flyer."

Puka nodded. "Yeah, it is interesting."

"And you find it interesting because you think it has to do with sex."

Now the other clerk stopped laughing, he seemed intent on listening.

Puka grinned. "Isn't it?"

"It is," said Jamie. "But this art," said Jamie, pointing to a Venus figurine on the flyer, "is a *cultural* expression of sexuality. Now, you might think this translates to a mere titillation of the senses."

Puka smiled widely now, the other boy giggled again.

"But anthropology," she continued, her tone firm, "demands we look deeper. We peel back the layers of the literal and unearth the symbolic core. Take, for instance, these Paleolithic Venus figurines. These figures, often dismissed as mere fertility symbols, reveal a far more complex narrative. Their exaggerated

A STICKY SITUATION

features – the ample breasts, the wide hips – speak not just to a desire for procreation..." The boy laughed even harder now. Puka just looked dazed. Jamie continued, unfazed "...but to a celebration of the female form as the vessel of life itself. They are a testament to a society that revered the power and resilience of women. Art—" her voice gained momentum now "—is not simply a pretty picture on a cave wall. It is a language, a code woven from symbols and narratives that illuminate a culture's deepest anxieties and aspirations. By understanding how sexuality is depicted and integrated into art forms, we gain invaluable insights into societal structures, gender roles, and even religious beliefs. You understand?"

Puka stared. "You're incredible," he finally said. Now the laughing boy guffawed.

Jamie laughed too, "Among its powers, let's not forget," she said, "always remains its ability to make teenage virgins laugh." That shut the kid up in the back.

After, she made sure to visit all the shops on North street. Every time she walked into a shop, she was greeted by people she knew from the local business association. "Tomorrow night?" many asked, "On such late notice?" She hadn't seen them since her mother died and they all seemed happy to see her, some curious, some downright nasty. "Oh. Jamie," said Irina, the owner of a soap and candle store, with a sneer. "I didn't know your store was still open. What a treat." Jamie knew that some of these people were a bust. They probably wouldn't hand out her flyers, but she thought it was worth the off chance. If one person came from these places it would be worth the embarrassment of having to face these people, their looks of pity, their rude asides. It occurred to her that more than one of the shop owners, especially the ones who assured her vehemently of attendance, might be going simply to watch her fail. Or to see what crazy idea she was up to now. Luckily, she had a pocket full of gum and that kept her from saying anything nasty in return.

Happily, she found Gregory at his shop. He told her he would pass out her flyers and he would definitely be there. He looked forward to the event the following night. Before she left, he said, "Sold that hat for double the asking by the way. It works, I tell ya."

As she entered the last store, she was so happy to see Martha, who ran a

Polish food goods store.

"You come. You try this," said Martha the moment Jamie walked into the shop. Jamie stepped forward, leaning over the counter, and took a bite of a leaf-wrapped ball of meat. It was delicious!

"Mmmm. Martha. That's so good. What is it?"

"You know galumpkis. Yes."

"Oh, yes. Of course."

Martha stopped behind the counter. Something had caught her eye about Jamie. "You different. Yes. Yes. Something different here."

Martha came from around the counter, her long hoop dress gliding side to side as she walked. "You do something different. Yes. I know. Different," she continued saying. Her dress moved gracefully, but it did give the impression of water sloshing in a glass. That energy seemed to transfer to Martha because she was a blur of movement and Jamie was surprised when she felt the woman grab her wrist. Suddenly Jamie was twirling, Martha making her spin like a ballerina in a box. "Yes, yes. Yes," said Martha as she examined her all around. "The hair is no, the same." Jamie nodded. "The clothes, no, nothing."

"Can I stop spinning now?" asked Jamie.

Martha let go of Jamie but planted her feet, her dress orbiting her, and examined Jamie some more. "Yes, but you different." She balled her hand into a fist and mimed driving it into her own belly. "You fire here, in your belly. You living."

"Oh?" said Jamie, confused about what to say.

"What has changed about you?"

Jamie chuckled nervously and held up a flyer. "I am holding a re-opening of my store. But that's about it." This last part she mumbled.

Martha responded ecstatically. "Party! Yes. See, you are more fire. I see. I go to party. Yes. I bring family, whole family to your store. But tell me now. You have boyfriend? That why you are so—." Here Martha made a euphemistic onomatopoeia, eh eh eh, and constructed something in the air with her hands.

Jamie scoffed. "Boyfriend? Me? No. Just excited about my shop."

Jamie and Martha, despite the many linguistic barriers, found a commonality. Jamie told Martha about the trouble to her shop and how she was re-envisioning the business. Martha exclaimed that this was it, where the fire

A STICKY SITUATION

was coming from, deep in her belly. So, Jamie thought, the fire was ambition.

Before leaving the Polish grocery, Jamie caught a glimpse of herself in the mirror behind the counter. Martha was right. There was something coloring her cheeks, she could feel it now like a warmth under her skin, and she smiled, proud of herself. Courage, she thought and then shushed the thought away. But no matter how much self-consciousness wanted to make her uncomfortable, she saw it, in that moment, an ambition she'd never seen before. When she had started the shop, ambition was the last thing on her mind. It was a romance, a haven for her interests, project for her and her mother. Now she saw, for a business, that was not the best or most logical approach. All this time, she had been simply surviving. But now...

When she was done handing out flyers, she went to the store. Luke called her and told her to text the list for the grocery store to him. He would pick the food up tomorrow while she compiled a music playlist for the opening and wrote out descriptions for the pieces they'd chosen. He reminded her that he couldn't buy the wine, so she made a mental note to pick up the wine before seven, when the party started. She thought about Luke. He had been so helpful so far, much to her surprise. She was glad for his help. She had to make sure she thanked him at some point to his face. She made another mental note.

The re-opening night spelled a new beginning for her. She felt excitement. She felt fear. But her idea was a good one. She looked round the shop and admired its new look. Yes, it would be a success, she told herself, as she set up the speakers she'd borrowed from the home entertainment system her mother had bought years before. This would all work out.

That night Jamie worked at the bar. There were still things she needed to buy for her re-opening and errands to run. But she had kept about fifty or so flyers and handed them out with every drink, using them as coasters.

"Just come," Jamie said to Ed, a regular, who sneered at the flyer under his pint of beer.

"Will there be liquor there?"

"No. Wine."

Ed grumbled and muttered into his beer.

"I need warm bodies, so you're coming. I'll make sure to bring you a little something."

There were no bus boys on. It was just her and a waitress. Jamie made sure everyone was set at the bar and then took a rack of glasses to the back. Ephraim smiled at her when he saw her. After she told him about the opening, he looked disappointed and said, "I can't go. Working tomorrow." She left the racks at the dishwashing station just as a rack of clean glasses came out of the sanitizer. She told Ephraim not to worry about it. One of the cooks said hello as she walked by.

Rinna, the server, came up to her as she was putting away the glasses at the bar. "Hello, sweet lips. I just had a seven-top come in. Can you make five rum and cokes, a dirty martini, and get me a Guinness?"

Jamie nodded. "Can you pass these out to your customers when they get their drinks?" Jamie pointed out the flyers under the bar.

"A party?"

"Of sorts, yes, come."

Jamie started on the Guinness first because it would take the longest. A few minutes later, Rinna looked relieved when she saw the cocktails made. "Thank you," she said. "You're the best. Heads up. That guy in the corner was asking about you. You know him?"

Jamie looked at the man. He sat with three other friends and right now they were laughing about something. His smile was very nice. He was a good-looking man. Just then he looked over to the bar and caught Jamie's eye. Jamie looked away. She didn't want to give the guy the idea that he should come over. "No, I don't know him."

Jamie covered all the bus boy positions, making sure to help Rinna clear the tables. At one point she walked by the table with the man that asked about her and they all turned to look. She thought she heard someone mutter the word, "beautiful." She ignored it and kept clearing and then went to drop everything with Ephraim. He provided her respite as he asked about her party and her store. She talked to him a while before returning to the bar, where more than one patron gave her a dirty look. Their glasses were empty. She refilled them and the crowd was happy again.

She had just set a drink down when the man who was asking about her came over.

"Hi," he said brightly.

"Do you need a drink?"

A STICKY SITUATION

"Actually, no," he said. "My glass is still full on the table. I was just wondering if I could talk to you a bit."

He was handsome. Very. But Jamie felt no attraction to him. Although she did like that he seemed nice, she had learned that first impressions with guys at the bar were usually inaccurate.

Jamie didn't respond. She just waited to see what else he might say.

"I heard you run that... shop. In the mall," he said.

"That's right," she said. "Tomorrow we're having a re-opening. You can bring your friends by," she said and nodded her head at the table in the corner. The group was playing quarters and chugging their beer. "Or your family might be better."

They both chuckled. She grabbed a flyer and handed it to him. Now he smiled wider, which just put Jamie more on edge.

"So, what's changing about the store?" He really did seem nice. He had green eyes, a gold haze in the center of the irises. His smile radiated. But, strangely, she thought about Luke. He just popped up in her mind. That made her smile and then she instantly regretted it because this man—"I'm Roger," he said—caught it and seemed to think she was warming up to him.

"Sorry, Roger," she said. "I really got to take care of the bar." Luckily, a patron on the other side of the bar grunted about another beer. "Duty calls," she said and walked away.

She could hear the table in the corner cheer as Roger returned. She caught a glimpse of him with the flyer in hand; he nodded at her. She wondered if he'd come to the event, but at least, if he did, there would be tons of people there. She wouldn't be alone with him. But it was more likely he wouldn't come by at all.

Soon she stopped worrying about that. She wondered more about Luke and why the thought of him had made her happy. She thought about his face. Particularly, she remembered his scars. The roughness there, for some reason, compelled her. She found it beautiful, to see a vulnerability on a man, right on the outside. Even more beautiful was that he seemed to not even notice it. It didn't make him shy. He was singularly focused on his dream. That's what drove him. And that was just something else to admire. She liked him, she was starting to feel. She liked him a lot.

CHAPTER FOURTEEN

Luke went to the grocery store with Jamie's list and bought everything she asked for. He couldn't help but indulge the fantasy that this list would supply their refrigerator, one they shared. He spent the whole time imagining they were a couple. Though, curiously, in none of these fantasies did he kiss her. It felt wrong. He wanted her permission. He laughed at himself for being so chaste even in fantasy.

His mother had accepted as an excuse that helping Jamie meant saving the mall just as much as securing cannabis dispensaries to lease the space did. At first Sheila had made the good point that Jamie did not rate as highly as the dispensaries in this scenario. They were much more important than she was. But Luke persuaded her that he wanted to be a certain type of landlord, like Pop-pop, and that meant helping people succeed if the opportunity presented itself. Not only that, but the dream was to have many stores making money and paying rent. A little business development, a little marketing help was time well spent. So he proceeded with this project as both a school project and a career move.

That morning he had woken up in high spirits. Spending so much time with Jamie had given him a jolt of energy. He had gone running, studied for a test his mother was giving him at the end of the week, and met with the architect and contractor to look at the drawings. The architect designed a smart remodel that amounted to strategic demolition, leaving the existing structures in place as much as possible, and the estimate for the ventilation upgrades to the farms were below Luke's projections. It was all on time and below budget. They could start at the end of the month as far as Luke could see. Now the contractor would apply for permits, buy materials, write a schedule and prepare his team. Luke felt elated. Pure luck had made it so that they could all start so soon, and he didn't question it.

A Sticky Situation

When he arrived at *The Cuckoo Cl*ck*, Jamie placed some printed index cards among the pieces she wanted to sell. She looked up when he opened the door and she smiled at the sight of him. This was the first time she'd greeted him with a smile. He suspected his outfit helped. He wore the slacks and shoes from his suit with a button up shirt. Jamie wore a black dress, simple and tight-fitting that reached just above her knees. He had the distinct impression she'd brushed her hair. It looked shiny and smooth, but some of the curls he loved had been straightened out. He wanted to compliment her, but he didn't want to make her uncomfortable.

"Jamie, I got the stuff you asked for."

"You can put it down at the table over there," she said pointing, she sounded out of breath, like she'd been running around before he came in. The table already had napkins, plates, toothpicks, and cups. "I put the wine in the freezer for a while," she said. "We can pull it out when it's really good and chilled."

Luke spent a few minutes making a charcuterie spread that looked pretty appetizing. "Jamie," he asked, "this look all right?" He tried to hide the smile that spread across his face. She gave him a funny look that told him she'd noticed his pleasure at her approval. He stepped away and went to look at the cards she had set up.

"So, I was thinking," he said, "that you could do a raffle, just to you know, get people excited." The shaking in his voice seemed unavoidable. He tried steadying it but failed. While she responded that it was a great idea, he pulled out a large roll of raffle tickets that he'd stolen from the school's drama club prop closet. "This should be enough," he said. "You just have to choose something to give away."

"Why don't you choose something?"

"Really?" He wished that he didn't show his feelings so openly. He remembered Pop-pop and how inscrutable he had been. "I think... I think..." He looked around the shop and his eye kept going to the tapestry of the reclining man—the tapestry of relaxation, he thought of it. "How about that?" He pointed.

"Why did you pick that one?" She was grinning at him. There was a joke at play somewhere there, but he didn't get it.

"It stands out to me. It's really richly colored and there's something about how relaxed he is. The pose—it's feminine, but he's not. I don't know. It's an interesting mix."

Jamie approached the tapestry and gazed at it. "OK," she said. "I agree."

He felt his stomach flutter. She watched him.

"What's up?" he asked.

"I've got an idea. Help me."

They each went to opposite sides of the folding table with the spread. "What are we doing?" he asked. She told him to grab the table and lift. Slowly they carried it out of the shop and put it along the shop's windows. "That's better," she said. Jamie propped open the doors and turned on the music. She looked around the shop, nodding. "We did good," she said and nodded at him too. "I agree," he said. Then she went to the door and switched off the lights, leaving him to follow in the dark.

"So we get them to congregate here at first, for fifteen or so minutes and then, poof, turn on the lights and surprise! Awesome new store. What do you think?"

"Drama. I get it. Two thumbs up," he said.

The first person to arrive was Ed, one of the regulars from the bar that Jamie had invited the night before. He went straight to the table with wine. Jamie was so happy to see him it made Luke smile. He watched her go inside the dark shop and come back out with a flask. "I told ya I'd have a little something for you," she said as she approached Ed.

Ed's little beady eyes lit up with the shine of a thousand suns. "Thank ya, darling. You sure know how to make someone feel welcome," he said and took a deep sip of the amber liquid. "I might say you look really beautiful tonight, kid."

Luke could've shot himself in the foot. Look how easy complimenting her was for Ed. He took his shot while Ed filled himself with cheese and crackers. "You do look really beautiful," he said to her.

Jamie turned to look at him. A confused smile almost crept across her face, but then voices from the mall's entrance grasped her attention.

"Hi!" She greeted people as they came in. She made sure they knew about the wine and food and then just chatted with them. Luke watched her smiling and laughing over her cup of wine. The way her hair kept falling in front of her face made her look so beautiful and soft. He wanted to grab her hair and clip it back so he could see her profile. She was beautiful and he studied her, saw how her buckteeth shaped her lips so they pouted. It made her look sensual. He listened

A STICKY SITUATION

to the small talk. Most of them knew her since she was a girl, either friends she grew up with or people who knew her mother. After about ten minutes at least twenty people arrived. Many came dressed in their best. They all drank, one couple danced to the music that blasted from inside. Luke overheard one woman say snarkily to her companion, "Oh, what a pleasant surprise. I didn't think anyone would be here."

"Why are we all out here?" yelled one tall, chunky, red-faced man.

"Just a sec," Jamie said and went inside. The music lowered. More people arrived. He recognized Martha from the Polish store. Jamie came out with a penis amulet and banged the glass at the front of the shop. It made a loud ringing noise. "Great." She smiled. "I've got your attention."

A few people laughed.

There wasn't a shy bone in her body, Luke realized. She stood up there and addressed her guests.

"Hi, everyone. I'm so happy to see all of you. So many of you were friends with my mother. She'd be so happy that you came. Thank you to my regular ladies for coming. You are the only thing that's kept me going all this time. I'm even glad to see you, Irina." He heard a few people laugh again. A few people turned to look at Irina, exposing her. It was the woman who was making the snarky comment earlier. "Most of you knew my mom. This was mostly her doing, *The Cuckoo Cl*ck*." Jamie made a flourish upward, towards the sign. "She did it for me, and I did it for her. Still, I want to make her proud, so I've made a few changes. That's why it's all in the dark. I want you to be surprised." A few people chuckled. "Also, I want to control how you interacted with it. Anyway, I hope you like the changes. Please let me know your thoughts, your true thoughts. No being nice." Luke had the feeling that at least Irina wouldn't have trouble with that. "So, just enjoy. There's food, there's wine, there's art. All the art you will see here was made by hand by people connected to old traditions and to their cultures and they come from all over the world. I'd love to tell you more about it. I'll be roving around talking about the pieces, but if I'm not around, I wrote some descriptions that I hope will illuminate all of it for you. Heads up. This might seem like a gallery or a museum, but everything here is actually available for purchase and the best part is you can touch it all. Oh, one more thing! There's a raffle. You can get tickets from me and I'll point out the prize to you in a moment. Again, thanks for being here. Have fun."

The people murmured and she disappeared into the shop for a moment. The lights sputtered on. A few people clapped; others whooped. Jamie definitely had fans, more than her sales numbers showed. They all walked into the shop, some stopping to refill their cups or plates.

An energetic deep canzonetta with cello and violin began to play. The first installation was a series of three Greek statues. In one, a muscular young man was draped nude over a boulder. In another he threw a javelin. In the last, he stood, lazy and bored. A shelf lined with an embroidered maroon and gold tapestry held variations of these statues.

On a card, propped up on a small easel, it said the following:

Oh, the Greeks sure knew how to spice things up! Their erotic art sought to cater to the male gaze, featuring gorgeous and fit male bodies that were just too hot to handle. That should tell you a lot about Greek proclivity. Meanwhile, women were usually depicted in more demure poses, which is a shame because we all know ladies can be just as saucy!

But wait, there's more! The Greeks weren't afraid to get down and dirty, as evidenced by their famous vase paintings depicting all sorts of sexual positions and acts. These naughty vases often showcased scenes of men enjoying themselves at symposiums, drinking and conversing while getting busy with each other. Talk about a party trick! Replicas of such vases are available here. With these talking pieces, you'll never host a dinner party with awkward silences.

Luke could hear the guests laughing as they read the card. The installations continued. There were carvings of the Sheela na Gig from Ireland, Japan's spring pictures, and a collection of handmade and limited editions of the *Kama Sutra*. Luke saw that the supply closet was open, light flickering inside.

He traveled through to that room. It was circular with a white tapestry hanging in the center, a film projecting onto it. Here an excerpt of a documentary about erotic American comics played on the tapestry, first discussing Tijuana bibles from the 20s and 30s and then R. Crumb followed by Penthouse comix. The walls were lit up with standing lamps. She must've brought these from home, he thought. The many shelves lining the walls were filled with erotic comics. When had she done this?

A Sticky Situation

Behind him a group had formed. He excused his way through the small crowd and saw her talking to another group by the pre-historical statues, replicas of goddess statues, huacos from Peru and other erotic art from central and South America. The people were laughing and listening attentively. Everywhere he looked people were engaged and laughing or inspecting statues. He found himself examining some of the art from Asia, tapestries with Dong Ho scenes, Filipino Sari-Sari prints, and Chinese erotic carvings in jade and bronze. A voice behind him asked, "See anything you like?"

He turned to find Jamie.

"When did you make that little instillation in your supply closet?"

She laughed. "I did that today. Inspiration struck!" Someone tapped Jamie on the shoulder.

"Can you tell me about that piece?" The lady, wearing a cocktail dress with beaded fringe, nodded towards a tapestry hanging above the Irish statues. "Just a second," she told the woman.

"Will you excuse me?" Jamie asked.

Luke shook his head. "No, of course," he said. "Go, go."

Jamie went with the woman and they talked. The woman nodded and smiled and pulled an item off the shelf.

Jamie came back over, hurriedly. "Do you think you can run a register?" she asked.

Luke shrugged. "We'll find out."

They both smiled.

It turns out the register was similar to one he'd used during the previous summer he worked at an ice cream shop. The woman who'd come to find Jamie walked up to him to purchase. She had picked one of the Greek statues and a copy of the *Kama Sutra*. He looked over the statue but there was no price.

"The statues are twenty-five according to the sign," she said.

Luke nodded, smiling nervously. He looked for a price list.

"The book I don't know," she said.

There was a sheet of paper under the counter. He grabbed it hopefully and, Yes!, it was a list. The book was twenty dollars. He rang up the woman and breathed a sigh of relief when she walked away. But then she was replaced by another person.

Just then Uncle Norman came in, shuffling with his cane. He made a beeline straight for Luke at the register. It was surrounded by bins of gum and people were digging in and exploring the options. A scale was on the counter to weigh out pounds worth.

"And you are?" Uncle Norman looked Luke up and down. "Besides adorable."

"Hi, I'm Luke," Luke responded, hunching automatically so as not to tower above the diminutive man. But Uncle Norman's diminutiveness applied only to his stature. Luke saw that the personality didn't follow suit.

"Oh! You're the mean old landlord."

Luke nodded, frowning. He passed change over to the customer in front of him.

"Boy, take a joke," Uncle Norman said waving his cane in the air. "You're also my landlord. I'm Jamie's uncle, Norman, and I am the manager at the Bullseye. Speaking of which, I have to get right back. I'm working tonight and I swear everyone forgets to how to do their jobs the moment I step out. But how good to finally meet you. Jamie didn't tell me how cute you were." Uncle Norman reached out and poked Luke in the belly. "Oof. Taut. Anyway, I must see the lady of the hour. I'm glad to see you helping. Carry on."

Luke blinked a moment, unsure what to do or say. He saw the man go and speak to Jamie. Immediately the group around her burst into raucous laughter.

"Can you ring me out?" A tall woman handed over a bag stuffed with gum. He weighed it and then consulted the card by the gum. He followed his instincts with the register and, luckily, it was easy. Uncle Norman left soon after, yelling, "How much for the boy behind the register?" Luke felt his face grow hot.

Jamie came over. "You're a godsend," she said, making everything in his belly ignite in flames. He grinned.

"No problems here?" she asked.

"Nope. I figured it out. Thanks."

"Ms. Davis here would like to purchase this Greek statue of an Olympian. The price list is under the counter."

"I'd already found it," he said. "Thank you."

"Thank you so much," she said, putting her hands together as if in prayer. Then she rushed away to talk to another group of people.

Luke smiled at Ms. Davis, who stood on the other side of the counter among

A STICKY SITUATION

the group of people filling bags with gum. "Ooooh, that looks fun," she said pointing to the bins of gum. "My grandchildren might like these. Oooh, dragon fruit? Maybe I'll like these too."

"You made it," said Jamie when she spotted the two young clerks from the copy place.

Puka laughed awkwardly. "Yes, we thought we owed it to you."

The other one turned slightly facing away and shrugged, hands in his pockets. Puka punched him in the shoulder.

"Dude."

"Yeah, sorry about yesterday," said the other one, his voice cracking. "We didn't mean to make fun. This store is actually really cool."

"What's your favorite piece?" Jamie asked, curious.

They both spoke at the same time, "The comics!"

"Yeah, definitely. I didn't know all that stuff about... what's his name again?" asked Puka.

"R. Crumb," said the other. "Very cool." He held up two comics from the display. "Buying these."

"Thanks for inviting us, Jamie."

"Thanks for coming, guys. I really appreciate it. But now that we're friends, I should probably learn your names too."

Puka turned out to be Devon and his conspirator was Kyle. Jamie made sure to take them over to the gum bins. "I'm sure there's something in here that will surprise you. Dig around."

"Awesome," said Kyle and then blushed.

Jamie walked away and immediately was surrounded. There were so many questions about her wares, the tapestries, the figurines, the books.

She was in her element, lecturing about the pieces, explaining their histories and how she came to sell them in her store. Listening to her you might've thought she'd traveled to all the source countries, but she was just relating her mother's stories of adventure. The crowd ate it up.

"Do you think this will rekindle our marriage?" asked one woman when the crowd around Jamie dispersed. She held a copy of the *Kama Sutra* in her hands, her eyes looked pained. Jamie wasn't sure exactly how to help, but she smiled and said that it would certainly be exciting at the least. The woman seemed satisfied with the answer because she nodded vehemently and said, "I'll take it!" Jamie led her over to the line that had formed at the register.

Jamie took a look at Luke, who was deep in concentration. Something about seeing him there, smiling and laughing with the customers felt right. He really was a sweet guy, she thought.

Her reverie didn't last long, however, because Lisa and Jack had found her. Lisa called out, "Honey!" from across the room as they got closer to Jamie. Jamie looked for Ben, but he didn't seem to be with them, thankfully.

Lisa held out a bright yellow saltshaker in the shape of a penis. "Honey, does this just work the normal way?"

Jamie laughed. "Yes, just put salt here," she said, taking the figurine and pointing out the hole at the bottom of it stoppered by a rubber plug. "Then you use it as normal." Jamie gave the salter a little shake. She handed it back into Lisa's hands.

"I'm not sure I want to shake around a—a—" Jack seemed at a loss for words, which didn't often happen.

"Don't worry, Jack," said Jamie. "It's just ceramic." He was holding a shaker too, this one formed into the shape of a vulva. She conked him on the head with it. "See? Just ceramic."

He laughed at that and seemed to relax a little.

"Yes," said Lisa. "Just relax, Jack. It's all in good fun."

"Jack, did you get any wine? That always helps," said Jamie.

"He's not drinking wine because his blood pressure has gone up," confessed Lisa.

"I'm more of a beer drinker anyhow," he said, looking over the crowd.

"Well, I'm glad you guys got to see my re-opening and I'm even more glad you found something you like."

"I'm taking these for sure," said Lisa, snatching the shaker out of Jack's hand. "They're so fun." She shrieked with laughter. Jack looked embarrassed.

"Don't forget to check out the gum, Jack. There's all kinds of flavors, even pineapple."

"Pineapple?" Jack was a pineapple fanatic. He'd try anything if it was pineapple flavored. She led them to the bins and soon they were digging like

A STICKY SITUATION

kids into the gum, looking for the perfect piece.

Jamie was pulled away to answer more questions. A woman was asking the correct way to hang a tapestry she was interested in. The tapestry was the image of a fawn amongst tall thin trees, the sun close to the horizon so that the creature was in silhouette. This was Jamie's favorite tapestry. It was the work of an artist from Vietnam, who typically wove scenes of sexuality, this piece, however, being one of the few that contained no element of sex. Jamie explained to her the best way to hang the piece on drywall. When the woman thanked her and bid goodbye, she heard a voice beside her, deep and warm.

"Hi, Jamie."

It was Ben, who, at the moment, was gazing at a tapestry of a flurry of wood nymphs dancing in a forest. He wore a black cotton tee that framed his broad shoulders. In his hand, he held a cup with wine. Now he sipped from it. His eyes crinkled as he smiled. He leaned in and kissed her cheek, as they had done countless times in the years growing up together as neighbors, friends, a couple. She kissed back automatically and then pulled back, smiled tightly. He looked handsome as ever. She reached into her pocket and started to unwrap some gum.

"Hi. Ben. You made it."

"Yeah, my mother insisted. My father did too. They said that you needed all the support you could get. Sorry. I know you probably didn't mean to invite me."

"No." Now Jamie felt badly for him. Then she wondered if this was his intent. She popped the gum into her mouth—cherry. "You're— you're welcome here too. Don't feel bad."

He nodded. "Place looks good," he said. They gazed at each other without breaking it. He smiled. She did too.

She found it strange to talk to him like this. They were no longer taking each other for granted, they were awkward, trying to figure out how to interact appropriately, yet they felt so familiar. She felt confused. The chewing began to soothe her.

"You have a lot fewer things. They really stand out now."

Jamie held his gaze a moment longer. Then she moved her attention to the tapestry above her. "You were looking at this."

"Aren't they girls?"

Jamie grinned. "No. They're actually hundreds of years old. They simply don't age on the outside anywhere near as fast as humans. It would probably take millions of years for them to look like us. They're a different species. Wood nymph."

His brow furrowed. He seemed to have more to say about that, but he didn't. He changed the subject. "My parents said something about you being…" he squinted "…challenged on your lease?"

"That's what this whole party is for really." She tried to avoid mentioning Luke. For some reason she thought that might create tension. She glanced over at Luke. He was at the register, still checking people out. She talked around him. "I needed to try and make the store work. Before I got closed down."

"I'm sorry to hear that."

There was a time when he begged her to leave the store behind. But he seemed sincerely sorry for her now. She regretted the conversation going down this path. "Went to Pat's the other day." She nodded her head, searching for something to say. "Had the curly fries." She nodded some more.

He laughed softly. Then he changed the subject.

"I'm glad to see the lamps being put to good use," he said.

"They were a godsend. Your parents are the best."

"You should keep them."

Jamie scoffed. "What? They're your parents."

"I meant the lamps, James." He winked at her. "They look great here."

Her cheeks went warm, her temples too; they thumped. He'd called her James. That was his secret pet name for her. In all this time, for some reason she couldn't explain, she'd forgotten that he called her that. The memories all came rushing back now.

She turned around and made eye contact with a few people, gave a wave. "It's good to see you," she said, turning back to him.

"I wasn't sure."

She put a hand on his arm. "I'm happy you're here."

He nodded.

"If you'll excuse me," she said. "I think those ladies have a question."

"Of course," he said. "Do your thing."

She walked away feeling as if she were on flames. She tingled all over. Then

A STICKY SITUATION

she recognized the sensation as blood rushing back into her once tense muscles. She had held them rigidly as she spoke with Ben. The woman she'd waved at had some questions. Jamie answered them automatically. She kept second guessing what had just happened with Ben. She hadn't meant to be harsh and she hoped she hadn't come off that way. Besides that thought, she was relieved. She'd survived the dreaded encounter virtually unscathed.

Throughout the night, she continued to move around and explain the pieces' significances and origins. People were responding well. They bought many pieces after talking with her. Or they credited her little explanatory index cards for their purchases. She was glad to see so many people embracing the art without being scared off by the sexuality. They were having fun, she thought. Her mother would have loved to see the store bustling, the customers so engaged. It's what she'd always wanted for Jamie, an audience for her ideas. She looked over at Luke. This was because of him. She felt the tears spill over. She quickly brought a hand to her eyes and moved into the supply closet, where everyone was looking at the flashing images. She wiped her face. She had surprised herself with that show of emotion. But she couldn't have helped it. For the first time since her mother passed, Jamie was certain her mother would be proud.

When she'd settled, she came back out of the closet and began to mingle again. Amanda came over and offered her a cup of wine. She drank it greedily. It burned in her stomach.

"I saw you talking to Ben," she said.

"It was awkward."

"Of course it was. He's still in love with you."

"Stop that." Jamie shook her head, her cheeks glowing red again.

"What? You saw the way he looked at you. Didn't you? You were there."

"He just wanted to congratulate me on what I'd done with the store and to assure me that his parents insisted he come."

"Likely story. He came for you."

"No, he didn't. He came to be polite."

"To be polite to you because he still cares what you think. Duh."

Jamie laughed. "OK. I can't argue with that."

"Your girl Amanda always knows what's up. Trust me."

Jamie wondered. No, their breakup had been mostly his doing, she thought.

Plus, he'd always wanted her to get rid of the store. The re-opening would be a strange time to have a change of heart. If anything, tonight symbolized a firm end for the two of them as a couple. She looked over at Ben. He was talking to Irina, the nasty woman from the local business owners' association. He looked over at Jamie, smiled and covertly rolled his eyes. Jamie chuckled. No, Amanda couldn't be right, she thought. Could she?

CHAPTER FIFTEEN

Luke had spent the rest of the night ringing up Jamie's customers. He hadn't expected the night to be quite so successful. Soon large patches of the walls became visible as tapestries were sold. Many of the shelves were emptying and Jamie had to refill the gum bins at least once. The gum, especially, was a huge hit.

The register's line had become interminable. But from this vantage point he could see Jamie flitting from group to group. He watched her, beaming with what he could only think of as pride as he saw her take command of the spotlight. And she was selling so much. She was more of saleswoman than her store had implied until now. She apparently just needed the right context, a chance to explain the work, to connect people with its story.

But what he was most impressed by were the candy sales. Almost every customer had a large bag of candy with them. Her idea to carry international gum was a hit. At least half the sales numbers would probably be from gum alone, he thought.

He had watched her talk with quite a few people when she was approached by a brooding man who kissed her on the cheek. Jamie and Luke had never talked about boyfriends, but he guessed that they had had some type of relationship, she and this man. He kept a covert eye on them, not wanting Jamie to catch him staring. As far as he could tell they seemed uncomfortable and that felt like a point in Luke's favor. Jamie had ceased to look that tense around him, so he decided not to be threatened by this unidentified man. He laughed at himself. He clearly felt he was in some struggle over her affections. He wondered what Jamie would think if she knew what he was thinking.

A couple hours later, Jamie said goodbye to her last customer, one of her fan club. They chatted a while and then the woman left. She turned to face Luke and let out a guttural scream that made him jump.

"That was amazing!"

Luke yelled too. "Yes, it was! Look how much money you made," he said pulling out the drawer. It was so full the clips couldn't keep in some of the bills. They rushed to each other and she grabbed his hands and started to jump and turn him in a circle. "We did it," she chanted. "We did it! We did it!"

"And you survived my uncle," she said, laughing. "He said you were a jewel in the crown of the evening." Luke blushed.

"That's the grandest compliment I've ever received," he said.

They took deep breaths and looked around the store.

"Clean-up will be brutal," he said.

Her shoulders fell and she sighed. "Tomorrow," she said. "I'm done for the night."

"Done? You can't be done. We have to celebrate."

"Celebrate?"

"Celebrate."

With that, they locked up and Jamie followed him out of the mall. They locked it behind themselves too.

"Where are we going?"

"You'll see," he said.

He was taking her to his favorite place.

"This is your car. Hmmm," she said, looking it over after she sat in the passenger seat. "It's really clean."

"I am a wonder."

"The way you worked that register, I'd say the term applies."

He turned the car on and a xylophone started to play a pop melody.

"Who's this?"

"Tiziano Ferro. Never heard him?"

Jamie shook her head. Luke started to sing in Italian with the man on the record. He sang animatedly and close to her face. She could smell his breath. Mint. She laughed watching his face twist and frown while he performed passionately.

"Do you know what you're saying?" she asked as he pulled out of the parking spot and drove.

A STICKY SITUATION

He kept singing loudly. "It doesn't matter what I'm saying. All that matters is if I say it right."

All that matters is if I say it right. She found that statement sexy, but she wasn't sure why. "Where are you taking me?"

"That will become clear in a moment."

"Who told you I like surprises?"

"You got in the car without knowing where I was taking you, didn't you?"

She narrowed her eyes at him. The next song also played in Italian but she recognized the word "sesso." She listened to Luke sing it too. He wasn't very good, but he showed commitment. She also recognized the lyric "ti amo." This was starting to feel slightly romantic. She didn't want that. She had said it already a bunch of times. She looked up at the sky. There wasn't a cloud in sight that night, the stars shining through. Was anyone up there listening to her? She said she did *not* want romance. But she didn't do anything to stop it. The car was hurtling forward to some unknown destination singing "ti amo" and she sat back, listened to Luke sing, and she let herself relax. Damn it, she deserved it. After all the work they'd put in, she deserved at least a moment to just let go.

Soon they were driving off the side of the road.

"Oh my god," Jamie screamed. "What the heck are you doing?" Jamie shot up in her seat, but Luke kept driving into a copse of trees.

"We can't have anyone find the car." It took a moment of confusion and terror, but she soon realized he was still in control of the car. He stopped in the middle of three trees, parked, lowered the music and turned off the lights. "We're going in incognito."

Jamie breathed. He looked so excited she became even more invested in learning where he was taking her. She thought they were near the high school in the neighboring town. "This is creepy," she said.

"Don't worry. The mall has cameras in the parking lot. The security company has video of us leaving together. If you mysteriously disappeared, I'd be the first person of interest." He flashed a devilish grin.

She took another deep breath. She admitted to herself that she was having fun. "OK. But I'm not easy to overcome, so watch yourself," she said as she started to exit the vehicle.

He took her hand and she turned to face him. She could smell his cologne and his breath. He smelled so good. She kept breathing him in. "I would never hurt you," he said to her seriously. Surprisingly, she felt herself relax. The sincerity rolled off him like a scent.

They exited the car and he led her through the tree copse in the dark.

"You know where you're going?" she whispered.

"I got lost about three minutes ago. I was just too afraid to say anything."

Jamie stopped in her tracks. Luke suppressed his laughter. "I'm messing with you," he said. "It's just a little further."

Not long after, they reached the tree line and a brick wall that went up at least thirty feet. It was the back of the school. He held a finger to his lips for silence. His eyes sparkled in the moonlight. She followed him as he pulled out a key and fit it into a door along the expanse of the wall. "You have a key?"

"Being in tech has its perks," he said as he turned the lock.

"They give you a key?"

"No, but I have access to the teacher's office. So...same thing."

"Wait," Jamie whispered desperately. "Isn't this a felony?"

"Well," he said looking at her with the door open to the darkness of the building, "I suppose it is...if you get caught." Then he stepped into the darkness and let the door start to close behind him. Jamie just had a moment to think. She jutted a hand out between the opening just as the door was going to close. She stepped into the darkness too and the door closed behind her.

"I thought you'd chicken out," said a voice beside her. She felt the hairs on her arms stand up and a chill ran through her. "I know the switch is here somewhere," said Luke amidst the sound of fumbling. Jamie felt herself strangely unmoored as if she were floating in the darkness, as if she weren't a body. She could hear Luke, she could hear the vast emptiness of the room they were in, as if the silence itself were echoing. Then the lights switched on, warm-colored bulbs high above her partially lit up the place.

They were in an auditorium, on the stage—behind the stage actually. She was seeing the seating through a part in the stage curtain. She turned to Luke. There he was, still grinning. "We did it," he said and then grabbed her hand and pulled her onto the stage.

On the stage stood a real-looking house with a miniature picket fence surrounding it. Their footsteps echoed as they walked. "I don't think we should

A STICKY SITUATION

be here."

Luke pulled her farther onto the stage and then up the steps leading into the back of the house. It was obviously all for show. There was nothing inside but bare plywood walls and a table for props. There was also a staircase that they climbed to the so-called house's second floor. There was a hole in the wall, and Luke let go of her and sat down on the edge of it. Jamie approached the hole carefully.

She could see the audience seating. It was mostly patched in darkness. He had only turned on some of the house lights. She touched the edge of the hole first and then sat down once she decided it was safe enough. She could see now that it was meant to mimic a balcony. "O, Romeo," she said.

"I prefer Luke," he told her.

Luke bumped her shoulder playfully with his own. "Hey, careful there, buster. I don't want to fall."

"I helped build this," he said.

Jamie was genuinely surprised. This guy did not lack for originality.

"Seriously," he continued and pointed at the joint of the walls. "See that nail? I put that nail there. I'm pretty much a carpenter."

"It's a perfect little doghouse. I'm sure a dog would be very happy in here with a few pillows."

"Doghouse? This here is not a doghouse. It's magic. Stage magic. That's right, apart from being a carpenter, landlord, and high school student, I'm a magician. For my next trick..." She hadn't even noticed that this whole time he carried his backpack. He reached into it and pulled out a small bottle of tequila. She reached for it."

"Oh, god. It's cold. You have a cooler in there?"

"Nope. I stuck it in your freezer when you opened tonight, then I swiped it before we left."

He pulled out a Tupperware container next and two shot glasses that clinked.

"You don't have a whole bar in there, do you?" she grabbed at his bag and looked inside.

"No, but I've got lime slices," he said shaking around the Tupperware.

"What are you a teen alcoholic?"

"OK, look I'm a teen, but I'm also officially a man, so watch it. I knew you were going to kill it tonight, so I wanted to celebrate. That's all."

"No salt?"

"Oh no, I've got it," he said and reached into the front pocket of his backpack for a penis shaped shaker.

"You little thief!"

"No, no. I bought that tonight."

"It didn't have salt in it."

"I brought that too," he said, pulling out a blue cylinder.

She laughed. "You're silly. I can't get drunk with you. You have to drive back."

"One or two won't make us drunk for long. Anyway, you *have* to mark the occasion."

She definitely didn't want any trouble, but he was right. They had to mark the occasion. "OK," she said. "I'll take one."

He set it up: the lime, the salt on the edges of their hands, the little glasses that read "Niagara Falls" full of cold spirits. They clinked glasses.

"To your success," he said looking at her.

"To ours," she corrected and then licked her hand, downed the spirit, and bit the lime.

It went down easy and she felt her fear start to dissipate.

"So," she said. "You definitely helped me perform magic tonight." She looked out at the theater.

"That was basically you. You are a marvel. Seriously. You know like everything about erotic art and you make it all seem really interesting and cool."

She felt slightly embarrassed at the compliment. "This is really cool," she said, banging on the floor of the house.

"I know. For some reason I just wanted you to see it. It won't last forever. Just a few performances before it gets broken down to become a set for next year. But you're changing the subject. How the heck did you and your mom ever come up with the idea for *The Cuckoo Cl*ck*?"

"Oh," she started then stopped herself. She wasn't sure she wanted to talk about all that. But the usual defenses were failing. "You know what? Let's have another."

"Shot? Yeah? OK then. Let's do it!" He served them and they clinked glasses. "To the drama club!"

A STICKY SITUATION

She laughed. "OK. To the drama club." They had another shot of chilled tequila.

"You're too young for this, you know."

"You're too old for breaking and entering."

Jamie coughed. "Yes," she nodded. "But I only did the entering. That's called trespassing. I think it's a misdemeanor. You, on the other hand, are on the road to the big house."

She was having fun. She couldn't remember the last time she felt like this. Maybe with Amanda. But no, this was different. She could feel something inside her, deep inside, relax. She had felt like such a failure the past year. She had felt inert, like a stone at the bottom of a lake. But now she saw, Martha was right, so was Amanda. Fire had erupted in her gut. She had faced the enemy, she thought, looking at Luke, looking at the delicate lines in his face. She had faced him and made him, she guessed, into something like a friend.

"Why don't you tell me what it's like to be Grand Sonny Warbucks?"

"OK. Don't be mean now."

"I'm a mean drunk."

"Are you really drunk?"

"No, but I am feeling it enough to feel way too comfortable up here."

Luke laughed and then helped her down to the stage. They sat across from each other in the front yard of the fake house, behind the mini picket fence, their legs crossed.

"OK. We're safe. Now tell me."

Luke sighed and looked away. "Honestly?"

Jamie nodded.

"It's so much pressure, oh my god. I feel like it's governing my life and crushing it at the same time."

"It must be hard to lose him?"

"Who? Oh, Pop-pop? I'm going to need one more sip for this talk."

"Deal. But last one."

Luke nodded.

They did another shot to Pop-pop.

"OK. Here's the thing. My grandfather was not warm or anything like that. I think we barely even had a conversation. He never asked me anything. Actually, sometimes I'd babble on and on when I was with him, hoping something would interest him, but I hardly ever got a word out of him. He just wasn't a talkative guy. But he prepared me for this. He made me work with him every Saturday, collecting rents, watching him interact with his tenants. Honestly, that first time you and I met was a disaster. He would've never handled it that way. Sometimes I'm just too blunt. Left brain. That's what I'm told. But he and I didn't really connect. So, no. It wasn't hard to lose him. It almost feels like he's still here actually. Maybe that's why I work so hard, to prove myself. I know that at least. That he wanted me to be successful and I think he'd like it if I were better at it than him. He taught me a lot though. Like how to be a good landlord, how to treat people. Our interaction excepted." He avoided her gaze. "What about you? I'm sorry about your mother. I heard you talk about her in the speech you gave tonight."

Jamie lay back and grunted. "Yeah." She sat back up and felt dizzy.

"Woah, you OK there? You looked a little sick or something."

"Good," she said, holding a hand out to steady herself, almost touching his knee. "My mother died in a plane crash."

"What? That's so horrible."

Jamie nodded. Had she really just said that? To this relative stranger? She didn't even talk about this with Amanda or her uncle. She'd kept that fact from her lips a whole year and now that she said it, it made her feel...nothing. It was the tequila, she thought. "Yeah. She was going on a trip for me, to buy stuff for the store. I've been terrified of planes ever since. I haven't even driven far out of the city. It just gives me anxiety. It was my fault."

Luke stared at her, but to her surprise he said nothing. The only person she'd admitted her guilt to was her uncle and he had immediately shot her down in trying to console her, asserting that she had no fault whatsoever. But the absence of that resistance made her feel light and empty. She had been so full of regret and guilt and now she had said it all and Luke didn't contradict her and that soothed her.

"You know, I'm not even sure I want this store," she said.

"What? I thought you loved that place?"

Now that he said it, she realized that she didn't. For a moment, it was all blazingly clear. "What made you think that?"

A Sticky Situation

"Can't imagine a store like that not being a labor of passion." He laughed. "No offense." She shook her head. "Also, you fought so hard. You were really impressive that day you kicked me out and then again in court and then with the re-opening. I just thought you were super passionate about the place."

Jamie suddenly felt a tinge of embarrassment. "Just forget I said that."

Luke nodded. "Look. If you want a space in my mall, you've got it. No hesitation."

Jamie nodded and looked at the floor. They sat silently a moment. Then she looked up and scooted closer. She felt him gasp softly. Then she reached out and touched his face. He didn't flinch. He just let her. So she traced the scars with her fingertips. They were so soft, so surprisingly soft. She felt like a god running her fingers mindlessly across a chain of mountains. "Wow," she said.

"That good?" He looked at her out of the corner of his eye.

"Sorry," she said and pulled her hand away. "I've just—well, I wondered." They looked at each other and Jamie thought he might kiss her and the thought didn't bother her. In fact, she was curious what that might feel like. His lips were thin and pink and soft-looking. Instead he let out a sigh and lay back.

"I'm tipsy as heck. I could take a nap right now."

This night filled with surprises had one more in store for her: she felt disappointed.

"Do you know when I was growing up," he said, "like when I was about four or something like that, I wanted to grow up to be a bunny?"

"What?"

"I wanted to hop around in meadows and eat those pink flowers that look like stars. I saw it once in a cartoon. *The Land Before Time*. The dinosaurs ate these little pink flowers and they looked like candy. Even now when I see them, I want to eat them, even though, yeah, I know they're not food."

Jamie laughed and then something sounded loudly at the back of the theater. They both jolted up and looked towards the darkness.

"Oh crap," he said and stood up. "Let's go." He packed his bag quickly and grabbed it and her. They rushed to the door and he flipped the switch right before they heard the creak of a far-off door.

"Hello," said someone into the darkness.

Quietly, Luke and Jamie left through the back door. Luke closed it gently behind himself and then they ran into the woods and didn't stop until they found the car. They sat in it and Luke rolled in his seat, laughing. "Oh, wow," he said. "I think we turned off the light before whoever that was saw it. Probably Jack the maintenance man. I didn't know anyone was there so late."

"I feel sick," Jamie said.

"Drank too much?"

"No. I'm just winded," she admitted. "I haven't run in like years. You sure you're OK to drive?"

Luke grinned again. She was growing fond of that look on his face.

"I'm OK. Really. I made sure to just give us half shots. But let's take a moment." He sat back and a minute later she heard him snore. Her mouth hung open in surprise at how easy that was for him. She decided she should just let him sleep, so she looked up at the stars and tried to relax. She couldn't believe this night. She had sold god-knows-how-much-more-than-ever-before and...

She turned to look at Luke, who slept peacefully.

After an hour, she nudged him with an elbow. "Hey," she said. "Wanna try?"

"Oh yeah," he said and sat up.

"You fell asleep there."

"Who me? Nah. I just shut my eyes a moment."

She shook her head. He took her back to the mall parking lot, where she'd left her car. She started to leave, and he reached for her shoulder, pulling her back.

"Hey," he said with a smile. "I had fun tonight."

"I did too," she said. "And I can't thank you enough for helping me. Honestly, I don't know how I'd've done it without you. And for the tequila too, thanks for that."

They looked at each other moment, but Jamie broke the gaze. "Night," she said and closed the door behind her. She got in her car and drove home.

CHAPTER SIXTEEN

Luke brought Jamie donuts the next morning. Through the plate glass windows, he saw her cleaning up the shop from the night before. The place looked a mess. Missing tapestries made the walls look messy, there were used cups and plates and napkins everywhere, on the shelves, the counter. The food table was still outside and littered with stale charcuterie.

He opened the door of the shop and the penises above his head knocked noisily together. She'd put them back. She turned to face him, surprised. "Morning. I brought donuts."

"Frosted?"

"Oh yeah, I learned my lesson from last time. I got strawberry, maple and chocolate."

"OK, then. You can stay."

"Why do I think you're not kidding?"

He put the donuts on the counter and started to clear it of detritus. Jamie, predictably, went straight for the donut bag. "What are you doing here?" she asked with a mouth full of dough.

He looked confused. Wasn't it obvious? He'd come to help. "You're not used to having friends, are you?"

She looked at him for a moment and then shrugged. "After we clean this up, want to help me hang some more tapestries?"

He had some schoolwork to do, but he could do it later, he thought. They cleaned up for the next hour. Luke teased her that she was hungover. Jamie teased him that he was too young to know what that meant. At one point she let out a frustrated shout.

"What's wrong?" He was alarmed.

"I just can't believe people left stuff on the floor. Like who does that? Who puts plates on the floor? There was a garbage can right there!"

He laughed and took her trash out to the dumpster. Together they hung some more tapestries to fill the blank spaces on the walls and they picked new pieces to display and sell. She complimented him on his idea of limiting what she sold. He was right about people needing to be led and also not overwhelming them with options. She made sure to say, "That doesn't apply to the donuts you bring me. Always feel it's necessary to bring a spread. Many options. Always."

He stepped closer.

She was biting her lip.

He got closer to her and closer and then bent down and pulled a napkin from under her foot. When he stood back up, she looked pale and nervous.

"You OK?" he asked, searching her eyes. She nodded her head. And it occurred to him that she might've thought he was going to kiss her. At least he hoped that's what made her all nervous and hollow-eyed. He wanted to kiss her, but he wanted her to tell him she wanted it. He shook the thought out of his head too.

Luke decided to tell her about his plan to travel the world as soon as things settled here. Fiji, Thailand, Vietnam, rural China. The food, the dance, the music, the art. He wanted to experience it all.

"Those are all my dream places too," she said. "I've always wanted to travel. I just never got to. When my mom was doing it, I was in college and I didn't want to miss any of it."

"Then that's settled," he said. "We'll travel the world. We'll surf waves in the south Pacific." He mimicked surfing a wave. "And we'll smoke ganja," he said in a terrible Jamaican accent, "in India, eat street food in Ho Chi Minh."

Jamie shuddered. "I'm going to tell you something, but you can't judge me."

She waited.

He nodded.

"I won't," he said.

She took a deep breath and searched his eyes for something. When she seemed satisfied that it was safe, he supposed, she started to speak.

"Whenever I think of it, getting on a plane, I have this like nightmare fantasy. I imagine myself on the wing of the plane. But not in a sweet cute romantic way, like look at me with the wind in my hair, traveling free like a bird. I imagine it realistically, like somehow I've ended up on the wing of the plane just as it starts

A STICKY SITUATION

to leave the ground and I'm too afraid to jump so far down so I just hang on for dear life, totally sure with this like childlike faith that a few hours hanging on to the side of a plane going over four hundred miles an hour thousands of feet in the sky is not only possible but probable if I just have enough determination."

He knew that it would be something like this. He hadn't known how to respond last night, when she'd told him about her mother. He didn't think that he loved anyone that much—to have their death destroy his world. If his mother died, he'd miss her, he'd mourn for her, but her death wasn't purely sad to him. He'd watched his mother's illness for so long, knowing that the medications and the other therapies brought her no relief. He'd thought for a while that death for Sheila would truly be rest. She'd said so enough times. The thought did make him sad and he tried not to feel it too much in the moment, not in front of Jamie. He didn't want her to retreat now, so he kept his own views to himself at the moment. The time would come, he thought, for him to tell her.

He decided a change of subject was in order, plus he was curious about something. "So, how much did you make last night?"

Jamie went to the register. "You know, I was too nervous to find out, so I left it for last." She grabbed the receipts and started to tally the sales. "We made about... $1,400."

"Respectable. That's a whole month's rent and more."

"Only because your grandfather gave me the cheapest rent in history."

"He was a surprisingly nice guy."

She continued to tally. "But, the highest seller was...the gum..."

"Really?"

"Yes, more than half of it was just from gum. People like it that much? Wow. No wonder I had to fill these bins a second time."

This gave Luke an idea. "What if..."

"I opened a gum store?"

"How did you know I'd say that?"

"You seem like a follow-the-money guy."

"What the heck does that mean?"

"Nothing. Just that you're practical. I'm not that practical."

Then a group of people walked in. Luke recognized them from last night. It turned out that the man was a regular at the bar and had brought his family to try out the gum.

"These little guys," the man said, rubbing the heads of two twins about age four, "couldn't get enough of it! They ate it all. We're going on a road trip in a few days, so I thought I'd get some more to reward for good behavior."

When the family left with their bags of gum, Luke and Jamie looked at each other wide-eyed. "It's a sign," she said.

"Yes, follow the money."

"We're a good team," she said.

Luke felt himself grow warm all over. He cleared his throat, swallowed, and nodded.

The amulets above the door rattled again. It was Norman, Jamie's uncle. Luke suddenly felt nervous.

"Well, if it isn't the happy couple."

Luke mumbled, "Hello."

Then he turned to Jamie who shot her uncle daggers with her eyes. "Uncle Norman? Why are you here? Shouldn't you be managing something?"

"Darling, is this how you treat a beloved uncle? With callous disdain?"

"No, Uncle Norman. Not at all. Just a little suspicion."

"I wanted to see how the opening went. I see you've cleaned up already. Pity I couldn't be of assistance."

"I'm sure."

Luke clapped his hands together and all eyes turned to him. "Sorry," he said, sheepish. "I got to go," he said. He had neglected his studies too much the past few days. He even skipped drama club.

"Don't leave on my account."

"No. It's not that at all," he said trying to smile. "I just got to go do some schoolwork."

He wished Jamie luck with the rest of her day just as a pair of people walked into the store, the amulets above the door banging loudly together. Both Jamie and Norman said goodbye and then he was out the door in the fresh air. He drove home with the windows open despite the cold. He felt a bit dazed and realized Jamie had that effect on him often.

When he arrived home, his mother slept on the recliner, her cigarette hanging from her lips, unlit. The house smelled rank. He started to clean before going up

A STICKY SITUATION

to his room. He washed the dishes and then he dusted and then he swept and mopped. His mother slept through it all. Luke had found a glass beside her that smelled like whiskey. He figured she'd be out another hour or so.

In his room, he lay down for a moment. When he opened his eyes, it was night. He staggered over to his desk and started to do his reading and his assignments for calculus. He spent a few hours under that desk light, trying to avoid going back downstairs. He could hear his mother fumbling around in the kitchen. No song trilled upstairs, so he figured it wasn't safe. At one point his stomach rumbled so hard he felt nauseated. So, he snuck down the stairs. He popped a head into the living room. His mother sat there, asleep again as the TV blared. He figured he should leave the volume alone or she might wake.

He made himself a simple sandwich and ate it slowly, his stomach still feeling queasy. Not too long after, he felt better and snuck back upstairs.

He moved his desk chair to the window and sat in it with his heels on the seat. He wrapped his arms around his knees and watched the sky.

He thought of Jamie, of all the time they'd spent together and felt happy. So far, their experiment with *The Cuckoo Cl*ck* had been fruitful and he hoped that he could convince her that the best thing to do was close down for the remodel and then be part of his vision for the mall. He had mentioned it before, that the mall would have to close for a while. But they hadn't discussed it directly. He worried about that. Jamie had proved herself to be a bit of a hothead. And while he found that attractive, he also didn't want her to fight him. A star shot across the sky then. *Make a wish*, his mind whispered to him. A wish...a wish... he couldn't think of anything to wish for. He had so much to be happy about. His plan, so far, was working. It felt like a waste, but he said it anyway. "I wish that this would all just work out...including the Jamie part."

He gazed at the sky a while longer. Then he went and brushed his teeth and showered. He got back into bed and he thought about Jamie. She had let him in, he thought. She had told him some of her darkest fears and thoughts. He had never imagined this, that he'd crush on a tenant, and he had scolded himself before about it. But now it seemed he couldn't stop himself from wanting to get closer and from trying to get closer. He could just give in, he thought. Then he thought about the mall, the deadline that the dispensaries had given him. It approached. He had promised himself that neither Jamie nor any other tenant would get in his way. But he was too overjoyed with all the time he'd spent around her, watching her laugh, catching her scent in the air whenever they were close to each other, examining her pouty lips, her buckteeth and how cute they made her look, and he felt little fear despite all the perilous thoughts that popped up. It would work out, he told himself. He could have the plan for his mall, and he could have Jamie—if she wanted him back. He could have both.

Then he fell asleep, dreamlessly, until morning.

CHAPTER SEVENTEEN

Luke woke up panicked. He got up to brush his teeth. Today he had a calculus test and he wanted to see Jamie. He wanted to see her not only because something in his belly asked him to, asked him to be near her, but also because he was worried about what he'd been thinking about last night. He had to talk to her about a realistic deadline for temporarily closing her shop so that the contractors could start their work. He kept thinking about how he'd confidently told the dispensary owners that there was nothing to worry about when he knew full and well that he hadn't discussed this with his tenant. But first, calculus.

He took a moment in front of the mirror and touched the scars on his cheek. Jamie had touched them last night. He could still feel her smooth fingertips there. He had always thought of his scars as an unfortunate circumstance, but feeling Jamie caress them last night, made him feel lucky. He had never felt that way about his scars before. He left the mirror and finished getting ready.

The test his mother had made him proved to be incredibly difficult. She was a stickler, so he was not allowed to use his textbook or any notes or sheets with formulas. Of course, he gave it his best and two hours later his mother was wrenching the test from his grasp.

"Hey," Sheila shouted, "let go. Time's up."

Luke growled. He had at least a few questions he had wanted to double check the answers of, but he gave in. He had the thought in the back of his mind that none of this mattered because he wasn't going to college. But, oddly, while he took his test, he had considered what it would take to open a gum store. He would need to use calculus for revenue and cost functions for the place. So, it was incorrect that none of this mattered; he ignored that part of him that wanted to decry all his work as pointless. It was important to stay positive as he tried to beat the odds and chase down success.

He had more studying to catch up on, but he was tired of being at home, so he went to the park. It was unseasonably warm. He sat out in the sun, with his wind breaker on, and read *The Great Gatsby*. His mother had chosen it for his English curriculum. He identified with Jay in many ways, the ambition, the struggle to prove himself when forces conspired against him. He thought of his lawyer. But he hoped to avoid the tragedy that befell Jay. Did that mean not pursuing anything further with Jamie?

Luke had fallen asleep dreaming of Jamie. It frightened him now. It wasn't so much that he had feelings for her. It was more that he had fallen asleep wondering if she'd be a detriment and the prevailing feeling had been that he didn't care. But that must've been the tequila talking. Now, in the light of day, he recognized that he did care. Very much. Nothing would stand in his way. But, at the same time, he couldn't imagine how Jamie could be a problem, other than getting angry once he made clear that he needed her to close down temporarily. She would understand him though, he thought. She would understand that needing to close down temporarily wasn't anything against her.

So, if this was true, why did he feel so nervous?

He texted Jamie. He asked her if she was free tonight. It turned out she was.

He had agreed to meet her at the mall. After he was done with his studying, he went home, showered, dressed and was off to see her. Luckily Sheila didn't ask any questions. She was so engrossed in what she watched on television. He saw Jamie through the window of her shop, his shoes echoing in the empty dark foyer of the mall. She had customers. A woman perused the pieces that Jamie had set out. Another couple was choosing gum. Jamie talked to another person over by the haucos and Luke couldn't help but feel some pride again. He definitely felt great that he had been so helpful to her, but it also made him happy to see that she had turned things around on her own steam. He had helped a bit, but really, it was her. She was passionate and interesting, and she made the pieces in her store seem interesting too. All she'd needed was a little guidance.

He sat at one of the picnic tables in the empty food court until the customers left. He admired the dome roof, that let in sunlight to make the intricate design in the dome sparkle. He went into the shop. The place had become so familiar already, he felt comfortable walking in.

"Hey, chica," he said. "Ready to go?"

A STICKY SITUATION

"Where are you taking me?"

"Just to get some of the best tacos in town." He felt a jolt of nerves. That had sounded like a date. While a date with her sounded like the best thing ever, that's not what he had intended. He simply wanted to break the news. Now, he was worried she'd see it as a date too. And he couldn't decide which possible scenario was worse: that she'd think it was a date and reject him or that she'd think it was a date and then felt bamboozled when he lay the truth on her.

"Sounds good," she said. She playfully pushed his shoulder with her own as they walked out of the store. She reached out and switched off the lights.

"My car?" he asked.

"Sure. You need all the practice you can get."

He started to recognize that he liked being teased by her. He opened the door for her, and she gave him an incredulous look before sitting. They sang Italian pop songs the whole way. Luke sang, Jamie just made noises, loudly and off-key.

They drove to the downtown, by the courthouses, where the food trucks parked. The spaces were all taken along the street and they were forced to drive a street over. But even there the spaces were sparse. It seemed that everyone wanted a piece of this preview of spring. They did find a spot between two other cars. He tried to parallel park, once, twice, thrice.

Jamie seemed to be unable to hold in her laughter anymore. "OK, let me help you," she said, giggling.

"You can help me if you stop laughing."

"OK. Done." She took a deep breath and composed herself. "Pull up to the car in front, side mirror to side mirror. Yup, exactly. Just like that. Relax, buddy, nerves aren't going to help you here. Now just cut really sharply and move in slowly. OK. OK. That's good. OK, stop! Now straighten out the wheels. More more more. Yes. You did it."

He felt a surge of excitement and jumped out of the car. She exited too. He shouted over the hood, "I did it! Thank you. I couldn't have done it without you."

"I noticed," she said and winked.

They started walking towards the courthouses.

"I've never parallel parked so smoothly before. It would have taken me, hmm... two more tries at least."

Jamie stopped him there and said, "Do you even have an ego?"

Luke tilted his head, thinking. "What do you mean?"

They continued to walk.

"The other night, at the place that shall not be named and that I'll deny ever going to—"

"You mean the high school?"

"I told you. I was never there," she said. "But anyway, the other night, at the place that shall not be named, I fully expected you to take credit for all the work we did. When you made your toast. You toasted my success. I said 'ours,' but you didn't seem to agree. I was surprised by that."

"Oh, well, you worked really hard and you had more on the line than me and all I did was push you. It was really all your doing. If you had set me up in that store exactly the same way and told me to run that opening, I doubt I would've sold a thing. But when you explain your stuff—your pieces, sorry—it really is mesmerizing. You convince people that they really want, maybe even need, a statue of two old Greek people going at it."

"See? Even now. You won't take credit."

"You're making me blush. Please stop."

Jamie laughed. "Sure. I'll stop."

When they arrived at a food truck with a small line outside of it, Luke told her this was the best Mexican food in the area, possibly the state. "Wait until you have the green sauce. Oh, the green sauce." He raised two fists and looked up at the heavens. "You'll see."

When they reached the window, the woman screamed. "Luquito!" The woman exited the truck and gave him a hug that literally lifted him slightly off the ground. Luke felt slightly embarrassed, but he also loved it.

"This is Edna," he told Jamie. "Edna has been feeding me for years. Edna, this is Jamie. She's my friend." Luke saw Jamie looking rapidly from him to Edna. She reached out a hand, but Edna pulled her in for a hug too.

"Luquito helped my son get into college with a scholarship. He's been tutoring him for years. He's so smart, this boy." She reached up and pinched Luke's cheek. Luke grinned.

"I had no idea," Jamie said. "He kept his good deeds a secret. But Luke does say you have the best Mexican food in the state. He made sure to tell me that."

"Oh, lo mejor. Eres lo mejor," Edna said to Luke with a hand on his elbow, the

A Sticky Situation

highest point she could she reach on him.

"You know I tell everyone about your tacos. I'm so hungry for your green sauce."

"OK. Tacos coming up. Your favorite?"

"My favorite times two would be perfect."

"Luquito, anything." With that the woman went back into the truck, the body of it lowering on its shocks.

"You're just the most loved boy in the world, aren't ya?"

Luke just waved a hand at her and looked away, clearly blushing again. When the food was ready, Edna made Luke lean in for her to peck his cheek. "You enjoy the food. OK? I put extra green sauce for you."

They sat on a bench by the library. The sun was setting already, and they watched the sky as they bit into their tacos.

"Oh my god," said Jamie gutturally.

"Right?"

"So good."

"Edna is a fantastic cook. Told you."

"You used to tutor someone who is in college now?"

"Oh, yeah. We used to be in drama club together. It's no big deal. She's making it seem bigger than it was. I just helped edit his essays."

"But you're younger. That's pretty unusual. Also, I thought you said you were homeschooled. But you have a key to the—place that shall not be named and you are in drama club?"

"Oh. I've only been being homeschooled for a couple months or so. Just before my Pop-pop died. I knew that I'd have too much going on, so my mother and I decided it was a good idea. But the principal let me stay in drama club. I told her it was important to me. She's nice."

"What's the meat in these?"

"Um...pork?"

"Are you not sure, little one?"

"Um...yes. I'm sure."

"What is it?"

"It's pork ears..."

"It's yummy. I don't care what it is. I'm eating it and no I'm not sharing just because you scarfed down yours already."

"How did you know I was going to ask?"

"You've been talking to my taco instead of me this whole time."

"I've got something to tell you," he said. His palms felt sweaty.

"So do I. You probably haven't noticed but I haven't been chewing gum the past few days. Whenever I've been around you, I just forgot about it."

"Oh. That's good. You don't want uh...cavities."

"No, you don't get it. I'm like obsessed. Well, not obsessed. It's just a sort of nervous tic thing that happened after my mother died. It soothes me. Anyway, I just noticed that I haven't been doing it when I'm around you, which I suppose is my body telling me it's OK to trust you."

"That's really cool. I'm happy for you and feel really honored," he said. Damn. He couldn't have picked a worse time for her to say that.

"What did you want to tell me?"

"Oh." He swallowed hard. "I'm thirsty as heck. I got to get us some drinks. I'll be right back." She nodded and he was grateful for the chance to think. He went back to Edna and ordered two guava sodas.

When he returned, Jamie accepted the soda gratefully.

"What did you want to tell me?" she asked.

"Hmm?"

"It sounded a bit serious."

"Oh, you know what? I don't even remember. It'll come back to me." He would talk to her about it, but it would have to be later. He didn't want to ruin this feeling of calm she had. He didn't want to ruin this moment, watching the sun fall in an orange and pink splendor.

"So, are you glad you came?"

"Yeah. I like hanging out with you."

"Hey, by the way, what's up with your Uncle Norman?"

"What do you mean, 'what's up with my Uncle Norman?'"

"He's quite a character. That's all."

"He is. He's a funny guy, really open. He's embarrassed by nothing. He's really been there for me, especially this past year with everything that happened, and he helped me with my store. Though he won't be doing that anymore."

"He won't help you?"

A Sticky Situation

"No. He used to travel for me and get the pieces I sell. After my mother died. She used to do it before him. I think I told you that. But once I developed this plane thingy, he stepped in. But I'll have to figure out some other way, I guess."

"Sorry."

"No, it's fine. It's just one of the changes I have to roll with. It has made me think a lot about my future and what I want to do."

"Tell me about it. I've had nothing but changes the past few months. And the hardest part was probably preparing for my Pop-pop's death. It felt cold or something to prepare myself to take over while he was still alive. But the lawyer insisted I think about it and he was right, I guess. No sense in letting everything just pile up on me at once. It was like I'd just accepted a job or something. You don't think about the guy who did it before you. Except to make sure your coworkers don't miss him. It kind of feels like that. Except, I have no coworkers. Not yet anyway. So I get how hard it can be."

"You don't feel anything about your grandfather?"

"I mean. We used to go out every Saturday and work together. So, on Saturdays I expect to see him still. But of course..."

"Yeah. I know that feeling. Like you forget for a second that they're gone."

"That does make me a little sad, but like I told you before, we weren't close. We never had a conversation, so I don't exactly miss him."

"Life is pretty messed up sometimes."

He agreed.

"Can I give you a hug?" Jamie asked, looking into his eyes.

Luke choked. Jamie started banging on his back as he coughed. He sat back on the bench and tried to breath once he stopped coughing. "Oh god," he said, coughing a bit more. "That was embarrassing."

"Not at all."

They laughed.

"Hug?" he asked.

"Hug."

He held her, feeling her warmth against his chest. She felt so small in his arms. She smelled sweet. He held her until she let go.

"Thanks," she said and smiled at him.

They got up and tossed out their trash.

"Ready?" he asked.

She nodded. They walked to his car, laughing about Uncle Norman all the way.

CHAPTER EIGHTEEN

After Luke dropped her off back at her car, Dean called Jamie and asked her if she could go cover for a couple hours. Apparently, Leah had gone home early because she wasn't feeling well. Jamie agreed.

The shift was only four hours, but it was grueling. The NBA all-star game had packed the bar to the hilt. It was pint after pint after pint and whiskeys with coke, with soda, with ice. Ephraim was in a terrible mood because the kitchen guys were spanking each other something fierce. It seemed that everyone was on full tilt. She wondered briefly if the moon was full—but only for a moment because she was too busy to think. At the end of the shift, she stood outside with the kitchen guys. They smoked, she chewed. She popped her gum non-stop.

"Do you ever take a break from that?" asked one of the line cooks venomously.

"Not when you're around," said Jamie and popped her gum. "You smoke and spank each other. I chew my gum. We each have our things."

That settled it.

Just then Dean came out back too. "Don't you boys have some scrubbing to do?" He was referring to the cooks who had to scrub down the kitchen every night. They put out their cigarettes and went inside. "Jamie, I want to talk to you."

"What's up, Dean?"

"I wanted to know if you'd given any thought to what I asked you a couple weeks ago."

Jamie knew this was coming, but she hadn't made up her mind yet. Things were starting to turn around at the store and she didn't want to make a quick decision she might regret. "Actually, I have."

"Tell me you've got some good news," he said and ran a hand through his salt and pepper hair.

"More like no news. Sorry," she said when she saw the look on her face. "It's a really big decision and I have to settle something with my landlord at the shop first. But I will get you an answer soon. Very soon. I promise."

Dean pulled out a pack of cigarettes and put one between his lips. He inhaled deeply through his nose and then lit the cigarette. "Why do we hang out by the dumpsters?"

Jamie chuckled. "Away from peering eyes? I don't know."

He smoked and she chewed for a few moments. The quiet made her nervous. She couldn't tell if he was pissed or not. Finally, he spoke up again. "OK. I don't want to start looking elsewhere, Jamie. I need an answer. Like in a week? Can you do that?"

Jamie chewed her gum. "I think I can figure it out in a week. Yeah. I'll get back to you. Thanks, Dean."

He nodded and then turned towards the woods to finish his cigarette. Jamie spit out her gum and went inside to do her side-work.

When she went back behind the bar, Rinna caught her attention. "I need five pints of Guinness, please. Also, heads up. Your ex-boo is here."

Jamie looked up and sure enough in the back corner was Ben with some buddies.

Jamie tried to avoid looking at Ben and was successful for the most part. At one point she looked up and he caught her eye. He smiled. For some reason, Luke kept popping up in her head. She remembered them laughing on stage, falling asleep next to each other. She thought about how calm and safe she felt with him.

She could feel Ben watching her and they made eye contact a few more times during the night. "Ugh, stop looking over here."

"Who, Ben?" Rinna had come over to the bar and was standing behind her as she filled another pint.

"Oh, nothing," said Jamie embarrassed. She made sure to fill all the orders and then she rushed outside to chew some gum. What the hell was Ben thinking coming here? Pop. First, he never came to this bar when they were going out or before. Pop, pop. Second, he had brought his friends to distract from his intentions, but she knew what he was here for. At some point in the night, he'd make an attempt to talk to her. She didn't know what about. They had broken

A STICKY SITUATION

up and made a clean break, for the most part. She definitely never initiated their conversations though. He sought her. Pop.

Later, during the rush, Jamie went to the bathroom. There was a line, but a girl she went to high school with took pity on her and let her cut the line.

"We need an employee bathroom," Jamie told Rinna as she stood behind her to go under the hinged countertop. Just as she tried to duck under the counter, Jamie felt a hand on her shoulder. She turned around and saw Ben. Oh, god, she thought. "Hi," she said.

They stared at each other awkwardly a moment.

"Can you talk?"

"Uh. No. I'm in the middle of a shift. It's really busy," she said, stating the obvious.

"I'll wait for you," he said and then he walked back to his table. His friends were mostly gone. Just he and one other guy talked over a beer.

The rush started to die down and when it was almost eleven thirty and they announced last call, the bar thinned out.

She started to do her closing duties after making the last drinks of the night. She brought bins to the dishwasher and started to wipe down the shelves with liquor. Looking over to the corner she saw that Ben now sat alone. He played with a coaster at his table. Then he looked around and almost caught her eye, but Jamie looked away quickly.

She went back to bring things to the kitchen again. When she came back out, Ben was waiting for her at the swinging door.

"Jamie Bell."

Jamie spun around furiously. "Shut your trap, mister." He should definitely not have been calling her that.

"OK," he said. "Come talk to me outside."

She could tell that she didn't really have a choice. She put up a finger to tell him to wait and then went and told Rinna that she was taking a break. She heard Rinna asking, "Where you headed?" as she walked out the front door with Ben behind her.

Jamie and Ben stood over by the potted juniper bush as cars streamed out of the parking lot. A group of people in the far corner were hooting and hollering and falling all over each other with laughter by a truck with the taillights on.

Jamie clasped her upper arms and rubbed them in the cold.

"Thanks for talking to me," said Ben. He took off his jacket and handed it to Jamie. She refused and he made a face. "Don't fight me," he said. "It's cold out."

She reluctantly put on the jacket. The jacket lining was warm and smelled like Ben, like leather and stained wood. She recognized his scent instantly and already she could sense herself relaxing into his jacket and his body heat.

"What's up?" Jamie tried to act as if she didn't just have a bit of a swooning moment putting on the man's jacket. But again, these feelings brought up thoughts of Luke. That confused her most of all.

"Talking to you was so good the other day."

True. It was good to see him. But their relationship ended for a reason and she tried to remember that, the arguments, the pressure. She let him continue.

"It got me thinking that maybe we should see more of each other."

It surprised her, this feeling that came up as he spoke. She'd never felt it before. She'd felt anger, frustration, sadness, depression when what happened between them happened, but she had never felt pity before. But that's what she felt now, looking at his earnest brown eyes, his handsome shy smile. He still looked amazing really, that masculine hard jaw line and those straight white teeth and that body, which she could smell on her now as she cozied unthinkingly into his jacket. But they were over. They had had irreconcilable differences, totally different visions of the future. She didn't want children yet if at all. And she didn't want to marry anyone, not yet at least. Exploring their relationship again, they both knew, would be an exercise in futility.

"I don't think that's..." she started.

Before she could say anything else, he leaned over and kissed her.

Familiar, warm, cozy. She had been kissed like this many times before, so many times she knew exactly what he was about to do with his tongue next. It would be a lie to say that this kiss did not turn her on. It sent sparks all the way up her spine. It made her want to melt, but it wasn't because she wanted to melt into him; she wanted to melt back into the past, into who he had been when they were together, she wanted to melt into a memory. But she maintained some of her senses and broke the kiss. In the background she could hear the group of tailgaters whooping at them.

"No, Ben," she said and stepped away.

A Sticky Situation

"You can't say that did nothing for you." His expression was hurt, a bit desperate.

Jamie wiped her mouth. "You can't just go around kissing people, Ben. We are broken up. You said you had no future with me and you were just wasting your time. So what are you doing now? Are you wasting your time now? Cause I am not as lucky as you. I don't have time to waste, especially on guys who can't decide if they want me or not. Why don't you just take your coat?"

The small group started to cheer.

"Yeah. You tell him, honey," said some drunk woman.

Ben held the jacket and looked over at the group and then back at Jamie.

"I'm sorry," said Jamie. "I can't do this anymore. Do me a favor, Ben. Don't come back here looking for me."

As she walked into the bar, she could hear the woman yelling from the parking lot, "losers. They're all losers. Girl, don't even sweat it."

When she was done with her shift, she asked Trent to walk her to her car. For some reason she expected Ben to be there waiting for her, but he was not.

The next day, Luke decided he would talk to Jamie no matter what happened. All night his stomach was a bundle of nerves. As he entered the mall's dead food court, his cell phone rang. It was his lawyer. He hadn't heard from him since they'd last yelled at each other outside the courthouse. He'd probably gotten wind of the plans for the building being ready. Luke could see Jamie from this spot. It looked like she was dusting and popping gum bubbles. He answered the phone.

"Hello?"

"Luke. I've been looking over—"

"Fred, I told you I'd call you once I got the OK to move forward. Rushing me isn't going to help anything."

"Listen to what I'm saying to you. I'm covering your ass here. The mayor won't give permits. Says the project is unsafe with tenants in the building."

Luke closed his eyes and took a slow deep breath. But his irritation still showed. "What are you telling me this for? I already know this, Fred. I'm handling my tenancies my way and in my grandfather's way. He trained me to do this for years and there's a method. I don't just go in guns blazing and that means you don't either. You represent my interests and my choices, not the other way around."

"I have your mother crying to me at eight o'clock at night on my home phone when my family's sitting to dinner. She's worried about you. Says you've been dating the mall tenant. Says you've not got your head on straight and I'm starting to wonder. This plan can't go through until we have a date for her to clear out and it's getting too close."

"She's going to leave when I ask her to at the end of the month. It's in her best interest. And stop talking to my mother about my personal business. The lines are getting a little too crossed here."

"You think I want to field her tears while I'm eating my stromboli—think again."

Luke looked up from the little corner of the small atrium at the entrance. He'd curled himself into it. Light streamed through the domed ceiling onto its coffers.

When he entered *The Cuckoo Cl*ck*, Jamie smiled up at him. He felt a familiar tingle in his belly when he heard the amulet penises above his head knock against each other.

"Hi," he said. "I brought donuts." He held the bag up by his shoulder.

"Playing that hand pretty often," she said nodding.

"If it's a winning hand…"

Her eyes darted to the corner of the store. Luke looked behind himself. There was nothing there. Was she upset?

"I heard you talking and sounded like it had something to do with me."

"Yes, you're right about that. I should have taken that call in my car. I didn't think you'd hear it. But that's actually what I was coming to talk to you about. You see, I forgot in the excitement of discussing your store to tell you that the mall project's plans are on a deadline. The project has to be approved by my partners in a couple weeks. They've told me that they'll only accept the plans if I have completely vacated the premises. That's because construction can't start while you're here. But I always intended to tell you this, I just. I wanted to handle the situation delicately. I'm sorry."

Jamie looked away from him and took a sharp deep breath. They were silent a moment. He could hear the low hum of the lights above his head.

"You said in court, under oath, that you intended to honor my lease."

"Or come to some mutual accord."

"Where's the mutual here?"

A Sticky Situation

"I'd hoped you'd see that this plan would make it possible for everyone to succeed and that you'd understand that closing down for a few months was worth it to come back with a stronger business plan that could thrive in a higher traffic environment."

Jamie calmly got up and went to the bins of gum. She started to dig, knocking a few pieces to the floor. She stopped when she found one in shiny red wrapping. She started to chew. He'd changed things. He was no longer a calming presence, he thought. He watched her eyes close. She took deep breaths. Her eyes opened and she looked into his with a softness he didn't expect.

"I understand what you want to do. You need me out of here, by when?"

"I didn't want it to be like this. I feel like I sprung it on you."

"Tell me when you need me out."

He wanted to keep telling her he was sorry, he wanted to say it until she told him it was all right, but he thought that that would probably piss her off. "Two weeks," he said.

Jamie nodded. "I want the ten thousand dollars."

What an idiot. He hadn't even thought of that. He was so busy trying to just tell her the truth, he hadn't even given her all the incentive. But it must've looked to her like he tried to shortchange her. "Of course," he said. "That's the deal. I meant to mention it."

"I'll be out by then."

"And you understand that I am guaranteeing you a lease when the *Shire Mall* opens again?"

"Yes."

"Would you sign this document, saying you will vacate by this date?" He lay the papers on the counter and pointed to a specific line. "It includes the ten thousand compensation and then that's it, the lease is dissolved. There's an addendum offering you a lease in the new *Shire Mall* too."

Jamie signed. She didn't look at him. She just chewed softly.

"I'm sorry for taking this long to make things clear."

She went back to the stool behind the register. She looked at him and then down at the document.

"Jamie?"

"What's up, Luke?"

"It seemed that we were building a friendship. It matters to me. I hate that I did something to put that in jeopardy."

"I understand. And I can accept that you didn't do it on purpose. This is your first time doing all this. It makes sense that you'd make some mistakes. I'm just going to need some time."

She was saying exactly what he wanted to hear, but he worried she didn't mean it.

"I have this idea for you to focus on gum."

Jamie nodded.

"Do you want to talk about it?"

"Luke, right now, I need to just take a moment. Do you understand?"

"Yes. I do."

Luke took the documents. "I'll get you a copy," he said.

"I'll talk to you soon," she said and looked at him.

He left and went to go collect rents.

He had taken to wearing a tie during his collections. He'd wanted to inspire a sense of professionalism and, hopefully, authority.

His hand grabbed the peeling paint of the bannister as he climbed the front steps of a single-family home he rented out to a small family. He knocked and the sound echoed into an empty hallway.

The door opened and Luke said, "Mrs. Henderson."

"Oh, Luke. Hello." The woman was in her mid-twenties. Her son came to the door too, a two-year old who clung to her leg. "I heard about your grandfather. He was a kind man."

"Thank you for that. I'm sorry about the circumstances of my visit."

Her eyes looked panicked. "Oh, you mean the late notices. I know it has been three months, but this has never happened to us before. We always pay on time. Have for years. But my husband lost his job and he's been having trouble finding a new one. But I assure you, he's on interviews. He's on one now. We want to pay. I swear."

Luke nodded and took a deep breath. "Think we can talk inside, Mrs. Henderson?"

"Yes, yes, of course," she said to him, picked up her child, and led them inside. Luke shut the door behind him. The apartment was dark, the lights were all off

A STICKY SITUATION

and this side of the building didn't get sun in the afternoon. They sat at a table and she asked him if he'd like anything.

"No, thank you," he said. "I had a coffee before heading over. I'm all set."

"OK," she said and sat down.

"Look, Mrs. Henderson—"

"Please, Luke. Don't evict us. We have no place to go. We are just on hard times. My husband will find a job soon and we will pay you all of it back. I promise."

"Mrs. Henderson— "

"You don't understand. This is killing my husband. He goes out and looks for work every day, but not many places are hiring, and the competition is so much that it's just taking a while. Please let us have some more time."

"Mrs. Henderson—"

"Luke please—"

"Mrs. Henderson," he said as quickly as he could. "Let me speak please."

"I'm sorry," she said. "Go ahead."

"I understand your circumstances." He thought about what his grandfather had taught him. Luke knew what to do. Listen and then start a payment plan or forgive the debt. It was simpler than eviction and made more sense when the tenants were actually trying. "Your husband is out looking for work and will pay me back when he's able. Take another month without worry for now. We can talk in a few weeks and you'll give me an update. After he gets work, we can talk about a payment plan. For now, just settle down."

"Are you serious?"

He nodded. "Quite."

Mrs. Henderson thanked him profusely. She offered to feed him, but he refused politely. "Let me know if your situation changes any," he said.

With that they said goodbye and Luke went to collect more rents. He spent the day keeping himself busy. He didn't want to think about how poorly things stood with Jamie right now. But no matter what he did, his anxieties didn't really settle. He didn't think they would, not until Jamie forgave him.

Jamie spent the night cleaning the house. She listened to "What About Love" by Heart. She dusted everything. Then she swept. Then she mopped.

She still processed the fact that Luke had left such important information out. She didn't want to have an angry response. She didn't want to regret her actions, so she tried to be understanding. Their time together had been so fun and easy lately that she forgot he was so young. He was a kid really. Even more than she was, she thought self-consciously. He could make a mistake. It didn't erase everything that came before it. She just needed some time to busy herself, so she could think about this new change.

It wasn't just that she couldn't operate her shop. She'd have to empty it. At least with the money she could put the things in storage, so they'd be safe. Just the thought of these things weighed heavily on her. Did she even want this store anymore? It seemed like everything was pointing to "no." But he had mentioned this idea about a gum store. She could run a place like that and run the bar. That could work out for her. The thought of working with Luke did feel like a good one still. He was smart and generous. He could help her. She could run a profitable business. A gum store wasn't a bad idea. No one knew gum better than she did and she might be able to expand into other international candy. That was something everyone could enjoy. Children would be fans, adults would indulge. It had broader appeal than erotica. That was for certain. It could be a money maker.

When she was done cleaning, she still couldn't quite relax even though it grew closer to her bedtime. She decided to go for a walk. The night was chilly and she pulled her coat closely around herself. The stars were hidden by cloud cover and everything seemed bright as the light reflected back on the ground. She stayed up walking for an hour until her calves ached, but she tossed and turned another hour before she gave up and called Amanda.

They talked for another hour, complaining about the things in their lives that were going poorly. They made each other laugh. The prevailing advice, however, was to see what the kid did next.

"Seems like maybe you like him now."

"He's really helped me. He has a good sense for business and I think he could help me more."

"But I mean the other stuff. That little taco excursion sounds like a date to me."

"I didn't call it that, but I'd be a liar if I said it didn't feel that way." She remembered Edna and how much affection he provoked in her. He was sweet. She

A STICKY SITUATION

figured the fact that she was thinking about it so much probably meant she liked him more than she'd admitted to herself openly. But now she thought that she should let herself feel it. It was OK to be attracted to him. Amanda encouraged it. That was something.

That settled it. She'd talk to him the next day.

CHAPTER NINETEEN

When Luke woke up, the house was quiet. This was not a good sign, so he took his time getting up and getting ready. He took a slow shower until he felt he'd washed away all the grogginess. Then he went downstairs to the kitchen. As he turned the corner, his mother threw a cast iron skillet at his feet.

"You left this in the sink. You don't have a maid here."

Luke jumped back. "Ma!" He picked up the skillet. "You broke the tile. You could've hurt me."

His mother staggered away from the sink and leaned on the table. "If I wanted to hurt you, I wouldn't have missed. When I want to hurt you, you won't have a doubt about it." She smoked a cigarette stuck between her lips and looked at him through her eyelashes. She looked dangerous.

"You've got to take your meds. Did you take your meds this morning?"

"No, I didn't need them today. I don't want to feel fuzzy."

"If you don't take them every day your symptoms become unmanageable. You've got to take them." He went to retrieve them from the living room. She kept all her meds in an old rolling-top secretary's desk.

"We need to prevent," he said as he went to the kitchen. "We can't play catch-up."

Sheila had a knife in her hand. She held the blade to her wrist.

"Ma?"

"I don't know why you want to control me. But I won't let you. You're not my father."

"You're right, Ma. I'm not. I'm your son and I love you. The last thing I want is for you to hurt yourself."

"Then stop screaming at me," she said and waved her hands and the knife around.

A Sticky Situation

"I won't scream at you, Ma," he said and stepped closer to her.

She began to sob. "I'm so tired," she said. "I need it all to stop. I'm not a good mother or daughter. I'm terrible."

"Ma, look at me."

Sheila looked up, tears covering her eyes up like a wall of glass. She blinked and the tears streamed down her cheeks.

"You're my mother and I need you. I need you. OK?" he reached out for her slowly and grabbed her wrist. "Let me have that." He put his hand around hers, the one holding the knife. She gave it to him, and he gasped as he moved it into a drawer. He led her away from the kitchen and she let him, sobbing and shaking. "Ma, it's OK, Ma. I promise. Everything is OK."

They sat on the sofa and he held her for a while as she cried. "I just don't understand why my father did it. He didn't trust me. I'm the adult here."

Luke held her and listened.

"But you mustn't think," she started and pulled herself away from him to look in his eyes. She touched his cheek with a sweaty palm. "Don't think that I don't want the best for you, honey. I want you to succeed. I do."

"I know, Ma."

"No, really. I want you to have all your dreams come true."

"I know. Don't worry."

"That's why I told him he could do it. Because we know it should really be my decision."

"Tell who?"

"Fred. He called me last night. I told him to do it."

"To do what, Ma?"

"He had the permits, he said. The mayor gave them to him. She wants that prison too you know. She's a very ambitious woman our lovely mayor. So, she let it all go through as long as the liability issues were cleared up. So, I said yes. I told Fred to go ahead and get rid of her."

Immediately it became clear to Luke. It had been her. Sheila had told Attorney Harris to sue Jamie, to have her evicted. For some reason he couldn't quite understand Attorney Harris had done it. He'd listened to her.

"I told him not to worry that I'd make you see sense, but ever since you met that girl you haven't listened to me. You keep just doing what you want and putting everything in jeopardy."

"You want the money that bad, Ma? You went behind my back."

"No. I know what you should be doing. My father spent years building this business and he didn't want you to do all this revitalization business. He wanted you to make sure we didn't need anything. That's only accomplished by selling to the state."

"What did you do?"

"I told Fred to make sure the contractor went through with it."

Luke's cell rang upstairs. He could hear its faint song. He'd answer it afterward.

"With what, Ma?" He grew impatient now.

"The construction." She started to laugh. "Now she can't go in, no matter what you say. It's a construction zone. I was always the cleverest one. See? He should have put me in charge. Me. Not a child. You're very smart, honey. But you're too young for these decisions. But I took care of it and now there's nothing to worry about."

Luke felt nauseated. He ran upstairs to get his phone. It was the contractor. He had left a message. Apparently, Fred had called him the day before and said that Luke had gotten the tenant out and the construction could start. They had started demolitions already when his assistant had found Jamie in her store. They had to stop construction and he had to pay his guys for a whole day. Luke called him back. The contractor explained the situation again.

"She's got to be out of there. We had to shut it all down, my guys are just sitting around collecting a paycheck."

"Why didn't you wait until you heard from me?"

"You told me the last time to work with Fred. He signed the papers himself, so we started. How should I have known he wasn't working for you?"

"No, you're right. I'll be there as soon as I can."

Now he had to do something with his mother. He didn't want to leave her alone. "Ma, you're coming with me." She complained but complied. He had her put on a coat over her pajamas and some sweatpants over her pajama bottoms. "It's cold out today, Ma," he told her when she protested. She was no longer as worked up. They drove together to the mall.

"Ma, stay in the car. I'll be back," he said as he pulled up to the opposite end

A STICKY SITUATION

of the mall from where Jamie was. He needed to talk to the contractor first. He took the keys with him.

Luke apologized to the contractor, Mike. Luke told him that Attorney Harris had made a mistake. It was nothing to worry about. He, Luke, would cover the costs the contractor had incurred for the day. He apologized profusely and told him that they could start as soon as Jamie vacated the space. He gave him the deadline she'd agreed to.

"From now on, please don't go on Fred's say-so. Run everything by me. I don't have any representatives in this project. It's just me. And I'll make sure Fred knows not to call you again."

Mike agreed. They would go forward and forget about this misunderstanding. He told Luke that things always went wrong in construction, even with the best planning. Luke thanked him. The men looked happy to go home for the day when Mike announced it.

Luke got back in the car. His mother seemed to be returning to lucidity.

"Luke. I messed up. Didn't I?"

"It's all right, Ma. You're just scared. But I'm firing Fred and from now on you have nothing to do with my company. It's mine. Pop-pop trusted me with it and you're going to have to do the same."

Sheila looked at him wild-eyed.

"Ma, you need more help. This medication isn't enough. I think we need to get you into a hospital."

"You don't love me?"

"Ma, you're sick. You went behind my back. You put everything I've been working for in danger. You lied to me. This isn't you. I'm so sorry. I didn't realize that you were having such a hard time with Pop-pop's death. I just worried about myself and all these changes and I didn't stop to think about you and if you were handling things. I'm so sorry. Ma, you got to let me help you."

Sheila looked at her hands. "I did do that. Didn't I? I want you to succeed, Luke. Not like me. I haven't amounted to anything."

"Ma. That's not. That's not true. Look how much you've helped me. You've given everything to raise me. Let me help you."

Sheila gasped. She was frightening him.

"Can we go? To the doctor? I'll take you to the crisis center. Ma? You got to say something. Ma?"

Sheila nodded. "Yes," she said so softly he almost didn't hear it.

He took her to the crisis center. He waited to talk to the doctor. She'd been growing paranoid over the past few weeks, they told him. She'd agreed to stay for treatment.

"I'm sorry. I know this must be hard," said the doctor. "The best thing you can do is go home and get some rest."

Luke didn't follow the advice of his mother's doctor, however. He went to the mall to find Jamie.

CHAPTER TWENTY

He entered *The Cuckoo Cl*ck*. He reached up and steadied the amulets.

He expected to see her dusting. "Jamie," he called out. But there was no answer. He checked the storage space, he checked next door, but she wasn't anywhere to be found. He sat on the stool a moment and took a breath. He'd really messed things up royally, he thought. He should have fired Fred a long time ago. If he had, this whole problem would've been avoided.

He shook his head. Where was she? She had left on the lights and left the door unlocked. It was unlike her to leave things unattended, he thought. He gave her a call. No answer.

He went outside to the parking lot. He didn't see her car. Maybe she had gone home.

He drove to her house. He wasn't sure this was the best thing to do, just show up at her house, but he was nervous she might not answer the phone or, worse, refuse to see him. He rang the bell.

He thought he heard faint footsteps. But he wasn't sure. Then he could hear the doorknob being fumbled. She was home. She opened the door and there she was in sweatpants with a blanket around her shoulders. Her eyes were red. She looked ready to climb back onto the couch or into bed.

"It's you," she said.

"Sorry to show up like this. I heard about what happened and I came to talk to you."

"Isn't there some privacy law that says you can't just look up my address and show up here, landlord? There should be."

She walked away, leaving the door open and disappeared around a corner. He guessed he was supposed to follow her. He stepped into the house. First there was a small hallway that looked like it ended in a kitchen and to the left was a staircase leading to the bedrooms, he imagined. It was a lot like his house. The living room must be around the corner. And there Jamie was on the couch wrapped up in the blanket like some Russian babushka. The TV was on low. The place looked immaculate. It took him back for a moment, how much it looked like he'd stepped into a magazine, everything in its place, and a stylish place for everything. Her curls stuck out from the makeshift cowl like rays. He looked at Jamie.

"Jamie?"

She didn't answer. She gasped for breath and the sound was weak and trembling.

"Jamie," he said and stepped closer. She didn't look at him, so he crouched down in front of her. "Jamie, I didn't mean for any of this to happen." She kept looking over his shoulder at the TV. He reached out and grabbed her hand and maneuvered his head to look into her eyes. She looked down at their hands and then slipped hers out of his grasp. "My lawyer made this happen. He told the construction crew to start today. It wasn't me. I swear to you, Jamie. I never would've done things like this. You can trust me. I wouldn't do this to you and I wouldn't do it like this. We already discussed closing down. If I needed you to clear out the space for some reason at the last minute, I would've talked to you about it."

Jamie inspired sharply as if she had woken suddenly from some uncommon noise. It startled him. "Jamie?"

"You made me sign a paper giving me time..."

"Jamie..." he started, but he didn't know what to say really. He waited for her to speak. She looked over his shoulder again, her eyes growing in and out of focus, lost in some thought.

"You took it away from me. Twice."

Luke grasped for something to say, but it all seemed empty or disrespectful. He didn't understand why.

"That was my mother's store." Now her eyes grew glassy with tears. "I thought you understood. Why would you just snatch it from me like that? After I promised to be gone in a few weeks?"

"I—I truly didn't. It was Fred. He keeps trying to force me to evict you and I've been refusing all this time. But he keeps going behind my back."

A Sticky Situation

"Fred?" She looked at him now and the tears escaped in tiny splashes down her blanket.

"My lawyer. Not anymore, he's not my lawyer. He told the construction crew it could start today. I swear that I didn't do this."

"Well, it doesn't matter anymore."

"It matters, Jamie," he said and reached out for her shoulder. "It matters to me. That's why I'm here. To tell you that it matters, it matters to me."

"It doesn't matter, Luke. It's a construction zone now. There's no turning back. You kicked me out. I can't even go in and empty it anymore."

"Who told you that?"

"Your lawyer isn't the only one in town, Luke. Though he might be the worst."

"I'll make sure to get your inventory safely into storage."

"I don't think I even care anymore. Do what you want, Luke," now her voice grew sharper. "It's not my store anymore. I don't care."

"Jamie. I never intended for any of this to happen. Seriously. I want you to open a store in the mall and I never wanted to do this this way. I'm so sorry I let this happen. This is my fault, but please know it wasn't my intention."

"I don't want to talk about this anymore. Did you get what you wanted?"

"I didn't want any of this!"

"I mean now. Did you get what you came over here for?"

She looked deep into his eyes again. He sensed heat behind them.

"I don't think so."

She tossed her hands up.

Luke sensed he had her close to an outburst. That's the last thing he wanted. He wanted to talk this out, to make her understand that he'd never try to hurt her. Last time she got angry, she kicked him out.

"I know what this store means to you, Jamie. I know it's not just a store. I know it's not something you do for money." She looked at him sharply now. "I just mean that it matters because of your memories and because you built it with your mother. Nothing can replace that, and you didn't even get a chance to say goodbye to it. I will never forgive Fred for that. I swear to you. He's fired. But I also need you to know that I didn't intend this. I never ever meant to do things this way."

"Maybe."

This word hit him like a boot in the belly. Maybe? Maybe I didn't mean to hurt her or maybe I did? Maybe I planned this, maybe I took away her only connection to her mother without any consideration? Is that what she was saying? That maybe he was malicious?

"Maybe you didn't, maybe you did. I don't know you. I just know that you kept things from me before and now it seems like you did it again."

"You can't honestly think I'd want to hurt you. I've done nothing but try to help you. And I thought we were at least friends."

"I don't know you well enough. I don't know what to think." She took in a breath sharply again, as if she'd forgotten to keep breathing. She sat up and that made him pull back. She stood up. She looked at him and then reached a hand up and touched his cheek. "So smooth," she said. After a moment, she began, "Look. I've been through this before."

"Through what?"

"This has brought it all back up and I just need some time. Just let me be."

"Jamie," he said. He felt desperate. "Will I see you again?"

She looked at him as if he'd said the dumbest thing possible, then she pushed him out of the house and closed the front door, so he stood a moment on the front step, staring at the red metal door. Then he left.

When he arrived at home, Luke found Ricky sitting in the living room with Sheila. Each of them drinking an amber liquid. Luke gave Ricky a look. "It's apple juice," he said and laughed. Luke was sure his mother could not say the same.

"Your friend came over, but you weren't here," Sheila said. "I got him all to myself."

"We've got to talk, Ma. We're going to go up to my room."

"Leaving me alone again. It's fine. I'm used to it."

Luke went upstairs to his room, Ricky trailing behind and then closing the door behind him.

"So where the hell have you been?"

"What?"

"'What?' What do you mean, 'what?' You disappeared for over a week."

"I've just been busy with work."

A STICKY SITUATION

"Too busy to come to drama club? Too busy to come work out with me?"

"Oh, c'mon. You don't ever workout anyway, it's just me doing the exercises and you watching."

"You didn't answer my calls. I called you twice and texted you."

"I'm sorry. I told you I was busy."

"I *texted* you. You always text back. You've been hanging with that girl. I know. Everyone does."

"Who is everyone?"

"All of drama club at least. Mr. Jack saw you, at least he thinks he did. He told Ms. Debby and she told someone and now everyone knows."

"Damn."

"She knows you stole her keys. She told me she suspected you. I tried to tell her that I couldn't believe you would do that, but she didn't believe me. And I know you did it. You had her with you, didn't you?"

"What does that matter?"

"Because since you started hanging out with her, you've been neglecting everything."

Luke knew that "everything" mostly meant Ricky. "She has nothing to do with it. I'm just trying to make *Shire Mall 2.0* happen."

"And she's part of that. She the reason you haven't been writing back to me?"

"Ricky?"

"You never ignored me before, man. We're friends."

"Yeah, we're friends. That's it." He took a breath. "Just because it took me a while to answer you back when I'm busy, it doesn't mean anything."

"It matters to me. You promised to help me with my workouts. That's our thing. It's our only thing since you left school. And I'm cool with that. I get it. You have a lot going on. But we're friends and you just ghosted me."

No argument presented itself to Luke. Ricky was right. He had neglected his duties and his friendship. Now Ms. Debby could probably have him brought up on charges. He hoped the fact that she hadn't done anything yet was a sign that she wouldn't involve the law. But worse than that, he'd hurt Ricky. They'd been friends since pre-school. He'd done exactly what he had promised himself he wouldn't. He let her get in the way of his responsibilities. He'd been busy trying to protect *Shire Mall 2.0* from her influence. And this had distracted him from what her influence was doing in the rest of his life.

"I'm sorry, Ricky." He opened his arms and Ricky hugged him. They held each other a long time. When they let go, Luke said, "I shouldn't have done that. I should've texted you back. You're right."

"I forgive you," he said. "But don't ever disappear again." He held a finger to Luke's face. Luke was so much taller that Ricky pointed almost straight up.

Luke sat down on the bed. He sighed. "I think I love her."

Ricky staggered back, but he quickly hit the wall. "You just met her."

"I know."

They sat in silence for more than twenty minutes. Ricky sat on the edge of the bed and then alternated between reclining and sitting up. Finally, Ricky spoke up.

"Why do you think that?"

"Do I really need to explain? I stole the keys from Ms. Debby. I neglected my friend." Luke stood up then and went to the window. "I can't get her out of my mind. I'm always thinking about bringing her something or seeing her somehow, helping her is a great excuse to see her. And trust me I take that opportunity as much as I can."

"Wow," said Ricky.

Luke grabbed a pack of papers from his desk. "Damn it. I got a seventy-nine."

"What for?"

"Calculus test. I just didn't get enough time to study because I was helping out Jamie. I've really made a mess of everything." He sat on the edge of the bed, next to Ricky. He leaned over and rested his head on Ricky's shoulder. "I'm so sorry, man. I messed up."

Eventually Ricky convinced Luke to go out for a jog. So they did. They ran around the block a few times until Ricky couldn't take it anymore and lay down on someone's lawn almost crying. "My chest—chest—burning," he gasped.

Luke bent over with his hands on his knees. "Yeah, let's take a break," he said.

They walked back to the house when Ricky was able to get up. They played WDC4 for a while, killing as many zombies as they had anxieties.

"So they're all talking about me, I bet."

"You know how it is. It's drama club. They feed off the drama to stay alive."

"Like zombies feed off brains."

A STICKY SITUATION

"It's worse. The drama kids know what they're doing."

Then they agreed to meet for their next workout in two days.

"But next time, I'm going to jog the whole distance."

Two days. That's also when he'd have to face Ms. Debby, Luke thought. They hugged one more time and then Ricky left and Luke went upstairs to shower.

He let everything be wiped away for a moment, relaxing under the hot water.

CHAPTER TWENTY-ONE

When Ephraim saw Jamie, he smiled. That's how she knew the boys in the kitchen were behaving today. He asked her how her week was going and she lied. "Everything's great, Ephraim. Thanks. How's yours?"

That started a fifteen-minute soliloquy in which he talked about everything from paying bills to getting along with his wife to teaching his kids how to play without hitting each other.

"Sounds tough," she said.

"You wouldn't believe. It's crazy. Kids are nuts."

The night was quiet. Only a few people sat at the bar and for a few hours no one else came in. Leah talked to her the whole night about her boyfriend and how he wasn't putting out and she couldn't understand why. "Maybe he's gay," said Terry, a regular at the end of the bar. She said this without looking up.

Leah scoffed. "Definitely not." Her face grew red and she excused herself, going out through the kitchen.

Terry looked at Jamie.

"You couldn't have spared her?" Jamie asked.

"Hey, someone's got to tell her."

Jamie shook her head. "You don't know that's true. You never leave this bar. What would you know?"

Terry hissed.

Eventually, Leah came back and avoided serving Terry. "I got her," said Jamie.

They finished out the night and after the patrons had gone, Jamie said, "Whatever," and poured herself a shot.

"Dean doesn't like that."

"Dean would understand this one time," Jamie said. "You want one?"

Leah hesitated, but then smiled. Jamie poured them both a shot and then

A STICKY SITUATION

downed it. "To men, may they all drown."

Leah whooped. "Yeah, screw 'em all."

Then Ben walked in.

Jamie stared at him. "What are you doing here?"

"He's here to get me," said Leah jumping up.

Jamie thought Ben looked really good. He was wearing a pair of jeans that cupped his butt perfectly and a leather jacket with a tight white t-shirt that showed off his chest. OK, obviously the shot was doing its job because she was getting a little too hot looking at Ben.

Leah ran off to get her stuff from the back.

Jamie and Ben were alone a moment.

"You look good," he said.

"You do too." Woah! That was the shot's magic doing the talking.

He lifted an eyebrow and stepped close. Jamie shrugged.

"You doing all right? If I didn't know any better, I'd say you were crying."

"What are you going to do about it?" The words were out of her mouth before she could stop them.

"What?" he asked.

"Nothing."

Leah came back, bouncing up and down. "OK, big brother," she said. "I'm ready." Leah caught the look Ben gave Jamie and said, "I can give you two a moment." Then she was out the door before anyone could respond.

"Do you need to talk, Jamie? It's me. It's just me, Ben. I can listen to you."

She meant to say, *no, it's fine*, but she didn't say anything and then he was walking behind the bar. He sat on top of it, looking down at her. He patted the bar next to him and stretched out a hand. She got up on the bar without his help.

Terry started to holler, "Sure, when I get on the bar I get kicked out for being a nuisance, but you guys can sit up there all you want. I see. The world isn't fair. Here's more evidence."

"Terry. Would you give it a break?" asked Jamie.

Ben ignored Terry. "What's going on?"

It all came out at once—how Luke had helped her with the store and then wanted to close it down, how he'd given her a couple weeks and then the construction crew came in and kicked her out. She didn't know what she was going to do with her inventory. She didn't know if she was even going to want the store. She told him that she felt lied to even though Luke was her friend. She was confused now. Was he her friend? Was it just a mistake or was he lying to her? She wasn't sure. But now she thought about her mother every day, all day. It's like it was all being held at bay, but the levee had now broken. She began to cry and Ben put his arms around her. She cried against his chest. All sense of self-consciousness melted away. It hadn't occurred to her all this time to talk to Ben. She hadn't really considered him a friend. She'd thought of him as an *ex* all this time, and now she was grateful for him. She sniffled against him and then sat up.

"Thanks," she said, her voice small and high.

Then Ephraim came in. "Everybody is done, we're leaving," he said. He looked surprised to see her on the bar with Ben, but he didn't say anything about it. "Have a good night," he said and left.

Ben lifted a hand to her face and wiped a tear. He was gazing into her eyes, as if he'd found something there and didn't want to stop seeing it. "Are you OK?" His voice was warm and rough. That was something she had always liked about him, his masculinity, his muscles, his strength. Those soft lips. She thought, *why not?*, what else could go wrong and she grabbed his shirt and pulled him closer and kissed him. His smell surrounded her, his warmth escaping from beneath the jacket. But she stopped herself.

She leaned back. "Sorry," she said, the back of her hand at her mouth. "Oh, god. I'm sorry. I shouldn't have done that. That's not what I want."

"Hey, hey," he said and hopped off the bar and stood in front of her. He grabbed her shoulders and looked into her eyes. "It's all right. You've known me a long time. It's normal to look for comfort in me. It's OK. You didn't do anything wrong."

She looked up at him, those eyes she'd peered into a million times and she saw something different. She saw that he was sincere. She had made a mistake because she was in pain—that was all; he was right.

"Thanks, Ben," she said. "You should probably go. Leah is waiting for you. We don't want to get her hopes up."

Ben smiled brightly. He shook his head. "You never take a break, huh?"

When he was out the door, she popped some gum in her mouth. She leaned

A STICKY SITUATION

against the bar a while, popping.

Then she remembered Terry. "Terry. I'm closing up. You got to close out your tab." Terry handed over some money and Jamie gave her a receipt. A horn sounded outside.

"That's for me," Terry said and got up and left.

Jamie waved goodbye. Then she cleaned the bar, wiped everything down, burned the ice. She thought about all the help Luke had given her. He'd shown her, directly and indirectly, what she was capable of, and what she could accomplish. Then there was the idea for a gum store, with her favorite gum and that seemed like a good idea, a great one, that would actually make some money. But she didn't know whether to believe Luke. He had seemed sincere when he told her this was the lawyer's doing, but Luke had hired the man and kept him on even after he had tried to sue her. It was his fault. She should have known better than to trust some eighteen-year-old kid trying to prove himself to a dead man. She could feel her stomach tighten at that thought. Was that fair? Was it fair to expect someone to know how to navigate all the things Luke was navigating and expect to never have his ship hit choppy water or sail near rocks?

She reminded herself that Luke was getting his mall. Everything was working out for him. It was she who was getting the short end. She had been filling up a bubble with her gum and now it popped so loudly it scared her. She looked around instinctively to find the sound before realizing where it came from.

She had kissed Ben. Luke had driven her to kiss Ben. Now she felt like a fool. She had kissed Ben, but now she saw that who she really wanted to kiss was Luke. He had gotten through all her barriers for him. Somehow, he had made her laugh and forget and relax. She had felt happy with him and the future seemed to hold more possibilities than she had allowed for since her mother died. This is what bothered her most of all, this pattern. Everyone leaving, one way or another, and the store closing had reminded her of that fact. Her father had left when she was a child, never spoken of, never to be seen again, and her mother had left too, not of her own accord, but life had taken her from Jamie and left her with an emptiness. Her uncle kept reminding her that he was next. It felt as if destiny waited for her, an empty room with a view and no company. Everyone would die or leave. These things with Luke, they were just the signs of that, she thought. All these ways he was hurting her, allegedly without wanting to, was just life rolling along at its normal clip, bringing death to every good thing.

She was tired. But something had just occurred to her, something terrifying and awful. She closed up the bar and went home. She sat in her tub a while, until the water turned cold. She felt unnerved, but somehow she willed herself to sleep. Then, the next morning she called her Uncle Norman.

CHAPTER TWENTY-TWO

The mall filled with dust, a poisonous cloud. Men wore masks and talked to each other in shouts. They wore goggles to protect their eyes as they filled the mall with loud banging. Luke watched from the side, trying to stay out of the way, as they removed the plate glass from the front of Jamie's store. Then the back room disappeared as they knocked down the wall. He watched as the place where Jamie once stood selling gum and erotica with that sweet smile, those beautiful curls, that nervous penchant for sampling too much gum at once, was now covered in rubble.

He hadn't heard from her. It'd been weeks since they'd spoken. He had hired a moving company to put her store's inventory in the garage of an empty house he owned. The house needed work before being rented or sold, so her things could stay there as long as she needed, certainly by the time the mall re-opened. He had sent her a text letting her know, but he'd never heard back. He figured she needed time. He definitely didn't want to rush her. He'd deposited the money from the settlement into her account and had hoped he might hear from her then, but it was radio silence.

He had faced the music for everything that he'd let fall to the wayside when he was spending time with Jamie. Ms. Debby the drama teacher had been lenient. She had sat him down in her office and closed the door.

"Now tell me why you'd go and do a thing like that?"

He had confessed pretty readily. He told her about the portfolio, about the pressure, and that he had met this girl that he wanted to work with desperately. Actually, he just wanted to be around her, he said almost tearing up. It was all coming out now. He had just wanted to impress her. He knew it was silly and foolish. He was sorry. And he would accept whatever punishment Ms. Debby saw fit. There would be no complaint from him. He had waited with his eyes tightly shut for her to pick up the phone and call the police. He figured that's how it would happen, but she didn't do that. Ms. Debby waited until Luke had calmed down and opened his eyes.

"Love makes us all idiots," she said. "Just make sure the next time you feel a brain wave going south, you don't include my keys as part of the experience. You understand me?"

Luke nodded. For the past few months, he had felt himself growing more and more adult and more and more capable, but in this moment he never felt like more of a kid. He'd remember this moment for years, as one when he was glad that someone still saw him as a kid and took pity.

He watched the store be demolished, his eyes wide. In just a moment it seemed, the place had disappeared.

Throughout the day, the developer tried to show Luke what he was up to, giving him regular updates. "See this is where they messed up building this place. They put up this wall here, but they didn't use the right beam to go across and we can't trust it to hold weight, especially not with heavy machinery here. So here is where we'll set up the new beam to replace the old one."

Luke nodded through this. He understood and was happy to be updated and explained these details, but he couldn't help but think of Jamie. It took everything in him at the moment not to show up at her house and just see for himself that she was all right. He could tell her how sorry he was, how bitter it felt to watch the walls of her shop be knocked down, traces of it only in the ever-present dust and a few stray pebbles. But that would probably hurt her, to imagine the walls of her shop fallen like Jericho's, the chosen victor someone who inherited his power, who was given influence by birth, who didn't have to try and build it from the ground up like she did. He felt like a fraud right then. He knew at the same time that he had had a great success, that a large economic plan that many people will depend on was orchestrated by him and that he should be proud. But he did it at the expense of Jamie, he felt. Jamie who had become a friend. More than that. She was undeniably special. Fun, strange, incredibly unforgettably gorgeous, a fierce fighter, a brave soul. She made him want to be better, to be more interesting, more helpful, kinder.

What a terrible price to pay—his success in exchange for her surrender and her trust.

A STICKY SITUATION

Luke stayed until close of the workday, letting the developer show him around and explain things. He barely paid attention to what the man told him, but it was enough to distract him from driving over to Jamie's house.

Next, he went home. His mother reclined in the living room, watching reruns of *Jersey Shore*. On closer inspection, he discovered she slept, a bowl of wheat thins beside her, her right hand still in it. He grabbed the kitchen towel on her lap and lifted her hand. He wiped her hand and placed it on her leg. He lowered the volume of the TV and watched her snore a moment. She looked so peaceful. He was glad to see her that way. Despair had changed and disturbed her. She had been like this since she had suffered a stroke six years before. It had changed her personality. She became overwhelmed by the simplest things. Ever since, she just seemed incapable of the simplest tasks, leaving Luke to fend for himself. That's why his grandfather chose him, he thought. His grandfather gave him the business so that Luke would be able to take care of his mother now that his grandfather could no longer do it. It felt strange to watch his own life get mapped out by another's hand. But he was too used to it by now to be bothered.

He went upstairs and tried playing a video game, killing zombies with a rifle. But it didn't distract him well enough. He still thought of Jamie. He tried to read a book. But all his books were about business and that just reminded him of Jamie. He called Ricky. But his friend didn't answer the phone. He had gotten a new job at a Mexican restaurant and had much less free time.

Luke remembered he still had a skateboard in the garage. From the age of twelve until he was sixteen, Luke was always on a skateboard. But one day he decided he was tired of it and left it in the garage forgotten. He went to get it.

Outside, the sun had just fallen, and the sky still had a bright bruised color. The stars shone brighter than usual through it. He stepped onto his board. His balance wasn't so bad. He gave himself a little push. Three houses down he leaned on his front foot and let his back foot drag along the street to slow him to a stop.

That was fun. He should have worn a helmet, but right then the wind felt so good in his hair that he forgot all about it. He pushed off again, feeling the wind spread through his hair and cool his scalp. He pushed more, going faster. A curve approached. He turned into it, his whole body leaning to the right, his knees bent, his toes pressing so that he didn't fall forward. "Woooo!" The sound escaped him. The board rumbled beneath his feet. He pushed off more, faster, faster. He could hear pebbles kick back, the repeated rumble of the wheels against the pavement. This felt good. This felt like forgetting. His mind had nothing in it, but *push, turn, push, slow, kick flip, land, push.*

By the time he stopped, he was covered in sweat and the moon had risen. It was fully night, and even though he felt tired, he was not sleepy. He went back to his house. His mother still slept on the recliner. This time he turned off the TV. Then he went into the shower. His legs were shaking as he soaped them up. It had been a long time since he'd used those muscles. They feel happy, he thought. He smiled. That made him think of Jamie. Damn it! He had gone quite a while without thinking of her. There she was again, popping up in his mind this time with a giant gum bubble growing larger and larger. He went back online, and Ricky was not on. He gave him a call.

"Ricky, you answered. Where are you?" He could hear lots of noise in the background.

"I'm at a party," he said. "Come by."

"No, you know that's not my thing."

"It's just a bunch of dorks who play *Dota*. Nothing to be nervous about."

Luke agreed and hopped in his car. When he drove up to the building, it was an apartment complex with probably about twenty apartments. It seemed like there were at least three parties going on at the moment. Ricky said to go in, turn right, go up the stairs, and turn left, last apartment on the left. He looked up at the window in the left corner of the building and saw lights flashing different colors. He went inside and knocked, but no one answered. He tried the doorknob and it opened. The music blasted and he could see that those flashing lights came from a massive television taking up a whole wall almost floor to ceiling. He could hear a group of people saying, "Awww," and "Got him!" As he entered, he stepped on a lost Cheeto. The group huddled around the TV. They were playing *Walking Death Com 4*. Ricky saw him and made him take a seat between two very large men, one of them furiously handling the controller, shooting zombies left and right.

"This is my buddy, Luke," Ricky said. "He's awesome at WDC4."

There was a discordant chorus of "Hi, Luke."

A couple people turned to smile, someone handed him a joint. Ricky cast

A Sticky Situation

him a look. Luke had never smoked before, but anything that got his mind off Jamie was worth a try. He took a hit, ignoring Ricky's look. He felt nothing. He took another hit, this one very long. It burned his throat and he coughed it up. People around him laughed and he passed the joint, still covering his mouth as he hacked.

He started to get a warm cozy feeling and he let himself sink into the couch between the two large men. He could feel their heat on either side of him. They didn't seem to notice him. He felt like he could sleep quite comfortably here.

He did.

When he woke up, he lay stretched out on the couch. Someone sat a few inches from the TV screen, playing a game. He noticed Ricky watching the game on a chair.

"Ricky," Luke said.

"Buddy, finally. I was starting to wonder if I'd have to wake you up."

"Where am I?"

"At my friend Frankie's. He said you can stay the night if you want, but I bet your mother would be pissed."

"That's right." Luke groaned as he sat up. He let his head and hands hang between his knees. He yawned. "Let's go."

They stumbled down to the car.

"Are you drunk," Luke asked.

"No. Just waking up." He yawned big and said "C'mon" before hopping in the car.

Luke looked at the car's clock. It was 3:30 AM. He dropped off Ricky with a hug. "Thank you for making me go out, even though all I did was fall asleep."

"Not to worry. That's very you to try weed for the first time and then just sleep through it."

When Luke got to his house, he snuck back up to his room, and once he was in bed, he counted to one hundred. He didn't fall asleep. He kept thinking that he had made a terrible mistake and that he had been right all along. *You don't have relationships with your tenants!,* his mind screamed at him. He tried counting again. It took three times but eventually he fell asleep. But in his dreams, like in his waking hours, he couldn't stop himself from thinking of her. She visited his dreams all night, appearing suddenly, leaving him in a perpetual cycle of anticipation and shock.

In the morning, he woke on a spit-covered pillow, the edges of the soaked liquid growing crusty and white. His first tragic thought was to go to her store, chat, buy some gum.

He spent half the day watching the construction. He had a meeting with his new tenants from the dispensary. All went well. They had all signed on the dotted line. They were happy about the project and pleased how quickly it seemed to be moving. And, he guessed, because none of them seemed to hate him, they had not heard any bad news from Jamie.

It was after the meeting, while the sun was setting that he drove up to Jamie's house and rang the bell. He rang it a few times, but five minutes later, no one had answered. Her car was in the driveway, but now as he looked up at the house, he noticed the windows were all dark. It started to rain and he opened the storm door. Magazines and envelopes poured out. He knocked on the door, hard. He knocked again. Nothing. She wasn't here. He called her. But he got her voicemail, no ring.

The only other place he knew to find her was the store. She definitely was not there. He had the distinct feeling that she was gone. But how? Jamie would never travel. She never even drove out of the city anymore. But it was clear from how he'd found things, that she had gone somewhere. His first idea was to go to the Bullseye. He thought he'd ask Norman about her. But when he asked for the manager, the person who appeared was not much older than him, and she was a woman. He asked after Norman.

"Norman? He's no longer with us," said the woman.

Did she mean that he had passed? That didn't make sense. Certainly, Luke would have heard about that. "You mean he went somewhere?"

"He's retired. I heard he was going on some big trip. I didn't know him sorry. I just came to replace him."

He thanked the woman. But he felt no better. That hadn't helped him at all.

Then he remembered the bar. He rushed over there and stood outside the door, trembling. Would they ask him for ID the moment he walked in? A woman came out then and gave him a look like she'd smelled dead fish. She pushed past him.

"Wait, wait," he said after her.

A STICKY SITUATION

"No, creep. No."

"I just wanted to ask if you saw Jamie in there."

"Look for yourself, you weirdo." She walked away, looking back as she got into her car and then drove off beeping and giving him the middle finger.

This didn't bode well for him.

He went back to his car. He stood outside of it, pacing by the driver's door. Seriously? He couldn't walk into a building and ask if they'd seen Jamie? Was he this much of a coward?

No, the answer was, no. He was no coward. He was going to find this girl, no matter what he had to do. He just started walking to the door when he heard a crash behind the bar, right by his car. He skulked over and peered around the corner. There was a man throwing out bags of trash from a large can into the dumpster.

"Hello," said Luke.

"HAAAAAAAIIIIIYAH!" screamed the man and jumped around into a pose like a martial arts fighter. He screamed again. "Man, you scared the crap out of me." The man backed up, his fists still up. "What are you doing being all creepy behind the bar?"

"Sorry, sorry," said Luke, jumping out from behind the wall with his palms up. "I just heard you back here and I was looking for someone. That's all. Didn't mean to scare you."

"Dude, you almost got my 'hiyah-chop.' You're so lucky."

"I know. I'm glad I was behind the wall," said Luke, trying not to laugh.

"Who are you looking for back here?"

"Ugh...Jamie...you know her?"

"Yeah, I know Jamie. She's like my sister. What are you looking for her for?"

Luke thought this was the perfect time to just tell the truth. "I'm her landlord, and I have a message for her, but I can't seem to find her. She's not home and the mall's closed. Her phone's off. Guess I got a little worried, so I came to check on her, and I heard you back here, so I just came to see if anyone had seen her."

The man looked at Luke suspiciously. "But you're really young, man..."

"Oh, yeah. I am young to be a landlord. I know."

"Hmmm...OK. Well, I don't know, man. Wait right here."

Then the man disappeared into the building. Next came out a man as tall as

Luke, older, with salt and pepper hair, the karate man right behind him.

"Luke?" asked the man.

"Dean?"

"Luke, what are you doing here?"

"Hi, Dean." They hugged and patted each other on the back. Dean was Luke's little league coach. Luke was also friends with Dean's son, Patrick, and had often been over to their house growing up. "I just came to find Jamie."

"Ephraim here says you're Jamie's landlord. What do you mean, you're her landlord? She owns the house." Dean put a hand to his forehead. "Oh, man. It just hit me. I had heard your grandfather died. So you must've taken over his properties, the mall. Oh, I'm sorry about your loss, Luke. He was a good guy, Zachariah."

"Thanks," said Luke, looking down at their feet. He forced himself to look back up, at Dean's eyes, like he'd learned from his books on business communication.

"Why you looking over here for her?"

"I have some info for her. But she's not home and her phone's off. It's like she's disappeared." He tried to keep his tone level, but now as he neared his object, he felt himself shake a little with anticipation.

"She's not here, Luke. She's in Peru. Won't be back for almost a week."

"Peru? But she's terrified of planes."

"I don't know what to tell you." He chuckled. "She's not here."

"Yeah, she's gone. Outta here," said Ephraim. Dean gave Ephraim a look. "Looks like everything is fine out here, boss. I should go back to work." And with that Ephraim went inside, looking back at Luke one more time before disappearing.

"Thanks, Dean. I just heard your guy out here and so I asked him. I didn't want to go inside. Still only eighteen. You know."

"It's no problem. I'll tell her you stopped by when she gets back. You get taller on me? You're looking taller."

Luke went home. At least he knew why she didn't answer him, she was overseas. But how was that even possible? She'd told him that she was terrified of planes.

He guessed there was nothing to do but wait.

So he waited.

CHAPTER TWENTY-THREE

When they got off the boat, Jamie and Uncle Norman were surrounded by ferns taller than them. The guide walked them along a path amidst the roundelays of rainbow-colored birds, the high-pitched creak of insects, the scurrying of invisible rodents until the group reached a building made of jungle stalks and dried grasses. In the path crawled something large that the guide stooped to pick up. He held in two hands a furry beige and black tarantula larger than his palm. The guide bared his teeth, all evenly spaced apart—his eyes crinkled.

"It does not bite," he said and placed the tarantula on the arm Jamie tentatively stuck out.

The tarantula gained its balance on its new perch, scratching Jamie's arm with its hairy little legs. Jamie looked into its big eyes, her belly quivering. "It doesn't have fangs or anything?" Her voice cracked.

The guide guffawed and the tarantula climbed up her arm a bit more. Jamie's eyes widened. "It does not have fangs. It won't hurt you. It's gentle." She breathed and steadied herself. After a few moments of feeling its prickly weight on her arms, she turned towards her Uncle Norman.

"Your turn," she said.

"Put it on my head."

Jamie knew her uncle well enough to know that he wasn't kidding. She placed her arm to his head. The tarantula climbed up towards her shoulders, closer to her face. "Oh my god, help me. Please. Please." Jamie tried to keep from screaming, but it took all her willpower. "Help!"

The guide chuckled and grabbed the tarantula from her shoulder. As the spider left her, they locked eyes. A shudder scurried across Jamie's back.

"Take a picture," cried her uncle, his smile full of glee. "Oh, it's crawling across my head. Ha ha ha. It's got a leg in my ear. Take a picture, niece. Take a picture."

Just the sight of the humongous spider crawling across him made it difficult for her to remember how to use her phone's camera. She eventually got video of the tarantula climbing across her uncle's face, him screaming happily as its leg slipped into his mouth.

"Can we stop with the tarantula?" Jamie meant to hold her composure, but she shouted this.

"OK, help me out here. Please," said her uncle.

The guide removed the tarantula from Uncle Norman's face and placed it back on the edge of the path.

"I know what I'm dreaming about tonight," said Jamie as she and her uncle climbed the steps of this structure.

The building was built above ground on stilts and reeds like bamboo, seemingly hand-tied, all of the reeds laid out side by side to form a floor. The reeds also rose in bundles to form large windows before holding up a raised ceiling, covered in thatch made of palm leaves. The first part of the structure opened into a foyer-like area that seemed to double as a dining area. Now there were small round tables set up for the group and a longer table presented a buffet of fish, palm heart salad, rice, cut vegetables cured in lime juice and sliced fruits.

"We'll take your things to your rooms," said the guide. "Now just sit and eat."

Jamie ate like a starved person, but she spent the whole time scanning the floor.

"Looking for tarantulas?" This was one of the men from the group who had sat with her and Uncle Norman. He was an older man, red-faced and excited, with dark green eyes. "I think they wouldn't come up here. There's no food for them here. They don't eat humans."

Uncle Norman laughed at this. "She won't get a lick of sleep tonight if you keep talking to her like that."

Jamie tried to smile and pulled her feet onto the seat and sat on them. The heart of palm was especially delicious. She shoveled it into her mouth as she kept scanning the floors and the frame of the windows. She smacked at the bugs that landed on her legs and arms.

It turned out that the man, named Terrance, was a manager for a big-box store too and he and Uncle Norman spent the whole lunch complaining about the troubles of running a place like Bullseye. Jamie ate until she was full. Then they

A STICKY SITUATION

were all escorted to their rooms. The room was the same, but these windows had screens and shutters. In this room she could hear frogs croaking and birds crying. It was a non-stop symphony. The room was dark and the screens kept out the bugs. She lay on the soft bed and before she knew it, she had drifted off to sleep. When she awoke, it was to her uncle hurrying into the room.

"Time for dinner. We went fishing for piranhas. They cooked them up for dinner. Come get some."

Jamie sat up. She'd never had piranha, but she was willing to try. She went to the dining room and there sat her Uncle Norman with Terrance. Her uncle signaled the chair and said, "Niece. You grace us with your presence." Terrence gave a small bow with his head. The rest of the group looked her way. Jamie waved and smiled.

She approached her table. She was feeling happy and lazy after her nap. "Thank you for the invitation to dinner, Uncle. I might've slept the day away. So, what's this I hear that we have you to thank, you and Terrance, for our protein tonight?"

"Your uncle was ferocious. The fish fought him like a whale. Almost took him under. But your uncle emerged victorious."

"I did. Didn't I?"

"Yes. Started jumping up and down in the boat. Almost tipped us over."

"Oh, Terrance. Don't go telling all my secrets now."

Jamie looked to her uncle and frowned. Was he crushing on this guy?

The piranha tasted like any white fish. It was bony and a bit dry. Jamie filled herself up with heart of palm salad. It was so bright and delicious, soured with squeezed lime. She drank papaya juice and hugged her knees.

"You'll be happy to know," said her Uncle Norman. "That we haven't seen any more tarantula. I don't think they're that common. I doubt you'll see another one."

She knew he was manipulating her, but it worked, and she let her feet down. "Where are you from?"

"We're from a little city in the Berkshire mountains. Jamie there runs a store."

"Actually, not anymore. I run a bar now. Or I will be when I get back."

She had made the decision without much direct thought when she had gotten off the plane. She could barely remember the ride or even getting off the plane, but she remembered that she had decided that she would no longer run the store. She would run the bar. The store had never really been hers, she'd thought. She didn't want to carry the burden any longer. But she hadn't thought about it much since. The decision was made and right now, in the Peruvian rainforest, everything seemed so simple, simple enough that she could just relax and enjoy her surroundings.

A screech from the dark jungle caught all of their attention. They peered out into the darkness, waiting. They chuckled nervously and went back to talking and eating and soon the din of them relegated the jungle noise back to the background.

"What was this store you ran?"

Jamie didn't want to get into this, but she couldn't see a polite way out of the conversation. "I ran a store of cultural erotica."

Terrance raised an eyebrow. "A sex store?" His voice lowered considerably, almost to a whisper.

"Yes, a sex store full of glory holes and lube dispensers," she said.

Uncle Norman roared. Everyone turned to look at him. "That's my niece," he said in between laughs.

"No, I'm kidding, Terrance. It was more of an art gallery, with artisanal erotica from around the globe. Mostly sculpture and tapestries."

"I've got to say I'm slightly disappointed. I feel like the other type of store might've given you a lot of stories to tell."

"With my uncle around there's plenty of stories to tell, not to worry."

"You watch your mouth, missy."

They finished dinner and stayed up a while staring at the night sky under a small gazebo-like area filled with hammocks. The beams holding up the structure had sconces with lit torches.

Terrence was in the middle of telling a ghost story. Jamie kept telling herself she wasn't afraid because ghosts weren't real.

"To this day," said Terrence. "It's said, 'If you enter that house, you can hear the old woman dragging her peg leg behind her.'" Then he imitated the hollow scratching sound of a wooden leg being dragged across a floor by scratching the side of his hammock. He whistled eerily.

Jamie shivered. Then she rolled her eyes and said, "Ghosts aren't real. Everyone

A Sticky Situation

knows that."

Uncle Norman said, "You tell him, Jamie."

He giggled.

Then they heard a loud sound. They all looked at each other. Jamie swallowed hard.

There it was again. It sounded like a slow scratching noise. Again, it sounded, closer and closer each time. It occurred to Jamie that it was the sound of something being dragged across the wooden planks beneath them.

Terrence whispered, "It's the woman with the peg leg."

The dragging sound grew louder and nearer.

Jamie hissed, "Stop it, silly."

The dragging sounded like it was beneath her hammock. She shut the flaps of the hammock and closed her eyes. Then she heard laughing. She opened one eye and peered at the hammocks around her. She could see them in the torchlight, trembling with stifled laughter. She popped out her head and looked beneath her. Right under her was a parrot with one leg. Then it started to move, dragging its body across the floor with its beak. The laughter roared out of the hammocks.

Jamie couldn't help but laugh too.

When they were done laughing, which took a while for Terrence and Uncle Norman who each inspired the other to full-bellied laughter with the slightest giggle, Jamie said, "what a coincidence that a one-legged parrot came around after your story."

"It wasn't a fluke," said Terrence, starting to laugh again, which made Uncle Norman laugh too. "I saw the bird earlier—" here he tried to breathe through his laughter "—and then I saw it a moment ago and came up with the story. I whistled and put down a cracker so it would come closer."

The two men roared again.

Jamie went to bed first, leaving her Uncle Norman and Terrence alone. She could hear them laughing still as she fell asleep.

The next morning, they had to trek through the jungle. Her Uncle Norman stayed behind on account of the cane, so it was just her and Terrence. Terrence mostly asked questions about their home life and about her Uncle Norman. She started to wonder if Terrence was sweet on her uncle. They hiked through a muddy trail. Monkeys swung from tree to tree, dozens of birds sang. They swung across a stretch of mud by vine. Terrence seemed pretty strong.

"You don't mind traveling alone?" Jamie asked Terrence as they followed their guide along the trail, sweat dripping from their foreheads.

"Oh, no. I always make friends. Like you guys. Do you always travel with your uncle?"

"No. I don't travel usually. My uncle had to drug me to get me on the plane."

Terrence looked at her. "Seriously? I can't tell with you."

"Oh, yeah. No other way to get me on a plane."

"Little tranquilizer?"

"I don't know. He called it a kway-lute."

"A Quaalude? You can't be serious."

"He said he was saving them up for retirement week."

"Your uncle seems like the right kind of guy to know. Was it fun?"

"You know. I mostly remember walking and then sitting and then waking up in Peru."

Terrence sighed. He looked lost in his own reverie for a moment.

When they returned, Uncle Norman was in a hammock with the one-legged parrot sitting on his belly. He fed the parrot nuts and pretended to squawk. "Isn't this the picture of a prince?" asked Terrence.

Jamie nodded and a look passed between them that made her feel embarrassed. So what if her uncle was flirting with some guy in the Peruvian jungle? She decided to leave them and go find a glass of juice.

The next morning, they took a canoe ride to a local tribe that still lived in the rainforest. They lived in huts and hunted with blow darts. They covered themselves with leaves and braided vines. Their faces were painted and when they smiled, their teeth were small and loosely set. The tribe also housed certain animals. Jamie, her uncle, and Terrence met an ocelot and held a sloth. They drank spirit made of various roots. They ate jerky made of large rodents. That night, after dinner, the whole group hung out in the hammock gazebo. One of the resort staff played the guitar, another sang. Her uncle had bought a couple bottles of the root spirit and they all took shots and tried to sing along. Mostly they mumbled in a broken patois of some imaginary drunken language and an impression of Spanish vowels. The forest sang more loudly at night and the stars here were so bright when they shone through the trees that they seemed fake.

A STICKY SITUATION

Her uncle and Terrence sat against a beam made of reeds, their arms around each other's shoulders, swaying side to side and singing drunkenly, the one-legged parrot dragging itself before them with its beak. Another couple got up and danced too fast for the beat.

Jamie tired before everyone else. The shots also made her woozy. She went back to her room. She spent a couple hours lying in bed, waiting for her uncle to come back. She listened to the group all sing until finally they just talked, their mumbling and excited trills punctuated with laughter. Her uncle never came back. She stood up at one point to go see where he was, but there was no longer anyone at the hammock gazebo. She went back to bed. She wouldn't worry about him. He was an adult, she reminded herself. And if he wanted to disappear into Terrance's room that was his prerogative. Though, it did make her giddy and nervous to think of it, her uncle falling for a man in the Peruvian jungle. Terrance was much older than her but, she thought, at least twenty years younger than her uncle. However, she definitely had no opinions on what should happen other than she hoped her uncle had some fun.

Since she'd arrived, she'd been able to keep thoughts of her store at bay, but tonight, possibly because of the alcohol, she imagined *The Cuckoo Cl*ck*. She stared up at the ceiling and listened, gratefully, to the buzzing of insects at the screen. The truth was that she didn't miss the store. She didn't want to return to it. She had wanted to just leave, to anywhere. She hadn't even told anyone that she'd left, except for Dean. She'd gone into the bar and told Dean that she was taking the position. But first she needed to take some time to travel. Dean had agreed immediately. Jamie could tell that his wife had put a lot of pressure on him to cover the bar and help her with her new shop. Jamie could see the relief on his face. Jamie had told her uncle to drug her, to knock her out, do whatever he had to, but she was going with him. He was so excited he kicked his feet up and immediately booked her a flight and added her to the reservation. Since he'd paid to be alone in a double room, it was no issue. She had done everything to run away from the wreckage of her life, but now things were settling and her barriers were faltering and her mind filled up with Luke. They'd left things poorly. They hadn't spoken in weeks and he had sent her a text asking how she felt, but she hadn't answered. Now that her mind had cleared and she no longer felt angry, it seemed to her that Luke was more credible than she'd given him credit for. Her uncle had told her to remember that not everything was perfect. That she couldn't expect perfection. She had responded that she didn't expect that, just honesty. He reminded her that she had no evidence that he did lie. She had left that conversation realizing that he was right. She remembered the hug he'd given her on that bench outside the library. She had felt totally at peace. This was the essential conflict: that he made her feel comfortable and vulnerable at the same time. Had she made a mistake? Had she jumped to conclusions? Then she heard something that sounded like a low growl. She'd never heard such a deep guttural sound; it sounded warm. It startled her to think that a large cat might be nearby. She fell asleep wondering about her uncle.

Her uncle didn't return until the sun had just risen. She woke up as he opened the door.

"What unmentionable thing have you been doing?"

"That question is a trap."

"Is it seemly for a lady to be seen going into a gentleman's hut in the middle of the night?"

"Is it embarrassing for a young lady to go to bed before her elderly uncle?"

"Did you shower at least?"

"Yes, actually, I did. That's what I was doing all night. Taking a long shower."

Her uncle fussed around his luggage for something. She lay back and listened to the jungle sounds. After a while, her uncle sat down on the edge of the bed. "Breakfast?"

"Let me ask you something."

"What's wrong?"

"Do you think I made a mistake?"

"You mean the boy. Well, I can't tell you that. I can tell you that sometimes you have to believe people. The only other choice is to believe no one. That's no way to live."

Jamie and her uncle ate breakfast. Terrence arrived in the middle of it, yawning. "Excuse me," he said.

"Sleepless night?"

Uncle Norman shot her a sharp look.

After breakfast, they packed and said goodbye to their guides and to the cooks before taking the boat ride back to the small city nearby. They spent the

A STICKY SITUATION

day eating and exploring shops. Jamie found a small musical instrument like a güira carved into the shape of a voluptuous woman. She thought about her shop and then remembered there was no need to buy more than one. It wasn't long before her uncle gave her a pill and they found themselves on planes, Jamie too hypnotized to do anything but sit back and sleep as they flew back home.

CHAPTER TWENTY-FOUR

"Oh, god," Jamie said when Luke's mother opened the door. The woman stood with her robe twisted up, her breast naked to the air. "Uh—hi. You must be Luke's mother. I'm Jamie—his...uh...tenant. Could I speak to him?"

The cigarette hanging from Sheila's lips fell as she spoke. "Oh, he just went out to get breakfast. You don't have any cigarettes do you, sweetie?"

"Actually, you just—" Jamie started. She squatted down and picked up the cigarette on the threshold. "Here you go."

Sheila smiled and her eyes crinkled at their corners into fans.

"You're a keeper," said Sheila.

Jamie assumed Sheila was under the influence. She decided it was better to wait outside for Luke and told Sheila as much, encouraging her to go back inside where it was warm. Sheila agreed, the cigarette hanging between her lips as she shuffled back into the house.

Luke arrived and pulled into the driveway. Jamie stood by the steps at the front of the house. Now that she saw him, she had no idea what she was going to say. She felt cold. She thought that when she saw him, she'd be overwhelmed with a sense of warmth for him. But now, with him right in front of her, exiting the car, his hands filled with a bag of, presumably, donuts, and a tray with coffee cups, she was unbearably shy. She felt embarrassed. The last time she had seen him she had behaved not so well, she thought. It was the best response she was capable of then, but it was far from smooth or pleasant. She remembered herself sitting in the living room, unsure whether she would scream. She forced herself to look at him.

"Hello."

"Jamie," he said, startled. He hadn't noticed her until now that they were face to face. "Oh my god." He put the food on the ground and grabbed Jamie into his

A STICKY SITUATION

arms, lifting her at least a foot above the ground. "You're back. You're back," he said as he squeezed her.

When he let go, her lungs expanded rapidly as she choked in air.

"I'm so glad you're back. You didn't say where you were. I had no idea when I'd ever see you again."

"I'm sorry. I had to get away."

Luke hugged her again. "I just can't believe you're here. Let's go inside though. It's cold and I have coffee for my mom. She's a zombie until she has the morning cup. Come on," he said, grabbing the food and going into the house. He couldn't stop looking at Jamie. "You're really here," he said and the excitement in his voice, the obvious pleasure at seeing her warmed her.

Luke opened the door and entered the house backwards. He never stopped looking at her. "Ma, come to the kitchen," he said, turning his face to the left, but his eyes stayed on Jamie. "Come with me," he said and stepped into the kitchen, put down the food. "Sit," he said, pulling out a chair. He sat beside her, capturing every move. "You're really here," he said.

Jamie smiled.

"Who's this?" Sheila's tone was more lucid now. "You wouldn't be Cuckoo Girl, would you?"

"Ma!" Luke broke eye contact for the first time to give his mother a shocked look. "*Jamie*," he said, smiling at her. "This is my mother, Sheila."

"Nice to meet you, Sheila."

"Honey, are you going to give my son what he wants? You've been confusing the heck out of him. Let me tell you."

Luke jumped up. "Uh, Ma, Ma, let's, uh, go into the other room and watch some TV," he said as he directed her to the other room with a sing-song voice. "Relax over here, not saying embarrassing things..."

"It was good to meet you, Cuckoo Girl!" said Sheila from her recliner.

When Luke came back, he was smiling sheepishly and mouthing *I'm sorry*. He sat next to Jamie, with his legs open, turned towards her as if he were closing her in between himself and her chair.

"I feel trapped," Jamie said, chuckling nervously, looking off to the sides.

"Oh, sorry," he said and closed his legs, turning towards the table. "I'm just so happy to see you. You have no idea." He stared at her a moment and Jamie looked away. "I'm sorry," he said. "I don't mean to stare. So, what happened to your fear of planes? You were in Peru?"

"Oh," said Jamie, pulling a lock of curls back behind her ear. "I was knocked out for the whole flight. Don't even remember it."

"Why did you leave? I don't understand."

Jamie looked down at her hands.

"Wait." He got up and grabbed the bag of donuts. He took one to his mother and then came back and offered the bag to Jamie. "You can't think on an empty stomach."

"Thanks. I haven't eaten breakfast." Jamie quickly bit into a donut, before it was even out of the bag.

"For someone who loves to eat this much, you sure miss breakfast a lot."

Jamie smiled with her teeth clamped shut, donut in her mouth. When she had had a couple bites, she spoke. "You know. I'll just tell you. I felt like I had to, like I was never going to face my mother's death if I didn't just get on a plane. It's like I needed to face it. When the store closed, I felt like I had no choice. I couldn't move forward until I faced this thing."

Luke nodded at her, a soft smile on his lips as he listened.

"The drugs my uncle gave me were sort of cheating."

"No," he said and reached out a hand to her, but he let it fall back into his own lap. "It was brave. That's one of the things I admire about you."

Jamie put down the bag of donuts. "It was a good trip. Good for doing a lot of thinking. And now I'm back and I have something to tell you."

"OK," Luke said. "But maybe I need a little coffee first." He reached across the table for his cup.

"Well, you know how the last time we saw each other, I was a little uncommunicative?"

"Yes."

Jamie chuckled. "I was just worried. I wanted the store's future to be in my hands. I thought it always had been. I thought I was losing something. But I wasn't. I never had any real control over that shop. I was just sort of going there and running it out of habit." She took a deep breath and continued, "But you came in guns blazing, telling me that the fate of my shop was in your hands and it—well, it pissed me off, you know?"

A Sticky Situation

They both laughed, Luke nodded vigorously.

"I just thought—just..."

"What?"

Jamie sighed. "This is harder than I thought."

"Talking?"

"Well, it's just a little embarrassing." She took a deep breath. "Can we go somewhere?"

"Let's go for a walk."

"Great."

When they were outside, walking briskly around the block Jamie, relaxed.

"Ah, this is cozy," he said.

"Quite."

"What did you want to tell me?"

She ran a finger through the tips of her hair. "I ran," she said.

"I figured that much. You disappeared. Didn't even tell me where you were going. And you got on a plane. But you were upset. Because of what I let happen. Listen, Jamie, I'm so sorry—"

"Stop. Stop being thoughtful for just a moment. God. I have something to say. Something I have to say no matter what. Let me just get it out."

"OK. I'll be quiet," he said nodding. He didn't seem upset. In the thousand different scenarios she had imagined earlier, she hadn't imagined this one.

She spoke slowly, as if every word were cautiously plucked out of the jumble spiraling inside her head. "I was scared. I'm scared now. People die and people grow apart. And sometimes you are alone so long that you just forget how to talk to people. I'm just saying that keeping everything together was taking everything from me and when it happened, when the shop slipped through my fingers, I just freaked. It was like it had all happened again, like my mother had just died."

"Jamie," he said softly.

She stopped and turned to him, looking up. "You like me?"

"Absolutely."

"Then can we keep trying to get to know each other? If nothing else, you are probably one of the most interesting people I've ever met."

"I could say the same exact thing about you."

Jamie closed her eyes and turned her chin up slightly, waiting.

But a kiss didn't come.

"Let me show you something."

Jamie opened her eyes. "OK," she said. They got into his car and drove toward the other side of town. He was taking her to the mall.

"What are we doing here?"

"You'll see," he said. He drove to the other side of the mall, the back, and parked near the entrance. He ran around to the passenger side and opened the door. "Excuse me," he said as reached between her knees and dug in the glove compartment. He pulled out two high quality dust masks. "You'll need this," he said. He put his on and winked at her. Then he went to the trunk. "You'll need this too," he said peeking around with a hard hat. "Construction zone."

They walked in and the place was dark and dusty. It no longer looked like a mall. There were no hallways lined with stores, no indoor promenade. Instead there was one very large room, reaching so high up she couldn't see the ceiling—not through the dust anyway.

"Come, follow me," he said and tapped her shoulder. He led her through the maze of sheetrock and flooring. "It's a good thing you showed up on a Sunday. That way we can come in here without getting in the way." Eventually they arrived where he was taking her, but there was nothing to see, just a big space with boxes piled in it.

"This is it," he said with a flourish.

She looked around but saw nothing that stood out to her.

"This is the spot. See this tape right here? This is your door."

"My—?"

"You have to use some imagination. This is your store. It can be a double, up to a triple. Whatever you finally decide on. But the best part is this." He ran over to another rectangle in yellow tape. He jumped in it. "This is the exit for the dispensary. It exits right at your store. Every single person who enters the dispensary will go by your store before they can exit the mall."

"That's amazing," she said.

"A majority of the people who smoke weed in the county will go by this very spot at least once or so every month," he said.

That was more traffic than she'd ever seen.

A STICKY SITUATION

"What is it? You don't look excited."

"I'm just thinking."

"Yeah? Tell me about it." He said this so warmly that Jamie felt her heart ache.

"OK, then. I'm thinking my shop wouldn't be quite the right place for this location. The rhythm is off. You exit the extremely cool store that sells you weed and end up at the museum slash erotica shop. It sounds cool but the vibe is wrong."

She could see little of Luke's face, but she knew he was getting excited. "Keep going, keep going," he said.

"Well...it seems this spot would be much better for a gum store than a cultural erotica store."

Luke punched a fist into the air. "I knew you'd get there. I think the same thing." Luke signaled some boxes with a flourish. "These are another surprise I have for you."

He opened one of the boxes, pulling hard at the stapled high-density cardboard. He pried the box open and then lifted it. It was about 3 feet long, but apparently not heavy, as Luke spun it around easily, he held the edges of the box and shimmied out the contents. It was an s-shaped container made out of hard clear plastic. One end was open, the other had woodwork, burned planks that looked expensive and had a small impression.

"What is it?"

"It's a dispenser," he said. "For gum. You put this plastic part in the wall and just this wooden part shows. So that it looks like gum is coming out of the wall. And it has this little peek-a-boo plastic part that sticks out so they can see the wrapper before dispensing. And right here," he said, pointing at the impression in the wood. Now Jamie noticed that it had a small plate of glass over it. "That's a scratch resistant plexiglass where you can display the gum description."

It was truly very nice. The dispenser was nice. The thought was as well. He had not only set out a place for her, he had set out a place with high-foot traffic. He had incurred the expense of—it looked like—fifteen of these expensive dispensers. He had guaranteed her a space to do something more personal. Here he was putting himself on the line, doing the same thing his grandfather had done: look at her young pretty face and throw his hands up saying, "The poor thing, we must help her." He was doing the same thing her mother had done, write her dreams. She had to stop him. Now. She'd have to teach him another way.

"You've got to stop this."

Luke looked at her, searching for clues to interpret in her expression. But he was at a loss. "Stop the tour?"

She took a step back, a bit wobbly. "OK. Get me out of here. Like right now. C'mon."

He grabbed her hand and led her through the dust maze and outdoors into the fresh air. She stumbled out into the sunlight, tossing her hard hat to the ground and lowering her mask right away.

"Are you OK?" He stood beside her, unsure what to do.

"My god," she said, gasping for breath. "I couldn't breathe. I couldn't stand it. I had to get out." She huffed and did a bit of a backbend, her arms raised. She seemed to keep herself from hyperventilating, so he stepped closer, probably thinking that he might need to catch her. But then she stood straight up with one deep inspiration. He stepped back.

"You all right?" Her eyes were shut tight as she took deep breaths, but she could feel his gaze.

When she opened her eyes, she looked up at him. "You are so open-hearted. It's really very beautiful." She smiled. "But I can't let you do this. I can't let you give me a store. I've already done this. I've already lived through this same scenario and I know how it turns out for me. Right now, I just need to find my own way."

"I can understand how you feel."

"So, I'm sorry, but I can't accept."

Luke shook his head. "No," he said. "I know where you're coming from, but you're making a mistake. This isn't my idea. This comes from you. This is your idea. This comes from your heart. I just want to help you make it a reality."

He was right. It was her idea. He wouldn't have thought of any of this without her. She had started the gum sales. She had curated her collection of them. It was hers. Then why did this make her so nervous? Why was she afraid?

But Luke seemed to be ready for this because he had answers.

"Maybe I shouldn't have jumped the gun and started things without you. But I saw an opportunity to get you these things cheap and I took it. You can pay me back if you want. But it's all yours. You don't have to turn it away. I didn't come

A STICKY SITUATION

up with this. This *is* you."

He was right. She guessed sometimes we all needed help, we all needed support. That's what it meant to be human. But this was different than her mother's help years before. Jamie had conceived of this idea. This was borne from her, from her grief, from her way of dealing with it. And the more she pictured her store, selling all kinds of candy from all over the world, not just gum, she got excited. She pictured how she'd decorate the place. She knew already where she'd source the candy from. He was right. This was *hers*. She nodded. "OK," she said. "I agree. I'll do it. It really is mine."

"It is all yours," he said. He smiled. She could see his eyes crinkle.

"Why am I still wearing this?" She ripped off the mask.

Luke took off the mask too and the hard hat. His hair was wet and plastered to his head. He took a big breath of fresh air, the sun making the snowy mountains behind the mall glitter. "Ahhhh. What now?"

Jamie looked at him. He smiled nervously. She reached for his shirt and grasped it in her fist and pulled his face down to hers. Her chestnut curls fell from atop her head and surrounded them with a smell like flowers.

"Actually," she said, "I've been thinking about this for weeks."

Her lips touched his. She felt her chest fill with heat and even her ears began to tingle.

They parted with a sigh. He rested his forehead against hers.

"I've been thinking about it since we met," he said.

EPILOGUE

Luke and Ricky walked into Jamie's job. She had promised to give Dean a few months managing the bar, just until her new store opened. After that she'd try to do both, but she made no promises.

Dean popped his head up from behind the bar. "You two," he yelled. Everyone in the bar turned to look at them. "Get out of here. Go to the back."

Jamie laughed.

Luke and Ricky went out back. Jamie came out of the back door soon after.

"Hi, Jamie," said Ricky.

"Hi, Ricky. How are ya, buddy?"

She pulled out some gum from her pocket. "Look what I found."

"Mango?! Grrrrr. Jamie, if you were a boy."

"Don't finish that sentence," said Luke. "Hey, I'm here too."

Jamie smiled at him. "I see you, buddy." She pecked Luke on the mouth. "So," she said hanging from Luke's shoulder. "You guys ready?"

"I was in the womb getting ready. I'm so ready."

"Ricky is serious about kicking your butt today. He's been talking about it since drama club."

The three of them drove to Jamie's house. When they arrived, Jamie said she would be right back down and went upstairs to shower and change.

"I made popcorn," said Ricky as she came down the stairs.

"Did you put gummy bears in it again?"

"You know it."

"Awesome," she said. "I'm going to get a drink."

She went into the kitchen and served herself some juice. Luke came up behind her then and kissed her cheek.

"That better be Luke," she said.

A STICKY SITUATION

"Stop trying to make me jealous."

"Ricky loves me more than he loves you. That is all I'm saying."

"That's right," yelled Ricky from the living room.

"When I taught you how to play *Walking Death Com 4*, I didn't expect you to get this cocky or to steal my best friend."

"Hey, first of all, I'm the *Walking Death Com 4* master. Second, it's not my fault you're boring and your friends have good taste."

"Remind me why I like you again." He wrapped his arms around her, and she spun in them.

"Because I keep you on your toes," she said. "And because my 'business model is pretty poor.'"

"That's right," yelled out Ricky. "Your business model sucks!"

"Good thing," she whispered in Luke's ear, "that my boyfriend is brilliant. He can help me fix it."

Luke felt his face grow hot. They kissed and then they went to shoot zombies and eat popcorn. Jamie chewed no gum. He could tell that she was totally at her ease.

* * *

If you'd like to join my newsletter and learn what I think about romance I'm reading, see behind-the-scenes looks at my work, or hear about release dates, follow this link:
https://subscribepage.io/piperireland

If you enjoyed this book, I would be incredibly grateful if you could take a moment to leave a review on Amazon or Goodreads. Your feedback not only helps other readers discover new books but also means the world to authors like me. Thank you for your support!

-Piper

More Entrepreneurial Romances
Out soon!

Together, from Scratch

Cristina has three constants in her life: her daughter Alma, her gifted hands in the kitchen, and a deep-rooted distrust of happy endings. When she finds refuge in the rolling hills of western Massachusetts, she's looking for safety, not romance – and certainly not the attentive gaze of Sebastian, her coworker.

Sebastian has spent years nurturing his garden in the rich Berkshire soil, dreaming of sharing its bounty with others. But it's Cristina's legendary tamales that finally open that door – and perhaps, his future. As their culinary collaboration blossoms into something more, he discovers that growing love, like tending a garden, requires endless patience and care.

But for Cristina, trust is a delicate ingredient, and even the sweetest romance feels like a risk when your whole world balances on protecting a precious daughter. Can Sebastian's steady devotion prove that sometimes the most powerful loves grow not from passion, but from the tender daily acts of showing up?

A heartwarming story of healing, hope, and the courage to believe in second chances.

Perfect for fans of slow-burn workplace romance where food, trust, and tenderness simmer together. This heartwarming second installment in the *Mountain Valley Entrepreneurial Romance* series shows that the recipe for success includes a dash of courage and a generous portion of love.

Box Office Rivals

Chris DaSilva has six months to prove he can save his family's theater—the Phenom—or watch it disappear.

Enter Tanya Mills, the elegant King Theaters executive dispatched to assess the competition. She arrives expecting a straightforward conquest, armed with precision and ruthlessness. But her rival, Chris, is full of surprises and a grit she didn't expect. When he puts up a greater fight than she anticipated, her admiration for him grows as does her hunger to take him down.

Chris knows exactly what Tanya represents—a threat to everything his family has built. Yet beneath her razor-sharp corporate exterior, he glimpses something more: a woman who's never allowed herself to be vulnerable, who's never experienced the kind of love that can't be strategized or controlled.

Tanya's calculated moves meet Chris's wily resistance. As they battle for market dominance, they lose dominion over their own feelings, unraveling the careful boundaries between business and desire.

A sweet, funny romance with a melting ice queen, enemies-to-lovers tension, millionaire romance, and small-town charm mixed with big-city sophistication. This enchanting third installment in the *Mountain Valley Entrepreneurial Romance* series proves that the greatest stories aren't only on the screen.

Acknowledgments

Thank you, Ricky. You are always taking care of me.

Thank you to Kallie Falandays and Tell Tell Poetry for all your help getting this book into the world.

Thank you to Jamie Mac Touré for your insight.

Made in the USA
Monee, IL
31 March 2025